A childhood best forgotten

August 1856

Harrison Hunt felt safe near his father.

Out in the Kansas dust lay the body of Frederick Brown, and if those Border Ruffians would kill the son of John Brown, then they would surely kill the son of Henry Hunt. When his father moved from one conversation to another among the men in the town square, Harrison moved with him, never more than five yards distant.

Until now, the farmers hadn't joined in the shooting. John Brown's thirty abolitionists had held off hundreds of pro-slavery Missourians for half an hour, and many of the invaders now lay dead in the outlying fields.

John Brown spoke. "We've almost no bullets left. If you men don't help us, the battle's lost."

"It's not our battle!" snapped Pratt. "We're farmers, not fighters. I don't like slavery - heck, none of us do - but you came into town uninvited, gave us your little recruiting talk yesterday and no one signed up. There's your answer. We fed your men and watered your horses. Can't do any more for you. We need to think about our families. You need to think about surrendering. Stop the fighting."

As the unofficial spokesman for the town of Osawatomie, Cecil Pratt's words carried a lot of weight. His property bordered the Hunt family farm, and Harrison knew about the bad blood between his father and Pratt over a fence line.

"It's me and my men they want," said Brown. "If we head out of town, they'll follow us and leave you folks alone."

"You don't know that. If you cut and run, maybe they'll burn the town."

Brown shook his head. "We're not surrendering. We'll fall back across the river and lose them in the woods. You can tell the slavers what you want. Blame it all on my men coming here uninvited. That way, you have a chance. We'll take the women and children into the woods with us for safety if you want. No? OK then, we'll get out of here."

John Brown turned to gather his men. The farmers now stood alone.

"Alright," said Pratt to the assembled farmers. "We'll declare an Open Town. Bertie, get everyone to put their guns on the dirt out the front of the store. Show them we're not looking for a fight. We'd better get a white flag out also. Hunt! You can carry the flag. We'll find one of the raiders to take a message to their general."

Harrison felt a surge of pride that Pratt chose his father.

Henry Hunt nodded. "I'll get a flag. Harrison, come with me."

"Best let the boy stay behind," urged Pratt. "There's still firing out there."

"He's right, son. Stay with the other men here."

"Pa, let me..."

"Stay here Harrison." Henry Hunt turned, and walked out of his son's life forever.

Harrison didn't find his father's corpse until days later, well after the raiders overran the town, stole what they could and then burned all that remained. The bullet struck Henry Hunt from behind, and the father he loved had fallen forwards over the white flag he carried towards the battle. After that,

2

"It is most true that this court will not take jurisdiction if it should not; but it is equally true that it must take jurisdiction if it should. The judiciary cannot, as the legislature may, avoid a measure because it approaches the confines of the Constitution. We cannot pass it by because it is doubtful. With whatever doubts, with whatever difficulties, a case may be attended, we must decide it, if it be brought before us. We have no more right to decline the exercise of jurisdiction which is given, than to usurp that which is not given. The one or the other would be treason to the Constitution."

- Chief Justice Marshall
Cohens v. Virginia, 19 U.S. 264 (1821)

***

Treason doth never prosper; what's the reason? For if it prosper, none dare call it treason.

- Sir John Harrington, 1600

***

"Silent enim leges inter arma"
(In times of war, the law falls silent)

- Marcus Tullius Cicero

his mother's wails and his younger brother's confusion took up all of Harrison's thoughts. A week later, he awoke in the night, suddenly remembering the smell of gunpowder on Pratt, from when the older man offered to take Harrison back to the farm after the battle.

Gunpowder on Pratt's hands. The bullet wound in his father's back. None of the farmers had been shooting back against the attackers. Harrison now knew the truth about his father's death. He also knew that he could do nothing about it.

***

March 1858

"Take your brother for a walk along the river. See if you can catch us some fish."

Sunset arrived on Friday night, and Harrison knew the routine. After he and Thomas took their bait and lines to the river, the men would come and stay for a short time. Then there would be some money in the house, until mother could spend it on gin. If the boys were lucky, there would even be food for a few days.

Harrison could fish and he could hunt, and thanks to the kindness of the schoolmarm, who stopped asking for school fees after he told her of his father's death, he could read and scribe.

He knew that he didn't have an instinct for the soil, and without his father to do the lion's share of the labor, most of their crops rotted in the fields. Their old farm went quickly; sold to neighbor Pratt barely six months after his father's funeral. Mother handled the discussions with the sheriff and the men from the bank, and her muffled sobs in the night helped Harrison understand that the Hunt family hadn't had the best of the negotiations.

The three of them moved into an old two-room shanty on the edge of the woods. The floor was dirt and the walls lacked windows and their only neighbors were the animals of the forest and the gnats and midges that rose from the river each night.

One Friday night it rained so hard, the boys needed to come back early from fishing. What Harrison saw and heard on that night made him determined to stay away until dawn. He hated the men who used his mother on those nights, and he hated himself for needing the food that came from his mother's immoral toil.

Harrison never blamed his mother for how she paid the bills.

***

September 1858

"Sorry Harrison, I just don't know. Sheriff says your mother thieved a customer's purse one night, and when he went there to talk with her about it, he found the house in flames and nobody there. Nobody's seen your mother or brother since then."

"She never leaves the house on Saturday night. Thomas didn't have nowhere to go neither. The man's lying! I'll find him and I'll kill him and I don't ca…"

"Harrison!"

Old man Peters had always been kind to Harrison. An older, stronger man could have done a better job helping to get in the harvest on the Peters farm last Fall, but that job went to Harrison. Every few weeks Missus Peters would leave a box of vegetables on the stoop of the shanty, and the Hunt family would have food for a few days. Harrison stopped talking, and listened.

"Son, life hasn't been kind to you. I know that. Dumb bad luck you were away helping move that raft downriver last week. You want justice, but you and your knife can't take on the world. You need to move on."

"I'm not moving on! This is my home."

"It's not your home any more, son. It's not fair, but that's the way it is. Do you have any money?"

Harrison shook his head.

Old man Peters and his wife fed Harrison, and gave him a bed for the night. The next day they put twenty dollars in the pocket of his buckskin coat, and sent him east.

At least it hadn't been Pratt who gave him the news.

***

April 1861

Harrison itched to draw his knife. In the two and a half years since he left Kansas, he'd learned a thing or two about fighting, and he knew he could take this swindler in a fair fight. The man's right hand rested on the butt of his revolver, while his left hand lay casually on the last of Harrison's money. Beyond the card table, another man pushed himself off the wall, and walked casually to the other side of the saloon, passing beyond easy vision. Now he needed to cope with two of them - at least two of them - and he carried only one knife.

The cheater spoke carefully, enunciating his words with apparent enjoyment. "Now young feller, you've been rather rude to me, calling me a cheater and all. You're darn lucky I'm an easygoing man. I'm letting you walk out of that door without giving you the thrashing you deserve. You go home to your mammy now, and let us men get on with our game. You can come back here when your pecker gets some hair 'round it."

The chorus of laughter told him the other man had won. The man cheated, but he sat among his friends, and they all wore guns. Harrison stood on his own, with only his knife. His heart ached for a remembered word of wisdom from his Pa, but his father's voice grew fainter with every passing month. Father, Mother, Brother, Home. He'd lost them all, and now he was penniless.

He had no chance of winning this contest. He needed to leave while he still had his life.

Outside the saloon, a group of men gathered around a tree and Harrison could never recall how his feet took him there to stand with those men. His eyes read and reread the poster. It took many minutes for its message to sink in. The President called for volunteers. A fort somewhere in South Carolina needed some help.

***

January 1864

Deep streams of gutter water, strengthened by weeks of constant rain, cut into the pressed earth sidewalks and the few islands of solid ground that remained were scarcely a half-inch higher than the dirty rivulets that flowed around them. Eighteen years of driving a four-wheeler over the rutted roads and potholed paths of Washington gave the leather-faced cabbie an unerring instinct about how quickly his taxi would bog down in one of those mud banks and when the cab's wheel squelched into the thick mud that flanked the footpath, he eased the reins, and allowed his steaming horse to cease its labors.

The cab stopped a dozen slimy steps from the stationhouse sidewalk.

"Fifth Precinct Police station! Like youse asked fer!"

Harrison Hunt squinted out from the cab, and studied the muddy distance he needed to travel to reach solid ground. "Get closer, damn you! I can't walk through that!"

"Can't do that, sir. Any further into that mud, and we'd bog right down."

Hunt's plan for a grand entry to the building died with those words. A thick coat of mud would now cover the shine he put on his boots the previous evening. He could do nothing about that now. He paid the man, and sloshed through the steady rain to his destination.

Washington City Hall commanded Indiana Avenue, and the Fifth Precinct police operated out of the basement in the east wing of the building. The heavy wooden doors parted at his push, and Hunt moved from the stench of the dung-covered rain-drenched street into the darker shadows inside the building where hanging oil lights dripped their overlapping pools of

6

illumination onto the hard floor of the vestibule. Two patrolmen with hands clasped around steaming mugs stood together in quiet discussion before a coal-filled fireplace at the back of the room. Angry voices, muffled moans and indecipherable complaints floated out from a half-hidden doorway near them.

The middle-aged sergeant seated at the charge desk, positioned barricade-like in the center of the room, interrupted his writing to examine Hunt. Hunt strode towards the sergeant, feeling the rain trickle from his clothes and the mud drip from his boots, but still meeting the man's eyes all the way. Hunt stood five foot ten, and he carried himself ready for a fight. His scarred cheek, dark eyes and long black hair added to his air of danger. He kept his hands visible, with his fists clenched at his sides. No one knew what to expect of that pose, and Hunt liked it that way. The sergeant sat entrenched behind his desk, with a low wooden barrier flanking his position all the way to the walls. He had reinforcements close at hand. The odds were even, but Hunt possessed both the initiative and the inclination to use it.

"My name's Harrison Hunt, sergeant. Where's Captain Price?"

The sergeant regarded the newcomer impassively, as a well-fed dog might regard a meatless bone, and his mouth twitched in anticipation of what might best be said to this uninvited stranger. The patrolmen by the fire stopped talking, and looked over at the impending confrontation. Hunt raised the ante. "William's expecting me."

The sergeant's face moved from bored indifference to a wary expression more appropriate for talking with someone who appeared to be on first name terms with his boss. Hunt could imagine the wheels turning in the man's mind. He would have witnessed all sorts and conditions of people walking through those doors, and on this cold January day, this new arrival wouldn't be worth thinking about. He had work to do, and this problem belonged with the captain, not with him.

"Ridley! Tell the captain there's someone here to see him."

Hunt kept his gaze fixed on the sergeant and heard the unseen Ridley rise and move away. He'd won the first round. Time to move in for the kill.

"That's a good fire you've got back there."

The sergeant put down his nib, and considered the visitor. Hunt knew the man would find it hard to guess his age. Twenty-five, thirty, maybe thirty-five at a pinch. His clothes were neat, but he wasn't dressed like a dandy. A worn buckskin coat over a newly boiled shirt. No hat, which would seem a mite strange on this wet day, but there wasn't much to be done about that until he'd paid the back rent and redeemed the missing hat from the pawnbroker. The question in the sergeant's mind would be whether Hunt could make his life in the Fifth Precinct more difficult. Could this stranger be the son of a friend of the captain, or of some big bug in the upstairs offices of City Hall?

In the end, prudence prevailed. "You want a seat back here then?"

Pause.

"Matthews will get you coffee if you want it."

Hunt smiled, and then moved through the wooden gate and towards the proffered seat. The lessons he learned in the Army also applied in civilian life. Win the first encounter and the other man will always be on the defensive. He'd achieved what he wanted, and it hadn't cost the sergeant anything. Matthews left his partner near the fireplace and moved to obey the sergeant. The coffeepot hung from a crane over the open fire and, with a skill indicating long experience in the matter, Matthews hooked it out and tipped a splash of the contents into a tin cup. Hunt watched him pouring it to see he didn't spit in the cup - a common army trick to even scores with a disliked officer - but Matthews poured it straight and passed the cup across with a smile of welcome. "Careful there. That'll be hot."

"Thanks."

The gratitude cost him nothing. The coffee smelt like tar and tasted much the same, but that didn't bother Hunt. During his time in the army, he'd survived a variety of beverages masquerading as coffee. Crushed corn, blackened peas, chicory mixed with a drop of molasses, and even tea made from boiling wild thistles. The Union might have all the food and firearms it needed to equip its armies, but sometimes the food stayed in the warehouses while the soldiers suffered in the field. Hunt nodded his appreciation for the coffee, and let Matthews return to the fire and his conversation. An empty chair against the wall beckoned, and he accepted the invitation.

Working as a detective hadn't been his first choice for a career, but he found only failure in all of his other job applications since leaving the Army. That difficulty ended when Superintendent Webb accepted him on the strength of his previous army commission and a well-spun, completely unverifiable tale of his early life as a deputy marshal out west. Hunt didn't like lying, but he liked starvation far less. The past didn't matter now. His appointment with Captain Price meant the beginning of a new and better life, and so, for the moment, he sat quietly, drinking his coffee and watching the flames dancing in the fireplace.

***

One floor above Hunt, William Price stood at a window, chewing on a dead cigar and watching the empty cab lurching away from the curb. It wobbled wildly as its wheels slithered from one rut to another, flicking lumps of slime onto luckless pedestrians with every bounce. That distraction lasted less than a minute, and then Price needed to return to the problem at hand. Standing at the window allowed him to reassert a measure of control over his emotions, but he suspected his feelings were no secret to the other man in the room.

In matters of organizational hierarchy and social connections, Captain Price outranked Detective Schultz, but in matters of intellect and powers of reasoning, Schultz definitely trumped his captain. Price turned away from the window and tapped on the notepaper lying on his desk, glaring at Schultz as he spoke. "You'll not get this approved."

"I've gone where the evidence leads me, Captain."

"Tarnation Schultz, even if it were Hobart…"

"It was."

"I say if - you've not proved that yet - even if it were Hobart, you'll not get a judge in this city to sign this warrant."

"That's true. I can't, but Superintendent Webb can. You need to talk to him."

Price chewed on his unlit cigar. They'd travelled down this road many times, and every time Schultz won the argument. Every goddarn time! Schultz's casual acceptance of his own intellectual superiority didn't help.

"You've got facts then?" he asked, already knowing the answer.

"Enough to satisfy me."

"Meaning you don't think I'll understand them?"

Schultz didn't reply.

Price felt himself getting into a fine pucker. Time to try a different tack. "You've discussed it with Sloan and Murphy?"

"Why would I do that?"

"Tarnation Shultz! You men are supposed to work together. You're not the regular sergeants or patrolmen. You're detectives!"

Schultz slowly raised an eyebrow. Clearly, his opinion of the other detectives wasn't any higher than his opinion of his captain. Price couldn't see a way to win the discussion. He knew he needed to finish it before he threw the other man out of the window. He dropped heavily into his chair and flicked a dismissive hand. "Alright then! Leave it with me. I'll speak to the superintendent."

The tight smile on Schultz's face could have been a sneer, but Price knew that his best detective wouldn't gloat over his victories. The man didn't bother tempering his brilliance with playing politics. When he was right, and he was always right, he told you so and expected you to own your mistake. Your personal pride didn't concern him.

Price watched Schultz leave, then stood up with a growl and paced across to the fireplace to help his temper settle. He used an ember from the grate to put a glow to his cigar. The chill of the room made removal of his overcoat and the unravelling of his muffler undesirable. He returned to the window to glare out at the miserable day and wish the conversation gone from his memory.

One day you'll be wrong Schultz. I hope I'm there when it happens.

The view failed to cheer him. The roads sucked at the traffic laboring to reach its destination. The bitter wind batted rubbish between the buildings. Price's eyes moved to the horizon, searching for good news about the weather. The freezing spray born on the Potomac would be pounding the docks, stretching its icy tentacles towards the heart of the city, and driving the rats and the birds back into their nests. The rain slackened a little, as if the day still needed to decide how to treat the people of the city. Washington normally endured a wet and cold winter, and this Monday in early 1864 remained true to that tradition.

A tap on the doorframe behind him prompted Price to turn from the window. Ridley stood there. "Capt'n sir, there's a man to see you."

Meeting Captain Price

"Mister Hunt, Capt'n says he'll see you now."

At the sound of his name, Hunt instinctively rose to his feet and stood at Parade Rest. Ridley had returned and stood beside him, pointing up the stairs. A small, old man. A runner of errands. Hunt felt foolish at responding so quickly to this messenger's voice, but took some comfort in the fact the other policemen hadn't seemed to notice his actions.

"Capt'n's in his office. Top of the stairs on the left."

Hunt nodded his thanks. Then Ridley left, and the desk sergeant continued to ignore him. Hunt walked with a measured tread, needing his footsteps to sound strong and confident for the waiting captain. The stationhouse walls on the next floor showed fewer marks of struggles, and lacked the smell of damp stone and unwashed bodies that permeated the entrance hall. The illumination from the downstairs oil lamps did not penetrate to the top of the stairwell, but sufficient light came through the open door ahead for Hunt to walk without stumbling. He stepped into the captain's office with confidence, but his salute died with the realization that he still held a coffee cup in his right hand.

A tall man stood at the window; an enormous white walrus moustache above a gray overcoat and a charcoal muffler, with a thick, fuming cigar in one hand. Cigars were a luxury in the north, and the curling tobacco smoke drew in Hunt's gaze. He smoked once, but like so many others gave up the habit when all legal trade with the southern states stopped, and the price of tobacco went through the ceiling. A pair of green eyes, framed between the moustache and thick bushy eyebrows, peered out at him. The cigar travelled up to the moustache and thick smoke curled around the eyes. "Hunt? Shut the door. Take a seat."

Hunt did that, noting that he now had his back to the door. The chair creaked loudly as he sat. Shifting his position brought forth another creak as the chair complained again. The cool air chilled the room and Hunt wished his coat were thicker. It seemed disrespectful to place his mug on the captain's desk. He carefully set it under his chair, wincing slightly with every creak from the ancient wooden seat.

"Superintendent told me you were coming," said Price, taking his seat behind the desk. "You understand the job? Twelve hour shifts if needed, on call seven days a week. No days off and no vacations."

"Yes, Captain."

They said that in the letter. Which is my desk? Where do I sit?

"We pay detectives four eighty a year. Same as the patrolmen, but detectives don't walk a beat. I give them assigned cases. You've done casework before?"

"Uh… Yes, I can do that, Captain."

The job's mine, right? But you're treating this like some kind of interview. Do I need your say-so before I start?

"We've got badges now. Didn't have those last year, but things are improving somewhat. You have a gun?"

"No."

The captain scratched his left eye, barely looking at him. "Detectives carry guns, Hunt. They told me you'd been in the army. Can you shoot?"

"I can shot a – shoot a gun!"

The captain looked up. The cigar shifted in Price's mouth as he studied his new recruit. Hunt gazed back, surreptitiously wiping his sweating palms on the sides of his trousers.

They didn't say I needed to bring a gun! Is he judging me for that? Should I let him outstare me? Be darned if I will!

"You'd be thirty?"

What number did I write down? Doesn't he believe I can handle the work?

"Just over."

Price raised an eyebrow and tightened his lips. Hunt had no way to tell the man's thoughts. It didn't look good.

I need this job! God! What do I do now? I've got to show him I can do it!

"Handy with your fists then? I need men who can fight."

Light flashed on metal, and Hunt's Bowie knife hurtled across the room to bury itself inch-deep in the window frame at the height of a man's head.

"I've killed men with that," he announced grandly.

The tip of Price's cigar twitched, and his eyes creased. Hunt couldn't tell if the captain fully appreciated his skill with the knife.

***

Price stared at Hunt through steady eyes.

Damn fool! You think your fancy knife throwing makes you a detective?

This young man - could he really be thirty - might be a problem. The thefts at the depot, the unexplained deaths at the soldier's hospital, the tavern riots every Saturday night that were too destructive to be unplanned - there were too many crimes, and not enough detectives to look into them. Price needed good material to fill his ranks, but old men waiting for retirement, or army dropouts with a chip on each shoulder like Hunt, were all he could get.

The situation exasperated him. If this recruit hadn't come in with the superintendent's personal recommendation, then Price would have thrown him out onto the street for that stupid stunt with the knife.

"Think you're the bee's knees then, Hunt?"

The look on the new recruit's face showed he realized he'd gone too far.

At least you learn from your mistakes.

A solution presented itself in Price's mind. Two problems solved with the one simple decision. "Let's put you with Schultz then.

He grunted to himself to confirm the correctness of his decision, then looked at Hunt. "He's getting on a bit. Reckon he could use a hand."

You two beauties can make each other's life miserable for a while. At least you'll both be out of my hair.

He jerked his thumb towards the knife embedded in the splintered woodwork. "Get rid of that."

***

Hunt walked to the window to retrieve his knife, twisting it from the wood and slipping it back into its sheath. Clearly, the captain hadn't been impressed with his knife handling, but he couldn't take that move back now. At least Price hadn't questioned the statement about his age. The name 'Schultz' didn't tell him anything. German, maybe? Possibly Dutch. That didn't really matter. Not knowing any of the detectives meant that none of the names could be preferred. All of them were strangers to him.

He settled himself back into the rickety chair in time to hear the office door creak open again. The unsteady steps behind him reassured Hunt that this new arrival posed no threat, yet he still needed to clench his fists to stop himself leaping up to face the newcomer. Battle habits die hard.

"She's a cold 'un today, Capt'n."

It was Ridley.

"Ridley, git yor hell-fired body in here and meet Detective Hunt," said Price. "Hunt, this is Ridley. He feeds the fire, delivers messages, and for two bits a week he'll git you a cup of coffee each morning."

The slow steps stopped beside Hunt, and a hand carrying a steaming mug moved into Hunt vision. Hunt turned carefully on his ancient chair to take a better look at the small man standing beside him. He decided the man's age sat somewhere between fifty and sixty. The empty left coat sleeve pinned to the shoulder, and the faint scars tracking up his cheek, showed the man's war hadn't been as forgiving as the one Hunt survived. Ridley set the coffee on the desk, then fumbled in his pocket and produced a crumpled piece of paper before turning to face Hunt.

"Morning, Mister Hunt. You want more coffee?"

Hunt still held the cup Matthews filled for him. He shook his head. "Finishing some now thanks. Might talk to you later when I get settled."

"Sure thing, Mister Hunt."

Ridley placed the paper next to the captain's cup and left, closing the door behind him. Price didn't bother to watch the old man go. It struck Hunt that Captain Price might be the sort of person who took most things for granted. Price held all of the aces in this job. It would be important to adjust to the captain's way of working.

Price retrieved Ridley's paper and scanned it. His free hand located his coffee cup and brought it to his waiting lips. When the mug descended, Price licked a stray drop of coffee from his tobacco-tinged moustache. The door behind Hunt opened again, and Ridley's voice returned. "Sergeant Bader wants a chat, Capt'n. He's in the duty room."

16

Price set down the paper and leaned back in his chair. "Roster changes?"

"Reckon so, Capt'n."

Price sighed. "Good enough Ridley. Tell him I'll be there right quick."

The footsteps retreated and Price unlocked a desk drawer and retrieved a badge and a revolver. "Schultz don't keep regular hours. Tarnation, none of us do. It's all about getting the job done. I want the results, not the darn timesheets. Come with me!"

Price stomped into the corridor and then through another door, leaving Hunt scrambling behind him. This next office had four desks and six chairs, and Hunt couldn't figure how people could occupy all six chairs at the same time within such a small space. Price indicated a desk in the far corner. "That's Schultz's seat. You keep busy reading his case files 'til he comes back. I'll tell him you're here."

Price thrust Ridley's paper, the badge and the revolver into Hunt's hand and strode to the door. "Give that note to Schultz. Robbery 'n murder at the Washington Herald. Right up his alley, I'd say. He likes the weird ones. I got things to do. You look at those files, and we'll talk later."

Price paused in the doorway. "Welcome to the Fifth Precinct, Hunt."

Price stepped into the corridor and Hunt found himself alone. He slipped the badge, revolver and paper into his pocket, and looked around at the four bleak walls that surrounded him. Drawings of unknown faces were pinned above desks. Scrapbooks of news clippings and reference works sat on old wooden shelves. The day-to-day toolkit of the working detective. Schultz's desk sat in a corner, away from the windows. That position gave him two walls on which to pin papers, but the position had poor light. Hunt settled himself into Schultz's chair, noting with relief it seemed sturdier than the one in the captain's office.

Hunt looked around at the rest of the room. Schultz's desk seemed more organized than its neighbors did. The files sat in neat stacks, and even the papers pinned to Schultz's part of the wall aligned vertically and horizontally. It seemed rude to disturb the symmetrical order of Schultz's work, but these files also belonged to him now.

Hunt picked up the first file and began to read. The files contained the darker side of Washington, described briefly on coarse, unlined notepaper. Newspaper clippings were scattered through the files, but many of them didn't bear an obvious reference to the case described on the cover sheet. A murder on the docks had a program for a play at Hassel's Theatre. Assault and robbery in broad daylight had a recruiting pamphlet for the Maryland infantry. Hunt sifted it all, replacing the papers in each folder as he read them. Schultz doubtless had some system worked out, and Hunt saw no advantage in messing it up. Partners needed to show respect to each other.

"You'd be Hunt then."

Hunt turned from the open folder to see a short man wearing an overcoat and a bowler hat standing beside the desk. Bright brown eyes stared intently at him and one hand held leather gloves. Hunt hadn't heard the newcomer arriving. That lapse in his concentration troubled him. "Schultz?"

At the newcomer's nod of assent, Hunt moved to get up, but Schultz waved him back into the seat. That suited Hunt. Let the other man stand. He leaned back in the chair.

Nature had not been kind to Detective Schultz. Five and a half feet tall with sloping shoulders and a pot belly. A broad bushy beard added to Schultz's troll-like appearance. Schultz slapped his gloves into his free hand as he spoke. "Read much of that yet, Detective?"

"I've made a start. Fair bit to read."

"I'll give you a hint, Detective Hunt," replied Schultz, waving a lecturing finger in Hunt's face. "Ignore anything more than three months old. If we haven't understood it by then, there's all but nine chances in ten we never will."

Hunt snorted derisively. "You talk like a man who's given up."

"No sir, I talk like a man who knows what happens in the Fifth Precinct. Moreover, I tell you for every seven cases without a firm lead after three months, we'll only ever solve one of them. Simple statistics. You want the

18

numbers? No? Suit yourself."

Schultz's eyes exuded energy and confidence, dancing over Hunt, noting details. The glove slapping resumed. "Gettysburg?" he asked.

Hunt twisted his mouth, feeling the tightness of the newly healed scars on his cheek. He'd heard that question too many times. Everyone knew about Gettysburg. No one remembered any other battle from 1863.

"Scott's Ford on the Rappahannock," he replied. "A week afore Gettysburg."

Schultz folded his arms, and the cannonball head retreated into his shoulders. "The Rappahannock, hey? Donohue died at Chancellorsville. Little bit west of Fredericksburg. Lots of good men dying in this war."

"Sorry for staying alive."

Hunt felt his dander rising. Since he'd left the Army he'd put up with plenty of comments about not being at Gettysburg, and he'd be darned if he'd apologize simply because he'd come back from the war and Schultz's friend hadn't. Schultz rolled his bottom lip over the top one and flexed his fingers. The silence grew.

"You're a westerner," Schultz announced at length. "From Arkansas I'd say. Confederate territory."

"Born in Tennessee and lived in Kansas! I'm a Union man, and I spilt my blood fighting them rebels. You finished with the comments, or you want to step outside?"

Hunt had height, weight, youth, and a couple of years of infantry fighting on his side. He might be the new boy here, but he'd have respect or someone would pay for it. Schultz looked to be the first buyer.

Schultz lifted his hands, palms open, to Hunt. "Steady on now. I'm not looking for an eye gouging. Your time in the army speaks for itself. I figured you for an Arkansas boy. Not many easterners wear that kind of buckskin coat."

Hunt looked at his coat. It once belonged to his father. "A buckskin coat doesn't make me a westerner. I could have bought it yesterday."

Schultz slipped his gloves into his coat pocket, then leaned over the desk and began restacking the folders Hunt moved. "You speak like a westerner, and I say you recut that coat to your size some years ago. Then there's two types of thread around the seams. A few months ago, you patched the collar, probably when you came out of the army. It's been your coat for years."

"You guessed!"

Schultz smiled at Hunt as he finished putting the desk back in order. "I don't go in for guessing, Hunt. Weakens the intellect and distracts the eyes from seeing what they should."

"Then how did you know I patched it? Could've been done by anybody."

"You're left-handed Hunt. Your coffee cup would be on the other side of the desk if you weren't. Then look at the unbalanced tension on those stitches. Stronger on the left than on the right. A lefthander did that patching, and an amateur one at that. No offense meant there. I'm not that handy with a needle myself. But it's definitely your coat, and you sewed it."

Hunt relaxed. Schultz showed to be a smart man, and probably didn't want a fight.

"It's my coat and I guess Tennessee is... was... rebel territory," he admitted. "Look, I'm sorry. I'm out of the army now, but it takes a while to stop looking over your shoulder."

Schultz smiled again, and spoke without sympathy in his voice. "Better hold onto your army habits. Life in the Fifth Precinct isn't exactly peaceful. It gets like Gettys... like a battlefield out there. That's why the captain thinks we need partners."

Hunt nodded, and let his voice loosen up a notch. "Captain Price told you we'd be partners?"

"Haven't seen Price since earlier this morning," observed Schultz, taking one of the folders from the pile. "We work best in each other's absence."

20

"Then how'd you know my name?"

Schultz pushed the folder under his arm, leaned back against the wall and steepled his fingers over his stomach. The thumbs tapped against each other. "Price is forever after me to take a partner. I come in here, and there's an ex-army man sitting at my desk looking through my files. Doesn't take much to figure out what you're doing here. Then you wrote your name on the back of your boot heels. That's left-handed work also. Probably need to mark all your stuff in the army. Mind you, it's not much better here at times."

Schultz cocked his head. "What do you think of Price?" His face gave no hint of the answer he expected.

Hunt took his time replying. Something political lay behind that question, and Hunt didn't want to take any sides on his first day in the job. "A bit straightforward maybe. He knows what he wants."

"Did you notice the chair?"

"Chair?"

"The one he made you sit in," replied Schultz, pushing himself off the wall and taking the folder back into his hands. "He always does his interviews in there, and always puts the visitor in the same chair. It creaks."

"Oh, that one."

"Yes, that one. It's an old trick. His guests are so busy worrying about whether they'll fall out of the chair, they don't pay attention to the questions he's asking them. He knows some of the ropes does our Captain Price."

Falling for that scam annoyed Hunt, but he shrugged it off. "Fine. Where do we start?"

"We don't start anywhere Detective Hunt," corrected Schultz. "I work alone. I'll leave a note for Price, and he can fix you up with a new partner when he gets back."

"Just like that?"

"Just like that." He picked up his folder and turned to the door. "Welcome to the Fifth Precinct, Hunt."

Schultz left.

A simple case of Murder

Hunt sat at Schultz's desk for a full five minutes, burning with anger at the other detective's dismissal of their partnership. What did Schultz expect him to do? Go back to Price with a request for a new partner because the first one didn't think he could do the job? Be darned if he would!

He stood up. Thrusting both hands into his pockets, he strode three paces to the window and looked out into the day. Across the road, a platoon of soldiers sought shelter under a rain-laden tree. His practiced eye ran over the troops, noting their worn uniforms and the old-style muskets. These were garrison troops, probably out on a patrol to find deserters. Two of their number stood guard over a prisoner.

Hunt spent no time thinking about the man's fate. His own army days were behind him now. The wound he took during the patrol across the Rappahannock became his ticket out of the Army. There had been a desk job waiting, but no chance to go back into the field. The colonel made it clear that Hunt would never receive another combat command. The words came back. *Better opportunities for you ... gift of organization.*

Hogswallop!

They didn't trust him. They'd never given him a chance to prove himself. Hunt shifted position to lean his shoulder against the window frame, and felt paper in his pocket rustling against his fingers. His hand withdrew from the coat and he held the paper Price asked him to pass onto Schultz. Another job he hadn't done properly. The paper unfolded and Hunt read the message.

Murder at the Herald Office.

An address on Eleventh Street up near Pennsylvania Avenue covered the second half of the note. Probably witnesses standing around waiting for a detective to interview them. A corpse that nobody could move until someone recorded all of the details. No one here could give him advice.

Hunt made his decision. Cramming some notepaper and a pencil into his pocket, he left the detective's room to make his way downstairs. The noise of angry voices grew as he descended, reaching an unintelligible peak as he reached the ground floor. The cells at the rear of the station were disgorging their contents. The stench of cheap perfume and stale beer washed over him as he pushed through the hookers, thieves and drunks preparing for their hearing in the nearby courthouse. Loud voices complained about injustice and wrist irons, but Hunt moved straight through the lawless pack and down the front steps. The chilled rain had eased during the last hour, although a sharp wind still blew along the street. His fast walk left the chill of the morning behind him. He had a job to do dammit, and Schultz could go to hell.

Less than five minutes later he came up against some fifty or so horses and their overcoated riders moving south through the city towards the Long Bridge and the battlefront. The rising wind stripped away the wavering mist of the breath of men and animals that trailed behind them. Few people stopped to watch the mounted horses. Washington had been at war for over three years and the sight of uniformed men no longer turned a civilian's head.

Those were fine horses. Strong of limb and eager to move. Most of them hadn't been born when the war began and most of them wouldn't live to see the war's end. Horses mystified Hunt. He'd grown up with them, and he'd seen cavalry ride through Maryland and Virginia, but he'd never taken to those animals. Although he admired the men who controlled the charging masses of horseflesh, he had no desire to be one of their number. The final pair of horses passed, and he joined the people surging into the street, all stepping carefully between the steaming horse turds as they continued on their interrupted journey.

Hunt headed for the small islands of firm ground dotting the unpaved street. Shuffling his way between likeminded pedestrians, he crossed the road and kept walking. The neighborhood changed as he came closer to Eleventh Street. The streets were less flooded, and the sidewalks busier.

Eleventh Street arrived, and Hunt stopped near Harvey's Oyster Bar to take in the picture. The Washington Herald occupied a three-story Brownstone, barely ten yards wide, positioned between two restaurants. A group of gapers, mindless of the rain, crowded the middle-aged policeman guarding the entrance to the office. There had been a time when Hunt might be one of them, but now he owned the voice of authority. He walked to the entranceway. It took longer than he would have liked to push his way through the crowd, but finally he stood in front of the policeman.

"Detective Hunt. Fifth Precinct," he said, fumbling in his pocket to find his badge.

The policeman stifled his initial reaction to block Hunt from entering, and instead saluted him. "Patrolman Hurley, sir. Sergeant Dawson's upstairs with the body."

That last word drew a collective "ooh" from the throng, and the idlers surged forwards, perhaps hoping to hear something new about the murder. Hunt left Hurley to deal with them and moved through the door, closing it behind him. The Herald ranked low on the list of popular Washington newspapers. Hunt read it once or twice, but he didn't like its style. If push came to shove, he would have said that the Herald seemed too highfaluting. Politics and business issues didn't interest him.

The office contained only a few items of furniture. Three small desks crowded into the front of the office, while the presses and printing paraphernalia sat at the rear. Harsh scorch marks scarred one side of a desk and, as he passed it, Hunt could see where the remains of a fire covered the floor between that desk and a large iron safe bolted to the floor. The smell of charcoal and ash hung heavily in the air. Two men and a negro woman were in the room, and they broke off their conversation at the sound of his entry. "Sergeant Dawson?"

"He's upstairs."

"That's fine. I'm Detective Hunt from the Fifth Precinct. Who found the body?"

Hunt felt out of his depth here, asking questions with no experience or rulebook to guide him, but he held the initiative. The taller of the two men half-raised his hand. "I'm Raymond Hackett, detective. I arrived here at six to open the office, and Mister Anderson lay dead in his room. Tom and Bessie here came in later."

Hackett stood a clear two inches taller than Hunt. An ounce or two less flesh and Hunt would describe him as cadaverous. His high-necked shirt and string tie sat comfortably with his Chesterfield overcoat, and Hunt mentally tagged Hackett as a man accustomed to wearing good clothes and enjoying the finer things of life. Not surprisingly, Hackett seemed to be in charge of the others.

"Six o'clock? Don't you need to get the presses working earlier than that?"

"We publish twice a week. Tuesdays and Thursdays. Today we get all the typesetting done and ready for tomorrow's issue."

Hunt had no reason to know that, but he felt uncomfortable with his own ignorance. He scrabbled in his pocket for notepaper to cover his embarrassment. "Go on."

"I went to open the office, but I found the door unlocked. When I saw the results of the fire, I went upstairs to see if there had been any other damage. John - Mister Anderson - lay dead in his room, so I went outside and found the policeman who sent for you."

The three of them looked at him expectantly. Hunt didn't know what to do next, but the woman saved him.

"I's here at six too! Met Mister Hackett here talking to the policeman I did.

Every day I starts at six, and I weren't late."

Hackett rolled his eyes. This dispute obviously carried a long history. "Fine Bessie. You were here at six. Don't worry about that now."

"That detective massa needs to know. You's always saying I's late, and you's wrong. Poor Massa Anderson. Kilt in his bed would you believe. Lord have mercy, a soul's not safe in this here city. And today I's gunna be late finishing, 'cause you won't lets me do my work."

Hackett turned to Hunt. "Bessie here cleans the office and makes coffee every morning. I thought it best to leave things as they were until you'd looked around."

Hunt thoughts cleared somewhat during Bessie's speech. "You did the right thing Mister Hackett. Bessie, could you make us all some of that coffee? I'd surely appreciate it."

"Why certainly, Massa Detective, sir. Anything to help."

With a sniff to indicate her contempt for Hackett's obvious inability to tell the time, Bessie flounced to the rear of the office and busied herself at the fireplace. Hackett's small smile showed he saw through Hunt's ploy to get rid of Bessie, and he gave an affirming nod of his head to show his approval. "I can take you upstairs."

"In a minute."

Hunt realized Hackett possessed even less experience of police procedure than he did. He could bluff his way through this. Hunt allowed his gaze to wander around the office. "No one saw the fire till you arrived?"

Hackett shrugged. "There's a police beat down here maybe twice a night. That fire probably burned for less than ten minutes, and the killers pushed the front door shut. Unless the patrolman walking past smelled the smoke or saw the flames, then he'd no reason to investigate."

"Did Anderson live here?"

"He has a house at Georgetown as well as the apartment upstairs.

Sometimes he slept there, sometimes he slept here."

Hunt turned and walked to the scene of the fire. The desktop nearest the fire sat empty before him, while the other two desks were untidy, with papers and books and nibs scattered across them. He squatted at the remnants of the fire and poked through the cold embers with the point of his Bowie knife. Fragments of charcoaled paper lay scattered through the ashes, charred and crumbled beyond deciphering. His knife's probing point exposed a cracked inkwell. This explained what happened. A sweep of the intruder's arm cleared the top of the desk, and assembled the fuel for building the fire. A strike or two on a flint would finish the task.

He could learn nothing else here. Hunt straightened and turned to the two men. "Has the safe been checked? Did they take anything?"

Hackett started, and turned to his companion. "Tom, did you check the safe?"

Tom spread his hands helplessly. "I don't have the key, Mister Hackett. You know that."

"Of course Tom. Sorry Detective, I'd have to get the key from upstairs."

"Best to check that, Mister Hackett. I'll look out the back."

Hackett left them and walked hurriedly to the staircase. Hunt paused, hearing Hackett's anxious tread taking the stairs two at a time. This would be a good time to look around. He moved past the assembly racks of lead type and the idle printing presses, toward the back of the office. The back door stood open, and a broken windowpane beside the door showed how the murderer, or murderers he mentally corrected himself, made their entry.

An intact padlock secured the inside of the double gates that bisected the rear fence, protecting the small courtyard from casual intruders. Hunt peered through the crack between the gates, and the thick mud of a narrow alley stared back at him. This would be where the newspapers were loaded and sent to the agents throughout the city. The walls around the courtyard were wood palings, well maintained and almost 10 feet high. He straightened up and moved back to the doorway to avoid the rain.

Stacks of raw newsprint covered by an oilcloth were stored against the back wall of the building and extended in a broken pyramid along the courtyard's side wall. The position of those stores would allow a thief an easy climb into, and out of, the yard. Pools of water puddled on the oilcloth and glass from the broken window lay on the ground beside it. It would have been simple enough to scale the wall, break the window and open the door. That part of the case seemed clear enough.

"Here's yor coffee, Massa Detective." Bessie's voice broke into his thoughts. Her dark face beamed up at him over the proffered coffee, and he took the cup with a smile. Bessie showed an age of barely twenty years, and her hands wore the calluses of a short life spent in hard physical labor. Her clothes were little better than restitched rags.

"You live around here, Bessie?" asked Hunt.

"I lives on R Street. It's a hostel for us colored folks. They finds me this job when I fust comes to Washington."

"That's right handy for you, Bessie."

Bessie cast a glance inside the office, then her face tensed and her voice became low and anxious. "Now don' you be listening too much to Mister Hackett now. Land sakes, he'd tell one soul one thing and a second soul another!"

Bessie's eyes locked on Hunt and the urgent tone of her voice shot a thrill through him. Through the open door, he could see Tom and Hackett at the front of the office conferring over a pile of papers. Doubtless, they opened the safe and were checking its contents. Hunt laid a reassuring hand on Bessie's shoulder. "You tell me the truth here, Bessie. Why shouldn't I be listening to Mister Hackett?"

"I's here at six. Every day I gets here at six."

"That's all right then. Have you worked here long, Bessie?"

"Ever since I been in Washington and that's a fact. But Massa Hackett, he's a bad massa, and that's not jus' Bessie talking. He always be arguing with Massa Anderson and telling him I's late to work."

Hunt suspected that Bessie didn't think much beyond her own personal needs. "I don't think Mister Hackett will have much to say about that now Bessie," he said. "We need to think about poor Mister Anderson. Did he talk much to you, Bessie?"

A dull crash from inside the office stopped Bessie's reply. Hunt looked up to see Hackett and Tom looking straight back at him. The sound came from somewhere between them. The three men moved towards each other, meeting midway down the office outside a stout wooden door. Hunt looked at the door, then at the other two men. Another small crash came from inside the cupboard. Someone, or something, waited in there.

"Printing supply cupboard," explained Tom. "Inks, dies, woodcuts, all that stuff." His voice trailed off and he stepped back. His sweaty hands massaged each other as he looked back and forth between Hunt and Hackett.

"The door doesn't open from the inside," added Hackett. "The lock's due for fixing, but we'd not gotten round to it."

Hunt could feel the tension of the battlefield returning. The killer must have inadvertently locked himself inside the cupboard. More fool him, but now Hunt would get the credit for solving the case. Even so, it would be best to get reinforcements. "Bessie! Fetch the policeman from upstairs."

She nodded; her hand clenched to her mouth, then ran to the stairs. Hunt examined the door. A stout frame anchored the door into the wall. No single man would ever break it down.

"There could be two, maybe three of them in there," suggested Tom, retreating a pace and wringing his hands.

"There'll be four of us," replied Hunt forcefully. His Bowie knife appeared and floated in his hand. "You in there!"

No answer.

"I'm a police officer, and I'm coming in."

No answer.

Hunt looked at the other men. The sergeant from upstairs joined them now with his nightstick ready for action. Through the front window, Hunt could see the crowds pressing in close, peering into the gloom for a picture of whatever might happen next. Hunt knew another patrolman stood outside, but he could not contain his eagerness. The door handle felt cool to his touch and turned easily. The broken lock clunked in its housing, and the door swung open. Hunt advanced into the storeroom, where dim light from the outside office revealed a small thin man cowering in a corner with his hands raised above his head.

"Don' hit me officer. I'll come quietly."

"Darn right you will!"

Two strides covered the distance to the felon, and Hunt easily hauled the pitiful wretch out by his collar. The unwashed down-and-out, wearing a week's growth of beard and a coat covered in splashes from countless messy meals, didn't resist. Hunt almost gagged at the smell of the sweat and the dirt and the cheap liquor that stained the miscreant's tattered clothing.

"Well done," breathed Hackett.

Hunt twisted the man's collar upwards, lifting the captive onto his toes. "Where's your friends?"

"- on my own - cain't breathe," gasped the prisoner.

Hunt held him while Dawson slapped the irons onto the man's thin wrists.

"Plenty of time for breathing and talking when we get you to the stationhouse," said the sergeant.

Hunt couldn't stop grinning. This would show smart-ass Schultz that Hunt knew how to be a detective.

"I'll get some transport sir," volunteered Dawson. "Can you hold him?"

"Not a problem. He's safe with me."

The crowd outside murmured approvingly when Hunt emerged with his prisoner. Sergeant Dawson commandeered a passing shay and Hunt left him in charge of removing Anderson's body and dispersing the crowd. The shay usually seated two people, and the horse struggled to pull its overloaded cart through the Washington mud. That didn't worry Hunt. He saw no reason to hurry, and the driver seemed strangely proud to have his original journey interrupted by this unexpected mission. Their captive, apparently resigned to his fate, didn't talk at all during the trip.

Greeley and Merivale

Horace Greeley's position as owner and editor of the New York Tribune gave him both wealth and political power, and in years past, he repeatedly demonstrated his willingness to use those assets to protect himself against threats. Merivale knew that Greeley would see today's news as such a threat.

For the last half-minute, Greeley said nothing, energetically cleaning the lenses of his eyeglasses with erratic movements that betrayed his worried thoughts. Now he turned his eyeglasses over and held them up, looking for a spot or smear to challenge him to begin the cleaning anew. Apparently satisfied, he returned the cleaning cloth to his vest pocket and perched the eyeglasses on his nose. "You said nothing about planning to kill Anderson."

Arthur Merivale sipped his tea and waited patiently. He understood that his news had been unwelcome, and he could see that Greeley needed time to absorb it, and to determine a response. Greeley's jerky movements indicated to Merivale that emotions, rather than thoughtful contemplations, were still guiding that response.

"You said that you had everything under control," continued Greeley. "Now this happens."

Merivale could predict the course of this conversation. In his many years of negotiation, he had been through countless similar conversations. There would be the indignant protests of offended morality, followed by the claims of personal innocence, and then the demand for guarantees of legal protection. At this point, they were still working through the first stage of the talking. There would be more irrelevant noises to come.

"I can't be implicated in this. I know – knew – Anderson. If people suspected my involvement with this in any way, I'd be ruined. Do you hear me? Ruined!"

Merivale studied the man. Horace Greeley competed ferociously in business, yet the white whiskers that framed his round face gave him an almost saintly air. The conditions of this blustery January day certainly justified Greeley's trademark full-length coat and brightly colored umbrella, however Merivale knew that they would be present on the hottest of July afternoons also. Eccentricity and genius frequently rode hand in hand.

Greeley continued in a firmer, commanding voice. "You must assure me that no-one will know of our conversations."

Merivale savored the faint tickle of the steam wafting from the surface of his tea. He disliked milk and sugar in the drink, believing that they polluted the fragrance and taste of the elegant herb. The time to steer this conversation to a safe harbor arrived. He replaced his cup onto the patterned china saucer. "You have that assurance. Our discussions remain private. As far as I know, nobody at the scene anticipated Anderson's death. The people there exceeded their orders. However, that won't alter the eventual outcome."

"But the man is dead!"

"Yes, he is. That unfortunate fact hasn't made my life any easier either but, as I said, it doesn't change the schedule of events."

"How did he die?"

"I don't have those details. I'm sure that Her Majesty's Government would regret the death of Anderson if asked, but since we had nothing to do with the events of Sunday night then our hands are clean in the matter."

"If they trace this to you then I could be…"

"There is nothing to trace. I didn't instruct these people in what to do."

The attaché from the British embassy spoke the truth. The orders for the fatal meeting with Anderson came to the killers from a place where the authority of the United States government had been somewhat restricted for a number of years.

Merivale understood Greeley's concerns, but the ship had already sailed, and there were no lifeboats for those whose nerve would fail at an unexpected death. The lure for the newspaperman had been too hard to resist. The removal of Abraham Lincoln from the White House would not be fatal for the nation, but it would provide Greeley with headlines for months to come.

The editor twirled the teaspoon in his cup for a half minute before speaking again. "What did they find there? Notebooks or letters or anything I can use?"

"I imagine the men would have destroyed anything they found there. Carrying around unpublished editorials would be dangerous."

"You promised…"

"I promised you nothing from the Washington Herald. You already have a good working knowledge of the plan, and you will have all of the documents that you need at the end of the week when the thing is done. It is agreed that you will see everything and then have access to all of the papers at that point."

"If I possessed more information beforehand, then I will be able to complete my tasks sooner."

"You will still be the first to know it all. You will have everything laid out for you while your rivals will be working with rumors and wild theories."

"Sometimes rumors can be enough."

"I can't give you something I don't have. For today, there is only that message from your friends. They thought you needed to know about Anderson."

"You won't tell me the names of these people. I would not count them as my friends."

Merivale did not respond to the comment. If Greeley knew the identity of his silent partners in this venture then he might pull out of the arrangement, and that would be unfortunate.

"They want my support don't they?" continued Greeley. How can they succeed without me?"

"Your assistance in the months to come will be of great benefit to them," agreed Merivale. "Yet there are others whose reach is almost as great as yours. Perhaps Mr Reid would…"

"No! That would not be possible. We all know Reid's politics. He would not be open to this. I am the best choice for these people. Yet you don't give me all of the details. Come now. I can understand why Britain is happy to conduct the orchestra, but tell me, who wrote the music? Obviously our friend Hamlin will benefit the most, but we both know he is not the energetic type of thinker who could put this scheme together. I'd be looking at General Fremont perhaps, or maybe even friends of Stephen Douglas carrying out a vendetta on the late senator's behalf. What do you say to that?"

This conversation could become uncomfortable. "Unfortunately the complete history of these proposals is not clear to me either," lied Merivale. "You will need to trust me for the moment."

Greeley considered his options. It may be that the Washington police would see Anderson's death as a simple robbery, but he had not risen so far by letting other people determine the course of events. He resolved to take some precautions. "More tea?"

Merivale accepted the offer and their talk drifted onto other topics.

Meeting Schultz

Hunt felt quite gratified that the patrolmen in the stationhouse, who ignored him when he first arrived for duty earlier that morning, should now respond so eagerly to his demand for assistance. Hunt couldn't wait to show his trophy to Schultz. The sergeant at the charge desk recognized the prisoner immediately. "If it isn't our old friend Adam Picard. What have you been doing now?"

"Caught him at the Washington Herald," explained Hunt with a satisfied tone. "Murder and robbery."

"Murder! I didn't kill no one! They left the door open. I went in there looking for stuff!"

"Explain it to the Judge," said the sergeant tiredly. "Well done there Detective - Hunt wasn't it? Captain Price told me you'd started with the men upstairs. That's a good start for your first day. I'll look after Picard if you want to tell the captain what's happening. He's upstairs."

"I never killed no-one," pleaded Picard. "I gone an' trapped meself in that room, an' I couldn't get out. I falls asleep. I didn't kill nobody!"

Hunt ignored Picard's protestations and bounded up the stairs two at a time. Sure enough, Price congratulated Hunt once he heard the news, and introduced Hunt to the other detectives, telling them all that Hunt showed them 'How It Should Be Done'. Hunt felt awkward that his first meeting with the other detectives should be at their expense, but they didn't seem too concerned. Murphy scarcely raised his head from his newspaper, while Osborne grunted then went back to sharpening a pencil with a knife. Only Sloan listened until Price finished his speech.

"Can you finish this one up today?" asked Price. "Sergeant Hawkins will help with the paperwork."

"Fine by me, Captain. Got anything a little more difficult for my next case?"

"Git out of here," retorted Price with good-natured disgust. "Reckon I did the right thing putting you with Schultz. The two of you seem a proper match for each other."

Hunt walked back downstairs to where Sergeant Hawkins addressed a gaggle of patrolmen clustered around his desk. Hunt caught the sergeant's eye and explained his requirements.

"Can't help you right now," answered Hawkins. "Maybe you could get some coffee or something. I'll fix up the forms and you can sign them later."

Hunt felt on top of the world. He walked out of the stationhouse and found a cafe where a few of his remaining coins bought him an early lunch. Even the sun managed to poke its way through the heavy clouds, almost in celebration of his victory. The lunchbreak led into a detour to a barber. Hunt intended to have his hair trimmed sometime this week, and he figured that a long lunch would be a fair reward for the morning's success.

The barber bordered a drygoods store, and Hunt kept out of the rain for a while looking through the range of hats on offer. Maybe he could now afford to buy a new one and let the pawnbroker keep the old Stetson. Ten minutes of inspecting the goods on offer helped him decide that purchase could wait for his second payday, and as he turned to leave Osborne, one of the detectives he met that morning, entered the store. That encounter gave him a good opportunity to talk with his fellow detective, and the two men retired to the Jefferson saloon to become better acquainted. Three hours had passed before Hunt returned to the station.

Sergeant Hawkins had the forms ready for signing. Hunt had barely laid down the nib when Schultz walked through the front door. Hunt took Price's original note from his pocket and nonchalantly passed it across to his partner. "The captain told me to give you this, but you left in such a hurry that I needed to look after the case myself."

Schultz scanned it before passing it back. "Price saw me in the lockup after you'd gone. Reckon I didn't give you much chance to tell me about that case. You'd gone by the time I arrived at the Herald."

Hunt felt his smirk returning. He struggled to keep his voice even.

"It doesn't matter now. I caught Picard and it's all done and dusted."

"You caught Picard there? Adam Picard?"

Hunt's widening grin gave Schultz his answer. Schultz gave a slow sideways glance at Sergeant Hawkins writing at his desk then, with a jerk of his head, led Hunt across to a corner of the room. "You're new at this, Hunt," he said quietly. "I should let it explode in your face."

Very well. If Schultz wanted to be a poor loser, then Hunt saw no problem in twisting the knife. "There's nothing to explode, Schultz. I caught Picard red-handed."

"That's what you say. Has he confessed?"

"He reckons he found the front door open. Says he walked in and then accidentally locked himself in the storeroom. He'll change his story. Only a matter of time."

"Time's on his side Hunt. When Price finds out you haven't a case here, he'll chew off your left one."

Hunt bristled under the attack. "I caught the man!"

"You caught a nobody," corrected Schultz. "Picard is a low-life who makes a living sticking his nose through any unlocked door, and selling what he finds there. He's been through three convictions for theft, and twice that many cases that haven't been proven. Any unlocked door will do for Picard, but murder isn't his style. Did you check his record?"

"No. Sergeant Hawkins was…"

"If you had, then you would have seen that Picard has never committed a crime of violence. Did you see Anderson's body?"

"No. Dawson offered to…"

"Anderson stood six foot six and weighed in at well over two hundred pounds. Picard is five foot nothing and half Anderson's weight, yet according to your theory, he overpowered and tied up the victim before killing him. Did you check the bedroom?"

"No. Tom and Mister Hackett…"

"Then you haven't found the motive. How did Picard get in?"

"Broke the back window and reached in to unlatch the door."

"Yet all the glass from that broken window landed in the back yard. There wasn't a shard inside the office. Looked to me like somebody broke that window from the inside. Come on Hunt, how do you explain that?"

Hunt stopped and let his thoughts backtrack over the morning. He could still see the sparkles of glass littering the back courtyard. He hadn't checked inside the office, but surely he would have seen the glass on the floor if it had been there. Hunt felt his cheeks flushing red with embarrassment. "How the hell should I know? Maybe that negro woman cleaned it up."

Schultz shook his head. "Bessie arrived late that morning, and when she arrived Hackett told her to touch nothing. Did you check in the neighboring yards?"

"No."

"There's only two ways out from the back yard and the intruders used neither one."

Hunt had his dander up right and proper now. Schultz's high-faluting questions didn't matter two beans, when he had the suspect locked up in the cells. "Give it up Schultz. You're guessing all of this."

"I never guess, Hunt. Explain this!"

Schultz's fingers were inches from Hunt's face, and they held something that Hunt hadn't seen before. A lapel pin, surmounted by an engraved triangle encasing an open eye.

"I found that on the floor of the bedroom, Hunt. It opens up a whole new book of questions about the reason for murdering Anderson, but I won't bother going through that conversation right now. You have a report to write. Don't let me hold you up."

Schultz stood back to let the younger man pass. Hunt saw his case in tatters, shredded by Schultz's superior logic. He yearned to sink his fist deep into Schultz's expressionless face, and feel the man's cheekbones crack beneath his knuckles. The urge bubbled and simmered inside him. Things were simpler in the army. You rode men hard, but you treated them fair. Schultz would prefer to let Hunt fail. He saw Schultz turning away, leaving him alone in his confusion. "Wait!"

Schultz waited. Hunt mentally ran through the points made by his so-called partner. He couldn't escape the conclusion that those facts made him into a gone sucker.

"If it wasn't Picard…"

"It wasn't."

"Then why was he there?"

"He's already told you. Check his record. Three convictions for theft and he made a complete confession in both cases where the patrolman caught him red-handed. In the other case, he owned the crime when his fence named him. There's no hidden motive. He's a small potato who's fallen into a very hot stew."

Hunt felt his stomach churning. The bitter pill caught in his throat, but he had to swallow it. He looked at Schultz, feeling his own heavy breath struggling through his lungs. "You're good at this, Schultz."

Schultz brushed aside the compliment. "I do my job."

Hunt looked past Schultz and swallowed uncomfortably. Captain Price asked for the case report to be finished by tomorrow. Schultz proved that Hunt possessed no case. He needed to ask Schultz for help. "What should I do now?"

Schultz laughed. It wasn't malicious, but it sounded like the laugh of a man who'd been asked how to boil water. "Hunt, you're heading for a fall. Trouble is, Price listed this case for both of us. I'm not one for taking home stray kittens, but my name's on the line here, and I'll not throw away my reputation in order to teach you a lesson."

"You'll help me then?"

The cannonball head moved from side to side. "No Hunt. You'll help me. I'll take the case back but it's my case from here on. We'll do it my way."

"We?"

"Only for this case, Hunt. Only for this case."

The men stared at each other for a full ten seconds. Hunt craved the victory; needed to know he made the right choice in arresting Picard. Schultz's unblinking liquid eyes stared back, denying him that answer. Hunt had to acknowledge the corn and take his lashes. His head sunk in a brief nod of acquiescence and he followed Schultz up the stairs to the detective's room. His imagination could hear Sergeant Hawkins's laughter echoing around the room. At least Schultz spared him a public shaming.

It took the senior detective ten minutes to outline the major points of the crime. There were three men involved apart from the unfortunate and irrelevant Picard. The misleading broken window at the rear of the office gave the only sign of a forced entry. The intruders tied up Anderson, then tortured and killed him. Opened drawers and scattered clothes showed where they searched the private quarters, but Mister Hackett and Tom reported the safe still held the petty cash and other valuables that were stored there.

"Then they didn't get the safe open?"

Schultz lifted his eyes from his notes and looked condescendingly at Hunt. "They opened the safe. They closed it again to make it appear as if it hadn't been opened."

"You're gues…" Hunt bit off his comment. Painful experience showed that he needed to respect Schultz's pronouncements of fact. "How do you know they opened the safe?"

Schultz passed a half sheet of business notepaper with a charcoal smear along the ragged edge of the last inch. Hunt examined both sides of the paper before he looked up at Schultz. "It's burnt."

"Hackett found that in a stack of papers when he opened the safe."

"Caught in the safe door! The fire destroyed the bit outside the safe."

"Exactly. Ask yourself, why would a letter be sitting half in and half out of a locked safe? If you'd seen Anderson's private rooms you'd have observed - probably observed - he presented as a man of neat and tidy habits and unlikely to treat his own business papers with such disdain. Can you imagine an employee treating his master's important documents so badly? I don't think so. More likely one of those ruffians carelessly slammed the door shut with that letter still partially exposed. Give it back now. I need to reread these letters then return them to Hackett."

"Why didn't they take the money from the safe?"

"It would seem that they weren't looking for money, and if their motives did not include petty theft then we can rule Picard out as one of the perpetrators. They tied up Anderson and tortured him to pass over the key to the safe. When they finished searching it they lit a fire to burn the building and incinerate Anderson's body, thereby covering their tracks."

"The building didn't burn."

Schultz chuckled and waved a lecturing finger in the air. "They may have been experienced burglars, but were only amateur arsonists. The papers they piled on the floor burned, but without sufficient heat to set the boards on fire. I suspect they poured printer's spirit on the floorboards, but mayhap the solution had been diluted and afforded the fire no assistance.

They'd have seen the fire start before leaving, but it only burned for a few minutes before dying out, so their crime scene remained largely intact."

"What about the lapel pin?"

Schultz tossed it on the desk. Hunt reached over to pick it up. The workmanship of the pin and device seemed superior to the everyday pieces of costume jewelry Hunt encountered previously.

"That symbol is the mark of a secret society called the Illuminati. Don't be surprised if you haven't heard of them. Not many people have. They don't advertise themselves."

"They've got lapel pins? Can't be much of a secret society if they go round wearing those pins."

Schultz's voice became more precise. "The pin is worn behind the lapel," he explained. "It is only revealed after the members have exchanged a particular handshake and performed other rituals of identification."

Schultz's schoolmaster tone irked Hunt. How the hell could he know where these people wore their pins? With an effort, he controlled his temper and tried to resume the original conversation.

"You think the murderers dropped the pin? Then we'll get a list of the members and find which one's missing their pin."

"The Lodgemaster's loyalty lies with his members, not with the law."

"That doesn't mean their lodge would protect them. This is murder."

"The Illuminati is more than a lodge. They are the guiding power behind dozens of lodges. They control the Alumbrados in Spain and the Societas Rosicruciana in England and France. They have many names, but it's the same skeleton under different skins. Murder means nothing to them."

Hunt couldn't see how to take the conversation any further. His own father joined the Freemasons before his death, but that seemed merely an excuse for a monthly meeting with neighbors and perhaps a few jars of applejack at the end of it. There appeared no harm in it.

"Well I've never heard of them. I'll allow I'm not a reading man, but it seems to me they couldn't be that all-fired powerful without the government figuring it out."

"If a government opposes them then they simply melt away and reform under a new name. It happened years ago when the Tugendverein were banned in Prussia. They reappeared as the Concordists within twenty years and are still going strong today."

Schultz rattled off those facts as if they were the news of last week's battles in Virginia, but his words didn't improve Hunt's understanding of the matter. He couldn't see how it related to a dead man up on Eleventh Street.

"So how do we contact these lodge people?"

"I'll work on it. Leave that to me."

"What should I do now?"

Schultz checked his watch. "I'd be obliged if you'd call at the Baltimore and Ohio depot next to the Capitol. The Baltimore Flyer is due there in an hour. Jane Anderson is the murdered man's daughter. She'll be getting off that train and expecting you to meet her. There's a reservation at the Belvedere Hotel in her name."

"A daughter?"

"The son is missing in combat, so she's the only relative."

"That's a breakthrough. She might know something."

"Perhaps. I sent her a message from the Herald's offices this morning. She confirmed her arrival time by return wire. Quite a prompt response for a woman I thought. Take this file. You can read it at the station."

Hunt took the file and gathered up his coat. "I'd best get moving then." He reached the door before he realized the import of Schultz's planning.

"Schultz ... you wired her this morning that I would meet her at the depot?"

"Yes."

"But you sent that wire before you saw me downstairs. You were planning this before I agreed to do things your way."

Schultz didn't speak. There was no need to speak. Hunt punched his fist against the doorframe, then spun on his heel and left, slamming the door behind him.

Meeting Jane Anderson

In 1835, the Baltimore and Ohio Railroad opened the North Capitol depot as the first railway station in Washington. The Washington Board of Aldermen initially required the steam trains to stop outside the city limits, and a team of horses would then pull the carriages to the depot. In 1864, almost 30 years after the depot opened, the railway still possessed little more than a single track and a few sheds, but the trains now rattled and smoked their way right up to the Capitol with confidence. A second depot also serviced Washington now, up on New Jersey Avenue and C Street, but the original terminus sat closest to the government offices, and its waiting room saw more politicians than any other depot in America. Diplomats, businessmen and other citizens all travelled to Washington to do business for one cause or another. This terminus had seen them all, and she treated all of her visitors with the same indifference.

Hunt reached the North Capitol depot in time to see the Baltimore Flyer moving at a fast walk along the single rail line that snaked in from Baltimore. Three volumes of assorted people, with an engine and a caboose for bookends. People on the platform were walking back and forth, eager to spot their visitor through the windows of the train. The baggage smashers waited with their hand trucks, trying to guess which passengers would give the biggest tip for the smallest baggage.

Jane Anderson. Daughter of John Anderson. Sister of William Anderson. The remains of the brother lay in an unmarked grave somewhere on the fields of Shiloh. Sergeant William John Anderson went into the Hornet's Nest with the rest of his regiment, but never came out. His name did not appear on the Confederate list of prisoners exchanged after the battle. No one recorded his grave.

Hunt hadn't been at Shiloh, but he'd been at Antietam. He killed his first Confederate on that day, a screaming bearded apparition that lurched like a broken puppet when Hunt's rifle punched a lump of lead into its chest. That battle ended with a march through Pennsylvania and back to Washington in time for Hunt to receive confirmation of his battlefield promotion to Lieutenant. Then, in the middle of 1863, Lieutenant Hunt went south on a patrol across the Rappahannock to scout the Confederate Army and record its deployment. Five men went south with him. Only Hunt came back.

Hunt jerked himself back to the present and looked around. The train arrived. He pushed himself off the rough wooden wall against which he leant. Flakes of whitewash stuck to his palms and he irritably rubbed them away. His eyes tuned out parties of men by themselves and examined other possibilities. Two soldiers and a woman. An old man and a woman. A woman with two children. Had Jane Anderson been married? Then her name would no longer be Anderson. Did she have children? Harrison cursed himself for not confirming these facts with Schultz.

Three women together. Another woman by herself, but far too old. He could see a woman talking to a railway official not ten yards distant from where he stood. Maybe thirty years old, carrying a carpetbag in one hand and a handkerchief in the other. She turned and walked down the platform. Hunt set out in pursuit, confident his longer stride would catch her within twenty seconds. He caught up with her, and raised his hand in greeting when she walked through a doorway, and Hunt found himself standing outside the women's Necessary. He hesitated for a second, and in that moment an elderly woman emerged, glaring at him for standing outside a room whose existence no one acknowledged in polite company.

Hayes moved to one side to let her pass, and then walked down the platform for another five yards to avoid further confrontation. He resisted the urge to look up at the doorway. A patrolman could arrest him for standing here. He'd heard of toilet lurkers before. He had nothing in common with them.

None would question his authority if he pinned his badge to his coat, but he didn't want to draw attention to himself. For the moment, he held the badge hidden in his hand. On the other side of the platform, a whistle screamed and white clouds spread upwards as the train vented its remaining steam. Women could take forever in those rooms.

"Detective Hunt?" The soft voice slipped through his head, and he spun around to see the face. The woman standing before him wasn't the one he followed down the platform. This one would stand five feet three inches in her stockinged feet, and Hunt suddenly knew an unexpected desire to see those stockings. His hands jerked together, crushing his badge between his clenching fingers.

"Jane Anderson?"

A rumble of steam escaping from the engine drowned her reply, but the tilt of the head and the gentle smile on her lips gave him all the answer that he needed. She wasn't wearing black as Hunt expected. Doubtless, her rushed trip from Baltimore made such preparations impossible.

"I'm Harrison - Detective Harrison Hunt, ma'am."

The lips moved over sparkling teeth, and her words flowed through the air between them. "It's Miss Anderson, Detective Hunt. I'm not married. Thank you for meeting me."

"Ahhh, of course not - my apologies - you're welcome Miss Anderson."

Hunt extended his hand for her carpetbag and felt the cool cotton of her glove glide across his palm as she passed it across. Her parasol moved gracefully to her other hand as she turned to walk down the platform with him. Hunt knew what his next two sentences were going to be, but after that, he didn't know what to say.

"Was your trip pleasant, Miss Anderson?"

"Pleasant enough under the circumstances, thank you. The train stopped once for rumors of Confederate raiders, but I have no complaints about the ride."

"And you are booked at the Belvedere Hotel?"

A graceful nod of her head gave him his reward. His fingers ached to stroke her cheek. Would she stop and talk with him?

"Would you stop and talk with me?"

The words hung in the air between them. She turned with a quizzical look and a half smile on her face.

"I mean after you've tidied - after you - when we get to your hotel. I can wait downstairs."

The smile formed itself into a small pout and her head tilted slightly. A ray of sunlight washed over her face and came back, somehow strengthened, into the day. "I am of course, at your service Detective Hunt. I have come here to arrange my father's affairs" - the light in her eyes clouded for a beat, but her voice never faltered - "but I will do whatever I can to help you catch these people. If you are in such a hurry, then perhaps you are close to finding them?"

The restrained hope in her voice poured guilt on Hunt. He had said too much of what he wanted, and too little of what she needed. "We have some ideas, but it will wait until tomorrow. Perhaps I can talk to you at say, nine in the morning? I - we - will call on you at the Belvedere."

She smiled again. Her carpetbag moved to his left hand of its own volition, and Hunt found himself offering her his arm. The parasol fluttered and her arm rested in his. They moved down the platform together where Hunt's badge gave them the first hackney on the rank. The trip took no time and the cab waited outside the Belvedere Hotel while Hunt saw her checked in and settled. He thought of tarrying and asking to meet her over dinner, but in the end he took the cab straight back to the stationhouse. Hunt saw no conflict of duty in pursuing a friendship with Jane Anderson while solving this case.

He knew he lacked skill in relationships, and often ruined any developing affinity with a careless word or a thoughtless act. Some men played the game with skill and nonchalance and repeated success. Hunt did not count himself among their number, but that didn't stop him trying.

When Hunt returned to the police station, he found only Schultz and Murphy, each engrossed with their case files. An open bottle of beer stood on the desk, close by Murphy's hand. Hunt took off his coat and flung himself into the chair beside Schultz's desk to report his success. Schultz tapped a pencil on the desk as he listened. The tapping annoyed Hunt, but he ignored it as best as he could. "She seems keen to help us."

"I would think so. Her father is dead. It would be curious indeed if she did not want to help us."

The tension in their conversation frustrated Hunt. On one hand, he strongly resented Schultz's treatment of him like a schoolyard brat. Yet he intensely desired to know the thoughts of the other detective. Since Schultz showed no sign of interest in talking further, it fell to Hunt to keep the conversation going. "What else has happened with this case?"

Schultz regarded him gravely and Hunt felt a level of patronizing amusement in the reply. "Happened? Nothing has happened. I have made further inquiries, and they will generate their answers in due course. For the moment, my attention is on another matter."

Hunt could think of no answer to that. He felt like the bootblack who finished the final spit and polish on the master's shoes, and received his penny in return. He determined to keep his temper, and tried another tack. "I told Miss Anderson we would see her at the Belvedere at nine tomorrow morning."

"That's appropriate."

"Did you want me to do the questioning?"

"I don't think so, Hunt. Your knowledge of police procedure is too rudimentary. You'll oblige me by staying silent during the interview."

Another rebuff. Hunt decided to cut his losses and go home. Before he could move, the door opened and Ridley pushed his nose into the room. "Mister Schultz, there's a fellow downstairs to see you. A Mister Singleton he is. Finely dressed fellow and all. Says he sent you a note."

Schultz turned to Ridley. "He did indeed, Ridley. Send him up."

Ridley gave a half salute of acknowledgment and retired, closing the door behind him. Hunt waited, uncertain whether he should remain for this next meeting. Murphy's voice broke the silence. "James Singleton the banker?"

"The same," replied Schultz. "Do you have business with him?"

"Not yet. Though I fancy I'll be serving a Treasury warrant on him one day. He's not too fond of paying his taxes."

"Mayhap he's bringing us a check to settle accounts. Hunt, you'll oblige me with the use of that chair for my guest. Stay if you want. There's no secret business here of which I'm aware."

Hunt scrambled to his feet as Ridley returned with their visitor.

"Mister Singleton," he announced, and once again left, closing the door behind him.

Their new arrival presented as a neat and tidy man. A sharply creased linen collar showed above his dark silk cravat and gold pin. His noble and dignified face, with its closely trimmed moustache and wire-framed spectacles, showed a life of no less than three score years. A fresh and finely woven woollen suit spoke of easy access to money. He spoke in a soft and cultivated voice. "Good day to you Detective Schultz."

"And to you, Banker Singleton," replied Schultz, rising to his feet and extending a hand. "You have met Detective Murphy before, but you are not yet acquainted with Detective Hunt, the newest member of our band."

"A pleasure sir, a pleasure," replied Singleton, shaking hands with Schultz, then Murphy, and finally placing his cold, flaccid palm in Hunt's hand. Hunt let go of the man's limp palm as quickly as possible, and resisted the urge to wipe his own hand on the leg of his pants. Instead, he moved aside to let the visitor sit down. Singleton arranged himself in the chair beside Schultz's desk and folded his greatcoat in his lap.

"You helped my bank in the Yeovill affair of two years past, Detective Schultz, and I found myself most impressed with your work. Very efficient. Very precise. Most unlike the work of many of our other public servants. You didn't retrieve all of the money, but I can't fault you for that."

"I'm glad we could help. I recall that at the time you offered to provide a gift to the Policeman's Benevolent Fund."

"Ah yes," replied Singleton, biting his lip and waving a dismissive hand. "The banking business has been poor these past few years sir, quite poor indeed. This war, you understand."

His voice trailed off and he sat for a moment, blinking rapidly. Schultz's wandering fingers found a pencil and began a rhythmic tapping on the desk. Both men speaking together broke the momentary silence.

"How can we..."

"You see, Detec..."

Schultz indicated for the visitor should speak first. Singleton refolded his hands over his greatcoat and began. "I am a man of some repute in this town, sir. It is by much hard work, and the smallest of profits, that I keep my clients. I could tell you their names, and you would be impressed sir, most impressed, but there are such things as confidences sir, professional confidences."

Singleton tapped the side of his nose twice to indicate the high degree of importance he placed on these issues. Schultz bowed his head slightly in apparent agreement and kept bouncing the end of his pencil off the desk as Singleton resumed speaking.

"Now here is the mystery for you, sir. Last month I received an invitation to the president's charity ball for this coming Friday and, of course, I expected it. Normally the President entertains on a Tuesday evening, but this is a fund-raising event and changes were made to attract more patrons. I have been to these events before, you understand. Quite a regular guest, I am. This town knows James Singleton quite well indeed, sir. At first, I thought I could not attend. Business in Philadelphia needed my attention. We have a branch office there, of course. We have branches in Philadelphia, New York, Washington of course, with another branch soon in - well it wouldn't do to say. Business is business."

"I told my clerk to decline the invitation, which he did late last week. Then this morning I discovered that affairs in Philadelphia do not need me until Wednesday week. So I sent a message to the Executive Mansion to say I could attend this Friday after all, and you won't believe what they said."

Singleton paused. It may have been for dramatic effect, but his immediate resumption of the narrative spoiled the theatrical moment. Hunt took the chance to glance at Schultz. A genial smile floated on his lips as if to encourage the progression of the man's story. The tapping pencil in his fingers showed as the only disturbance in his silent, statue-like poise.

"They said I already paid, and assured me of my reserved place at the top table! I protested I wouldn't pay for such a thing. You probably haven't been to these events, and don't realize the way they are organized, but there are different grades of seating. To dine at the top table requires a donation of perhaps thousands of dollars to charity. Middle seating may require a gift of hundreds of dollars or so, but I never bother with those seats. I have the same food and meet the same people for only, well, for a smaller amount. Yet they wrote that I secured a seat near the President as requested. I never requested it, I tell you!"

Singleton paused, and looked expectantly at Schultz. The detective's response came at a leisurely pace. "I don't see the problem. If you don't want the seat, then let them know, and I am sure they'll sell it to someone else."

"There is the problem. "They say they already have the money and have issued the ticket. A thousand dollars sir, for a ticket in my name!"

"Where is the ticket then?"

"I don't know! They issued a receipt to a James Singleton of Singleton's Bank for one thousand dollars, and someone paid for it and took the ticket. They will go to the banquet pretending to be me, and who knows what business they will do there."

"Did the money come from your purse?"

"Heaven's no!" exclaimed Singleton. "I can account for all of my cash, and all of the bank's funds. I assure you that the money came from neither of those places."

"Then to me, it seems like a simple confusion in their bookings. I cannot see a law broken. Those banquets are there to raise money for charity. If someone else is willing to pay a thousand dollars of their own money to sit near the President, then I cannot see why the President, the charity or you should be concerned. By your own admission, you are a well-known man in those circles, so I doubt you should fear someone would misrepresent himself as you. What do you think, Murphy?"

The Irishman had been worrying a fingernail with his teeth. He paused in the assault, and regarded the offending cuticle carefully. His relaxed demeanor indicated he didn't see much of a problem with Singleton's issue.

"I'd say Schultz is right with that. Someone's surely made a fine mess of the receipts. Get Monohan to look at it."

"There will be guests there who don't know me. New people who have only recently arrived in Washington. I wouldn't want them confused."

"You'll need to speak to Bill Monohan then. He looks after those things at the White House. He doesn't work out of this stationhouse, but the sergeant downstairs will know how to contact him. We also have one of our own assigned to protect the President on these occasions. John Parker his name is. You'll need to talk to one of them."

"Then you'll not help me? My good name is at stake here."

"Show us the felony and we'll investigate it! As yet, we have no crime."

Singleton shook his head, clearly amazed at Schultz's refusal to assist him.

"I'm sure it is a simple error," continued Schultz, standing to escort Singleton to the door. "Either way, it's Monohan's responsibility to investigate such things. But while you're here, did you want more information about the address of the Policeman's Benevolent Fund?"

The subtle prompt worked. Singleton gathered his coat and left without another word. Schultz waited until the footsteps faded down the corridor then gave a low chuckle. "I hope the Fund isn't desperate for that check."

"It wouldn't have too many zeros on it I'm sure," laughed Murphy. "I'll be seeing Monohan tomorrow after work. I'll give him the story, in case 'tis something to all of this. Remind me about t'other case then. Didn't Yeovill get away?"

"Went to Europe with a couple of thousand dollars in cash. We stopped the rest of the money before Yeovill could move it offshore. He'd sent it by third class mail to England. A risky move perhaps, but fairly safe from casual inspection."

"Ah, that's it," exclaimed Murphy, snapping his fingers with the recollection. "'Twas that handwriting thing. Couldn't see the difference in the signatures meself, but you was right enough."

"That's yesterday's news. For the moment, I'm content to let Monohan do the worrying about who sits where at a White House dinner party."

Schultz turned to Hunt. "We get all sorts in here. If the duty sergeant isn't sure, he sends them up to us. Singleton is a small-time banker who thinks he's God's gift to Washington. Fond of his pennies perhaps, but still harmless. Frankly I can do without hearing his problems, but being a detective means upholding the law, all of the law..."

"...not just the parts we like," broke in Murphy. "Yes. Yes. We know that, Schultz. Heard it all before."

"You disagree?"

"Surely not," said Murphy, reaching for his beer. "Just tired of hearing you say it."

Schultz closed the folder on his desk and reached for his coat. "I'll be back here at a quarter after eight in the morning, and then we'll see Miss

Anderson at the Belvedere. Tomorrow may bring us some better information."

Hunt gathered up his own coat and followed Schultz out into the evening air. The rising wind bit at his face as he turned for home.

The Belvedere Hotel then the Docks

Yesterday, white fluffy borders softened the edges of the massed gray clouds. Today's clouds were missing those borders. The clouds hung low and heavy, and the air smelt of the returning storm. Hunt knew the bitter wind would soon return but, for the moment, he enjoyed the stillness of the chilled air on his walk to work. The night had been difficult. Sleep eluded him for hours, while he struggled with the unreasonable fear that Schultz would seek his dismissal, then an early morning rooster roused him well before dawn. It would be a long day.

Streets iced over again during the night, and the smooth roads were vicious and deceptive. Fortunately, he'd made an early start, so the leisurely pace required by the iced roads did not create a problem.

At the side of the road, laborers rolled barrels of beer off a cart and into a saloon in preparation for the evening's trade. Hunt endured a few months of that kind of work himself in years past. The breath of the horses steamed in the cold morning air and they stamped the occasional hoof in the mud as the work progressed behind them. He moved on towards the stationhouse, glad that his life now held more meaningful duties.

Clammy brown slime splashed up the legs of those early morning travelers careless enough to put a boot through the surface of ice-covered puddles. Hunt moved carefully across the road, avoiding those traps as he went. The shouts of a nearby huckster selling hot chestnuts started up and faded into the background as Hunt made his way to the stationhouse and then upstairs to the detective's room.

Sloan sat at his desk, still wearing his coat and muffler. Ridley's duties included lighting the fire at six, so the room would be warm by the time the detectives arrived. This morning, the fire grate remained empty and cold. Apparently, Ridley preferred a flexible interpretation of timekeeping.

"Morning Sloan."

A half-hearted grunt emerged from the muffler as Sloan turned the page of his newspaper. Hunt moved to read the headlines over Sloan's shoulder. The other detective stabbed his finger into the page. "Don't see why we can't take Richmond! Grant's got close on a million men, and those darned Confederates are only 75 miles away!"

Sloan had been too young for the Mexican War, and his advancing age protected him against conscription for the current conflict. He never served in uniform, but judging by his comments, he didn't consider that inconvenient fact as a limitation on his strategic genius. Hunt looked at the map displayed in the paper. Washington and Richmond sat at opposite ends of the rough map, and halfway between the two cities sat the Rappahannock River and perhaps the unmarked graves of the five Union soldiers he commanded in his last battle.

"Gather them up and march them south, and the war will be over in a month," fumed Sloan.

"Tried that last May. Lee stopped them at Chancellorsville."

Sloan either didn't recognize, or chose to ignore, the sarcasm.

"Huh! What did you expect with Hooker? If they'd left McClellan in charge, them Confederates would soon have packed it in."

Hunt's eyes drifted across the paper and focused on another article. He smiled to himself. "I see the Senate's going on about slavery again. Now Henderson's talking about abolishing it everywhere."

"Senate's always talking. That's what they're paid to do."

According to Osborne's ramblings in the saloon on the previous afternoon, Sloan owned two slaves, and worried constantly that the government would take them away from him. The Senate abolished slavery in Washington many months previously, whereupon Sloan employed his two former slaves as housekeeper and gardener. Osborne suggested to Hunt that Sloan never told the slaves they were now free.

The door opened and Murphy's voice launched itself into the room. "Sure, 'tis cold enough to freeze a snowman's willy. Where's that fire?"

A muffled thump recorded the landing of Murphy's bag on his chair as the Irishman made his way across the room toward the fireplace. "Ohhh, not again! Ridley!"

Murphy disappeared downstairs to find Ridley. The clock struck the quarter hour, and Hunt moved back to the window. Two troopers on horseback edged their horses around a rubbish cart while mongrel dogs sniffed at the cart's wheels. Hunt stared at the morning. He decided that he would live forever in this city. From the waterfront to the wagon yards, he would learn it all. Other towns from his childhood and younger years were only painful memories now.

Hunt lived in Washington before the war for a few months, but in those days he'd been a private citizen. Now that he carried the badge of a detective he could peer beyond the building facades and see the real lives of the Washington people. He had no time for the politics and the politicians. The commonplace crimes of the commonplace people would be enough for him. He turned back to Schultz's desk to see a familiar shape sitting there, sorting through folders.

"Schultz!"

"Morning Hunt. We leave for the Belvedere in five minutes. Then there's something I need you to do."

"Fine by me."

Captain Price came through the door. Schultz spoke without turning.

60

"Captain, the Halliday case is completed and on your desk for your signature. The burglary at Spauldings is waiting for news from Pittsburg and I still maintain my conclusion about the finances at City Hall."

Price glared at Shultz's back and slumped into a chair. "Tarnation, Shultz! I told you I can't just go to the court and get a warrant for Hobart."

"That's your choice, Captain. I've documented the evidence to convict Hobart, but if you don't want to proceed, then I'll leave the matter as pending."

"I'm telling you to leave it alone now. You've got the newspaper case."

"Hunt is handling that."

"You stay with it also. I'll talk to Superintendent Webb about Hobart."

"Thank you." Schultz stood and faced Price. "I'd like to keep Picard in the cells for a few days."

"Has he confessed yet?"

"No, but I spoke to him this morning, and he's agreeable to staying in the cells for a while."

"Agreeable, huh? I don't think I want to know what you said to him. Get along now. I'll talk to you about Hobart later."

Hunt followed Schultz downstairs and into the street. The wind had risen in the few minutes Hunt spent in the stationhouse, and the first drops of rain were falling. A cab answered their wave. They climbed in, and soon were pushing through the mud to the Belvedere Hotel.

"Who is Hobart?"

Schultz turned to look at Hunt. His head swayed in time to the rocking of the moving cab. "Percival Hobart is a councilman for the waterfront borough. He's married with three children, and he has a close personal relationship with a number of other women apart from his wife. Those relationships are expensive, and he's taken to supplementing his wages by some creative accountancy with the city's money."

Hunt leaned back in his seat. "Why not arrest him?"

"Unfortunately Councilman Hobart has friends in very high places. One of the benefits of his position I suppose, and those friends want this case closed quietly."

"You don't want that?"

Schultz snorted derisively. "I don't care how the courts deal with Hobart, but I do care the case isn't marked 'Unsolved'. I have my failures from time to time, but this wasn't one of them."

The cab lurched to a stop as the driver failed to maneuver around a trio of feral pigs rooting for garbage in the mud of the streets. The pigs ignored the danger from the horse and cab, perhaps having ears only for the sound of a hog-reeve who would gather them for sale and slaughter. The sudden halt forced the passengers to grab the straps to keep their balance, and when the cab resumed its journey, Hunt found that the conversation ended. He sat silent for the rest of the trip digesting their discussion.

He could see that Schultz possessed a thinly disguised contempt for those whose reasoning lagged behind his own. Apart from yesterday's disagreement about working together, Hunt wasn't yet sure how he felt about the man.

"Belvedere Hotel!"

The cabby's shout roused Hunt from his contemplation, and he scrambled from the cab into the rain. Hunt followed Schultz past the deferential doorman and into the lobby, where he knew he would see Jane again. Hunt wore a freshly boiled shirt for this day, and he thoroughly inspected his buckskin coat to remove any splashed mud before travelling to work.

The Belvedere did not pursue the high-spending customers who carried risks of scandal. Its preferred clientele consisted of genteel travellers who desired clean sheets and pleasant food, while avoiding the political dramas that kept Washington turning.

A young negro bellboy faced them. "Morning, Mister Schultz, suh. Nothing to report. I'll tell the lady youse here."

A nod from Schultz dispatched the youth, and Hunt followed his companion to a pair of leather armchairs beside an open fire.

"Nothing to report, suh," mimicked Hunt. "Did you have Miss Anderson watched all night?"

"I instructed Barrington to note whether anyone asked after her. If those ruffians didn't find everything they were after at the Herald, then Miss Anderson is a potential target for their attentions. I thought it best to take precautions."

Once again, Schultz's thinking surpassed what Hunt would have considered. He found it difficult to dislike the older man.

"Consider this," continued Schultz, arranging himself in one of the armchairs. "The criminals were searching for something. Why tie up and torture Anderson unless they were asking him questions? The fact they searched the safe without taking the money showed they sought some physical object, and not merely a piece of information."

Schultz shifted his coat under himself and crossed his legs before continuing. "We know they built the fire from materials found in the office, when it would have been easy enough, and more sensible, to bring their own flammables if the arson had been premeditated. The fact they sought to destroy the evidence of their presence... destroy the evidence... destroy the evidence..."

Schultz's voice trailed off and his eyes lost their focus. Hunt watched him staring into space, with only his regular breathing and the rhythmic tapping of a forefinger on his lips to show his life hadn't ceased. What thoughts were moving through that mind? A minute passed.

"Detective Hunt?"

The soft voice sliding into his ear sent a jolt through Hunt. He jerked to his feet. "Miss Anderson!"

Jane wore mourning clothes today. She stood before them in a gray jacket bodice with a flowing black dress supported by crinolines. Her hazel eyes shone out from the high cheekbones he remembered from yesterday, but the puffy cheeks and red eyes told of her night of lonely grief. "I'm sorry. You startled me."

"I seem to do that a lot."

The slightest of smiles, and a twinkle in her eye tempered her comment. Her eyes moved to his right.

"Miss Anderson. I'm Detective Schultz. You already know Detective Hunt."

Schultz stood beside him now, roused from his contemplation, and Hunt felt control of the conversation move firmly into the other man's hands.

"A pleasure to meet you, Detective Schultz."

"As it is for us to meet you, Miss Anderson," replied Schultz. "I wish it could be under happier circumstances."

Her lips tightened and her chin lifted higher. Hunt could see Jane holding her emotions in check for this meeting. He stepped back to offer her an armchair, but Schultz beat him to it. She settled her skirts around herself and smiled up at the two men. "I should like to know how my father met his... his death," she began. "After that, I am prepared to meet your questions."

Schultz sat in the armchair opposite Jane, leaving Hunt standing at the fireplace. The wood-paneled walls and the dull red carpet combined to give the tableau a rich heavy atmosphere.

"We know very little at this point," admitted Schultz. "Three burglars captured him at his newspaper office, and that's where it happened."

"His office?"

"The Washington Her...", began Hunt, before Schultz's upraised hand bade him keep quiet.

"I thought it happened at home. That is why I stayed here the night. I could not bear the thought of sleeping in the same house where... where..."

"I'm sorry my message wasn't clearer," apologized Schultz. "I should have

64

been more informative."

Jane nodded her forgiveness. "I will return home tonight then. How did father ... what happened?"

"We are waiting on the doctor's report. I fear his heart gave out under the stress."

Her right hand crushed a handkerchief, and Hunt could see her eyes moistening with anguish. "I'm sure it happened quickly," lied Hunt, uncomfortably watching Jane blink away her tears.

"Was your father distressed?" asked Schultz gently. "Did he say anything unusual in these last few weeks?"

Chestnut hair flared around her collar as her head shook twice, three times. "Since I moved to Baltimore we corresponded on alternate weeks. I wrote to him on Friday last, so I know nothing from the last two weeks. He rarely talked business with me. He wrote about family issues, and memories of William, my brother."

Her voice faded as strong emotions surfaced briefly, but then she found her words again. "They never located William after the battle. That hit my father hard. Never knowing for sure. No grave to visit."

Hunt knew that feeling. Sergeant Slater and the rest of the patrol never turned up on the rolls of Confederate prisoners. Hunt never found out what happened to the members of his last command.

"Did your brother's death cause a change in your father's political views?"

"My father had no time for this war, Detective Schultz. He saw no reason in it, and he blamed both sides evenly. I know his business suffered because of that. Readers wanted to know they were fighting for a just cause, and my father never called this war a just cause."

"Was he a Copperhead? If you'll forgive the expression."

"He did not sympathize with the Confederates, sir. He often said those states had the right, but not the reason to leave the Union."

Schultz leaned back in his chair and hooked his thumbs in his waistcoat. The man had a distinct style about himself, decided Hunt. Short and argumentative he might be, but his manner put people at ease.

"Did you know that your father corresponded with George McClellan?"

"No I didn't. I do know the name of course, Detective Schultz. There is talk in Baltimore of General McClellan challenging Lincoln for the presidency in November."

"I have heard that rumor also, Miss Anderson. Did you discuss the General with your father?"

The hair shook again. "No, my father never mentioned him in his letters."

The questions flowed freely from Schultz. Hunt found it difficult to predict the direction of the conversation. Schultz moved between many topics in his interview, and never dwelt too long on any one item before moving on to another subject, or giving a compliment or even rephrasing an earlier question while all the time adding comments into a small notebook.

The picture unfolded of a loving relationship between John Anderson and his daughter. Washington had been her home, but she moved to Baltimore to study, and still lived there with an aunt who provided lodging. The death of her mother brought her back to Washington for a few months, but then she returned to Baltimore. Hunt felt his lack of sleep catching up with him, and needed to stifle a yawn three or four times during the talk.

At length the interview ended and Schultz rose to his feet. "You've been extremely helpful Miss Anderson. How long will you be staying in Washington?"

"I need to attend to my father's affairs. That will keep me in town for at least a week I suspect. Will you keep me informed of what you know?"

Schultz bowed his head in assent. "Detective Hunt will be your main point of contact with us while you are in Washington, Miss Anderson. His calendar is less cluttered than mine."

Jane looked at Hunt. "That would be fine. I feel safe with him around."

Hunt's heart bounded, and he smiled at her. The two men escorted Jane back to the reception desk. With a swish of skirts, she departed, and the detectives left the hotel. The rain set in while they spoke with Jane, and it took the doorman a full ten minutes to find a cab for the trip back to the station. The wind howled around them now, and the darkness of the day set a grim backdrop to the streets. During the short dash from the hotel awning to the shelter of the cab, Hunt managed to get water into his boots from the running streams splashing around the cab wheels.

They settled side by side on the single bench seat, each man instinctively drawing away from his window where the raindrops splashed around the canvas curtains. Hunt looked forward to an opportunity for a rest in front of the fire in the detective's room, and maybe some coffee. Surely Ridley would have lit the fire by now.

"Water street docks first, then the Fifth Precinct stationhouse," called Schultz to the cabby before resuming the silent battle for the center of the seat. The cab pushed into the road and the rain beat into the exposed faces of the two passengers.

"I want you to check on the shipping arrivals," shouted Schultz over the crashing of the rain and the sloshing of the carriage wheels through the mud. "Go to the Dockmaster's office and ask for Albert Lachlan. Tell him I sent you. Get a copy of all movements into the harbor for the seven days before Anderson's death. He'll give you some notepaper, but you'll need to write it out yourself."

"Shipping arrivals?"

"Make sure you get both passenger and freight movements. That's two separate lists."

"Why do we need the shipping arrivals?" challenged Hunt. He could feel that warm fireplace at the stationhouse slipping away. "What do they have to do with this case?"

Schultz turned his body on the seat to look at Hunt. He grimaced in frustration, then spoke in an even voice. "Let me put it to you plainly, Hunt. No event occurs by itself. There is always a reason, and there is usually a consequence. On Saturday and Sunday, the Herald stayed closed. Therefore, the burglars would have planned their visit for Friday night if they wanted the maximum time for their getaway. Yet they waited until Sunday night to attack, so something happened on that day to make the attack both imperative and possible."

"Anderson could have been away on the Friday or Saturday."

"Could have been, but wasn't. He dined alone at Rosselli's on Friday and attended the Palace Theatre with a lady named Beatrice O'Conner on Saturday. He slept at the Herald office on both nights, yet the burglars made no move on him. Therefore, they weren't ready to move until Sunday."

"Wait! How do you know all of this?"

"I visited Rosselli's yesterday at noon, then I spoke with Anderson's lady friend while you were meeting Miss Anderson at the station. The lady is a new acquaintance of Anderson's, so it's quite conceivable he hadn't yet mentioned her to his daughter."

"You think they came into Washington by ship?"

"The evidence so far indicates that is so."

"What evidence?"

"Evidence you would have seen at the Washington Herald if you did your job properly. We're not there now, so I can't show it to you."

Hunt mutely conceded the point, and settled back to endure the ride as best he could. The trip felt long and miserable. The rain stayed heavy, and by the time the cab drew up at the dock, both men were wet and cold from the intrusive sleet. Hunt stepped out of the cab without a word, and it sloshed off into the rain behind him. The gates were open and he found the Dockmaster's office with no difficulty. Hunt entered under its sheltering roof. No one paid attention to him at first. He stopped a passing clerk to ask the whereabouts of Albert Lachlan.

"Can't say. Not upstairs. I've only now come from upstairs and he wasn't there. Try the lunchroom."

Hunt followed the clerk's direction, and found an old man reading a paper spread over the broad table that took up most of the room. "Albert Lachlan?"

It seemed the man hadn't heard. Hunt prepared himself to repeat the question when the white-whiskered head lifted and turned to face him. "Who'd be asking then?"

Hunt moved into the room and shed his still dripping coat. "I'm Detective Hunt. Detective Schultz sent me to talk to you."

At the mention of Schultz's name Lachlan leaned back on his bench and chortled to himself. "Heh heh. You knows I bet meself this morning I'd be hearing from him sometime this week."

"Really?"

"Oh yus, I've been on the docks these forty years, and I knows a wrong 'un when I sees it. That ship's not quite right. Oh, her papers are fine and her cargo's nothing special, but to keep the crew on board like that after crossing the Pond is more than strange."

"Pond?"

"Ah, the Atlantic," answered the man dismissively. Hunt knew he lost some of the man's respect.

"Detective Schultz wanted me to get…"

"I knows! I knows! He wants the berthing books. It's always the same for him, but you tell him he'll be looking at the *Angelique* afore he's finished."

Hunt followed Lachlan back out to the work area and, at the old man's invitation, sat at a vacant desk to jot down the required information. It took a half-hour to complete the simple, but tedious, task. At length, he could stow the list into an inner pocket and return the books.

"Now you be telling Schultz what I said, young fellow," said Lachlan.

"I'll do that sir," replied Hunt deferentially. Letting the old man enjoy his condescending turn of phrase didn't cost much, and could yield valuable information. "Could you point out the *Angelique* to me?"

"I'd say there's no need for me to get wet right now. You'll find her easily enough. She's sitting by herself at Pier Four. She's moved no cargo since she's docked, and there's been no vittles taken on board."

"Maybe they're doing repairs?"

Lachlan snorted derisively. "I doubt that. They'd be carrying half a hold of spares on board since they haven't been near the chandler, nor the wood yard, since they berthed. Yus, I'll wager that's the ship you'll be wanting."

Hunt took his goodbyes and left the office. The rain paused, though dark clouds and the heavy smell of the storm showed it would be a brief respite. Hunt turned towards Pier Four. The *Angelique* sat rocking gently at her berth with her bow pointing downriver to the open sea. The rigging hummed and clanked in the breeze as the ship butted the pier fenders. The fore and aft moorings were secure, the ports shuttered and the hatches firmly battened. There seemed no sign of life aboard. Gold letters across the stern picked out the name *Angelique* above the homeport of 'Brest'.

Hunt resisted the urge to climb aboard the ship and search its secrets. Seagulls sheltered in its rigging, and the wind whipped swell slapped against the hull. As Hunt watched, a shadow detached itself from the foremast. Light from an opened hatch bathed the moving man for an instant until he descended into the ship. The light cut out as the hatch closed. Hunt turned and quickly left the dock. Had the shadow seen him? Would the *Angelique* leave port before Schultz could search it? He cursed himself, feeling like a foolish schoolboy, and ran through the rain until he found a cab to take him back to the stationhouse.

Picard is missing

Hunt found Murphy sitting alone in the detective's room when he arrived back at the station, and the Irishman seemed more interested in the enormous sandwich and bottle of beer on his desk than in making conversation. Hunt, in return, had no problem in leaving the Irishman to his solitary lunch, and settling himself by the fire. The trip back from the docks confirmed Hunt's suspicion that his left boot leaked. His wet sock dripped on the floor as he removed the offending footwear and stretched out his legs towards the warmth of the flames. Dark rain pelted against the windows and the growl of thunder circled the building. This seemed a good time to sit inside.

Hunt inverted his offending boot over the poker stand, and left its partner remained upright close by. He stood up and removed his buckskin coat, draping it over an empty chair, which he turned to face the fire. He hadn't had any lunch yet, but that could wait. The list of shipping arrivals sat in his pocket, well protected from the rain, and he now unfolded the paper then smoothed it flat. Schultz's folders sat in their neat piles. Hunt easily found the Anderson file then added the new paper to its contents. The fire beckoned. He took the folder with him to resume his seat in front of the flames.

The file had grown in the short time since Hunt took it to the railway station on his assignment to meet Jane. Now he had the opportunity to catch up with his partner's thinking. Setting aside the shipping list for the moment, Hunt worked his way through the other papers. The description of the crime scene ran to six pages of notes, interspersed with simple sketches.

The intruders tied Anderson to a chair, indicated by the chafing on his wrists and ankles. Marks on the floorboards showed how they dragged the chair to near a sideboard. Spirit stains on the sideboard around a circular imprint denoted the hand lantern used for illumination. Hackett found Anderson lying on the floor next to his bed, clothed in his nightwear. His body had been untied after his death.

Hunt felt a rising excitement as he followed Schultz's deductions through the pages. He cursed himself for not examining the actual murder scene in detail, but the capture of Picard seemed to end the need for further investigation, and he promised himself not to make that mistake again. Schultz's bland narrative of Picard's interrogation described how the prisoner tried doors along the street until he found one that opened. After entering the Herald office, Picard claimed he lost his bearings in the dim light, almost immediately venturing into the storeroom on the mistaken assumption he had found an inner office. The rest of the page detailed events Hunt already knew, but none of it related to the cryptic note at the bottom of the page where the word "RALLY" sat alone in Schultz's bold copperplate. Hunt read that word repeatedly to himself. It made no sense being there.

Had Schultz decided to cheer up Picard by offering to drop the murder charges? Could that be how he persuaded Picard to agree to stay in the cells for a while longer? He hadn't yet figured out why Schultz wanted Picard to stay in the cells. The man freely confessed to his trespass and intent to steal, but that remained a matter for the courts to settle with a fine or a term in jail. Either way Picard didn't belong in the Fifth Precinct's holding cells.

Hunt shut the folder and stood up. Since Picard remained in the cells he could check the answer with the prisoner himself. He slid the folder slid back onto the desk and tugged on his still damp boots. Murphy's sandwich had disappeared, but the Irishman still held onto his beer with one hand and turned the pages of the journal in front of him with the other. Hunt strode out of the room, cheered by the thought he owned the opportunity to do his own investigation, rather than merely reading Schultz's notes.

He descended to the basement to reach the holding cells. Scars and scrapes on the damp bricks of the corridor to the cellblock showed where prisoners struggled. Three paces down the corridor, Hunt stopped before a massive door of steel bars.

The scene on the other side of the bars took his breath. Dim light from oil lamps gave a faint light to the hallway of cells stretching out before him. Occasional groans and shouts echoed up the corridor and the heavy foul stench of unwashed bodies and open drains clung coldly to the wet bricks. The police could keep their prisoners in these holding cells for an indefinite time before transferring them to a permanent penitentiary. In this scene of human desolation the spirit of a man would be destroyed, not by a sudden conflagration, but by being worn down over weeks and months into dismal subsistence. Yet there were worse hells in Washington.

"Can I help you then?" The unexpected voice at Hunt's side startled him. He turned quickly to face the person who appeared there. A watchman emerged from an unnoticed nook in the wall, and stood there with a ring of keys clasped in his hands. "Sorry to surprise you."

Hunt straightened himself. The Invalid Corp badge on the man's lapel showed his status as a wounded soldier pensioned out of the army. Hunt couldn't imagine this small man ever pulling on a uniform. This inoffensive turnkey should not be able to startle an ex-army man. He found his voice and spoke sternly.

"I'm Detective Hunt. Fetch the prisoner Picard. I need to talk to him."

The turnkey shook his head, and bounced the keyring off his thigh.

"Can't help you there. Picard's not here."

"No, he's here. It's Adam Picard I want. I brought him in yesterday for the Anderson murder."

"That's right, and we released him earlier today."

"Released?"

"Released this morning, as instructed by Detective Schultz."

The man retreated to his annex and retrieved a thick cloth-bound book. Maneauvering the heavy tome to under a sputtering lamp, he pointed to the appropriate entry. Schultz's signature and the terse phrase 'Charges dropped' were inscribed opposite Picard's name. Hunt stared at the words.

"Was there anything else?"

Hunt looked at the man standing there, neatly uniformed with his small moustache and precariously balanced eyeglasses. If not for his IC badge, Hunt would have guessed the man spent his entire working life in this sewer, signing prisoners through the barred gate. The turnkey would treat both Adam Picard and Jefferson Davis with the same efficiency and lack of interest. Asking further questions would not yield additional information. "No."

Hunt walked back through the corridor and into the main police station. Schultz proved Picard hadn't committed the murder, but only this morning Schultz asked for and received permission from Captain Price to keep Picard locked up. Then four hours later, he released him. It made no sense for Schultz to release Picard. Hunt found his way back to the detective's room and resumed his seat in front of the fire. The flames danced before him, but they provided no answer. Patterns formed and dissolved in the heated air, mocking his attempt to see the final resolution of this case. He sat for a long time staring at the flames, until the fatigue of his sleepless night finally claimed him.

Greeley is alarmed

When Henry and Edwin Willard took over the lease for the inn at the corner of 14th Street and Pennsylvania Avenue in 1847, they opened a metaphorical gold mine. Within six years, they did well enough to buy the inn, plus the adjacent land and buildings, from the heirs of the recently deceased owner. Major remodelling of the six contiguous houses followed, to create a hotel that dominated the social landscape in Washington. Abraham Lincoln stayed at the Willard on his first night in Washington following his election victory. Julia Ward Howe penned "The Battle Hymn of the Republic" after sleeping in one of the Willard's rooms. It claimed the reputation as the best Hotel on the eastern seaboard, and charged accordingly. The same rain that hammered down on the Fifth Precinct Police station also vented its fury on the more elegant Willard hotel.

A new summons, arriving so quickly after the previous meeting, surprised Merivale. However, he had no objection in attending another meeting in these halls. The Willard served an excellent blend of tea, and the crackling of the logs in the fireplace gave a comfortable ambiance to the setting. Greeley waited for him in the lounge, and their first two minutes of conversation exhausted discussion about the weather, and allowed other patron's eyes and ears to forget about his arrival.

"I'm afraid I have no further news," said Merivale at last. Greeley's eyes behind the immaculately clean eyeglasses blinked.

"I didn't expect anything from your side. I need to tell you that Anderson's daughter has come to Washington."

Merivale pursed his lips. "They certainly moved quickly. He only died yesterday."

"Too quick. If the detectives ask her the wrong questions..."

"Calm yourself. She knows nothing."

The eyeglasses came off and the cotton cloth stroked the lenses. "How can you be sure? Her father found out. He might have told her."

A passing waiter disturbed their conversation long enough to take an order. Merivale made sure the man moved out of earshot before continuing.

"I'll pass the word to keep a special watch, but I still see nothing to fear. Anderson worked as a newspaperman and his daughter paints portraits. That's chalk and cheese. Why would he tell her what he knew?"

The cleaned eyeglasses were back on Greeley's face now, and framing the unblinking eyes that stared at Merivale. "Anderson's reasons for telling his daughter would not matter. The question is whether he actually did so.

"Very well. I'll pass on your message."

"Tell them not to think of harming her. One death is bad enough. After Friday, it will be different. The police will have far more interesting issues to consider than investigating Anderson's death."

Merivale had no disagreement on that point. He knew that presidents of the United States died in office in both 1841 and 1850, yet the young nation continued onwards to even greater glories. The Constitution provided a process for filling a vacated office, and that process worked well for Henry Harrison and Zachary Taylor. It would work just as well for Abraham Lincoln.

The waiter returned to set their places for tea.

Hunt confronts Schultz

"You have the list?"

Schultz's voice broke into Hunt's slumber. He struggled to escape his wretched dream; he was alone on a ship where every corridor he travelled took him further away from the sounds of Jane screaming. He needed to get to her, but no one would guide him.

"What?"

"The shipping report from the docks. You were meeting Albert Lachlan."

"Oh, the list!"

Hunt hobbled to his feet, massaging the dead muscles of his thighs, as Schultz hung his coat and muffler on a nail in the wall. The afternoon shadows battled their way through the clouds, and Hunt knew he slept in front of the fire for some hours.

"I put the list in your folder. You released Picard. He's gone."

Schultz drew the Anderson folder towards himself as he settled himself in his chair. Murphy had left, but Sloan sat at his own desk writing in a journal. Hunt cursed himself for falling asleep.

"Good work."

"Lachlan said to look for the *Angelique*. He had suspicions about her."

Schultz thrust his tongue behind his top lip and ran it into his left cheek as he perused the list of ships. Finally, he nodded in agreement.

"Yes, that fits. Her, or the *Hill of Grace* would be my choice. Doubtless you're well rested after your nap so you'll be able to help me tackle her tonight."

"Tackle her?"

"Meet me opposite the dock gates at ten tonight. Wear old clothes. I'll need to make some arrangements."

"Yes. Yes. Fine. Tell me why you released Picard."

Schultz began writing notes in the folder and answered Hunt without looking at him. "We don't need Picard. He's more useful on the streets, and I've given him a few jobs to do to help me with the Spaulding case. I can get him again if I need him."

"Then why did you ask Price to keep him locked up if you were going to release him? You're playing me for a fool!"

Schultz clenched his fists on his desk and gave a long exhalation. Sloan looked up from his notes then returned to his jottings.

Hunt felt angry. He felt angry with Schultz for leaving him out of the planning in the case. He felt angry with Picard for not being the murderer and robbing Hunt of his earlier glory. He felt even angry with Sloan for being an unwanted witness to this confrontation. A glimmer of late afternoon sunlight forced itself through the dull clouds, but that gave no joy to Hunt. The silence grew. Schultz flicked the folder closed and drummed his fingers on the desk. "The Jefferson saloon does a passable beef pepperpot. It would be good to eat before we head out."

Hunt bit out his reply. "I ate earlier."

The rejected invitation hung in the air between them. Hunt recognized the

78

older man's tact in trying to move their confrontation to a more private location, but for the moment he felt no desire to concede even on that small point.

Schultz turned his head to face Hunt. "Fine then. I'll see you at the dock gates at ten."

Schultz's impassive face and cold demeanor told Hunt that the conversation was finished. Hunt's mouth opened, then shut, as his brain searched for a response. The rhythmic scratching of Sloan's nib on the notepaper seemed a metronome ticking away the few seconds left for Hunt to find an appropriate answer. Schultz's face grew in his vision. The cannonball head. The bushy beard and the shining eyes. A previously unnoticed scar running from his right ear down the line of his cheek. The pen held loosely in Schultz's hand. None of it gave Hunt an opening. The only safe response lay in a withdrawal with as much dignity as could be salvaged under the circumstances.

"The dock gates at ten," replied Hunt. "I'll talk to you then."

He grabbed his coat from the chair and stalked to the door. His stomach growled to him as he took the stairs two a time, pushing his way out of the police station and into the cold of the Washington streets.

The Docks at night

Harsh starlight gleamed down on Washington, reflecting itself from the myriad pools and rivulets flowing through the streets. Hunt kept his shoulders hunched against the cold and his hands stayed deep in his coat pockets. The only persistent noises were his own steps and the gentle gargling of cold droplets falling from eaves and gutters onto the pavement. From time to time, raised voices or bursts of laughter filtered into the streets from the saloons he passed along the way.

A dull anger replaced his earlier fury. Schultz held all of the aces in this game. He had years of service in the force, and enjoyed the well-earned respect of his peers and his captain. On the other hand, Hunt blundered badly on his first day by charging Picard with Anderson's murder. Anyone could have made that mistake. Anyone but Schultz.

Was the problem simple jealousy on his part? He pushed the thought away. If Schultz couldn't share his thoughts, and give him the opportunity to be a partner in solving the case, then other detectives would forever perceive him as a fetcher of coffee and runner of errands. That reputation could follow a man until his death.

The winds of the day still gusted an occasional zephyr, pushing away the dark clouds, which retreated to replenish themselves for whatever weather the morrow would bring. It lacked a quarter of ten, and a bare half a mile separated Hunt from the dock gates.

A regular beat of footsteps alerted Hunt to the passing of an army patrol. They came from a side street; twelve uniformed men with their rifles sloped across their shoulders. They ignored Hunt; probably hadn't even seen him, he realized. They marched straight into the mud of the aptly named Water Street. Within a few steps, the sucking mud outfought their marching rhythm until each man lost the pace and wallowed his way across the road as best he could. The patrol re-formed on the sidewalk and marched off. Probably on their way back from settling down some soldiers rioting at a saloon, decided Hunt. Brawling would happen wherever soldiers could find a drink.

A final turn in the road and Hunt reached his destination. The closed wooden gates of the dock and the adjoining fence were both too high for a man to climb over without difficulty. A brace of lanterns hanging from the dockyard wall washed away the starlight, and created strange shadows among the few remaining trees bordering the street.

Earlier in the day, Hunt sprinted through those gates on his way to see Albert Lachlan, and at the time no one ventured out into the rain to challenge him. Now the only entrance lay in a small sally port to the right of the main gates. A dim illumination showed the shadow of a man, doubtless the gatekeeper, ready to contest any intruder. Hunt grinned to himself. Should he try to brazen his way in? His badge sat in his pocket but that would be a last resort. How would Schultz do it?

The last thought jarred slightly, but Hunt knew wisdom dictated following the example of those more capable than he was. Schultz would have a disguise, or perhaps bribe the gatekeeper. Did only one man keep watch there? If so, then nature must eventually take its course, and the man would leave his position for a few minutes. He could see the gates clearly and Schultz wasn't waiting there for him.

"They offered you a desk job."

The voice whispered at his right shoulder and for the second time that day Hunt felt a claw of fear grip his stomach. He spun to face the voice. Schultz stood in a shadow, two paces away.

"What?"

"The army offered you a desk job after you were wounded. Instead of accepting it you resigned your commission and three months later joined the Metropolitan Police Department."

Hunt moved back against a tree, keeping his head turned to face Schultz. Water slowly dripped on his shoulder as he stood there. He had to answer. "I joined up to fight. They wouldn't let me fight."

"You resigned your commission. Didn't you see a desk job as part of your duty?"

"I did my duty, dammit! No man says otherwise!"

Hunt felt his anger burning. He balled his fists ready for a confrontation, but Schultz's calm voice offered no provocation in itself. Only the meaning of his words carried a threat.

"Calm down. Why didn't they offer you another field command?"

Hunt would be thrice cursed before telling Schultz the story of his last patrol. Those events were none of Schultz's damn business. "The Colonel wouldn't say."

Schultz smiled wisely. He showed the look of secret knowledge. "Oh Colonel Lukey said it all right. He wrote it all in his report, but I wanted to see if you knew the answer."

"You saw Colonel Lukey's report? How the hell did you get that?"

"There are ways," replied Schultz, pushing past Hunt and surveying the dock gates. "You'll pardon my reading that report. However, if I need to work with you for this case, then I need to know your measure."

The air of a snake grew around the senior detective. A deadly reptile about to penetrate into a rabbit warren and snare its prey, confident its abilities would see off even the most determined defender.

Another gaggle of soldiers passed the dock gates, holding their weapons casually while they murmured among themselves. Bad discipline, thought

Hunt. The detectives watched them until they passed out of sight. The strangeness of the moment both exhilarated and disoriented Hunt, all at the same time.

Knowing what Colonel Lukey wrote in his report would set Hunt's mind at rest, and perhaps bury some of the ghosts that kept him awake at night. Once again, Schultz knew all of the facts, and Hunt needed to beg for information. It seemed mad to be discussing his army career when the *Angelique* sat waiting for their attention, but Hunt needed to know the answers. "Did he mention... did he write about...?"

"Scott's Ford, Rappahannock River, June 6th 1863," interrupted Schultz. His eyes stayed focused on the dock gates and his voice slipped into a monotone as he recited the report in a voice that uncannily echoed the way Colonel Lukey would describe an event.

"Lieutenant Hunt and a detachment performed a scouting patrol of the Confederate positions west of Fredericksburg, and confirmed the absence of those units of the Army of North Virginia which were previously encamped there. During an encounter with enemy troops, the Lieutenant became separated from his command. Despite serious wounds, he killed two enemy soldiers in single combat, then returned to Union lines by himself. The other men in his patrol are missing, presumed prisoners of the Confederacy."

The monologue finished and Schultz turned to face Hunt. "That's exactly what he wrote and it sounds all very positive. Tell me then, why didn't they offer you another field command?"

"I told you. I don't know."

"I think you know why, Hunt. You don't realize you know."

"That's stupid, Schultz. I told you Colonel Lukey wouldn't tell me."

"Very well then. He said you were too impulsive for a combat command. Too much bayonet charging, not enough leading, that sort of thing. Not that he considered you a dullard though. He described you as intelligent, just a little too quick on the trigger."

Voices grew from near the dock gates, and a rambunctious party of seven drunken sailors stumbled into view, headed towards their hammocks. One at a time, they entered the sally port and disappeared. "Too much bayonet charging," repeated Schultz. "Mind you, bayonets can be useful sometimes."

Hunt could think of nothing in reply.

"Pay attention now," said Schultz with a sharper voice. "Once we're past those dock gates, then we're in enemy territory. Councilman Hobart and the Port Authority control these docks, and they are not our friends. We go in and see what we need to see, then we leave."

"Enemy territory?"

"This city has many petty kingdoms Hunt. We're crossing a border into one where the local monarch has a price on my head. He'll take yours also if they catch you. Stay close and keep quiet."

Schultz looked up and down the street, then stepped from the duckboard and into the mud, picking his way towards the dock gates, and forcing Hunt to run a few paces through the mire in order to catch up. The sally port, barely a man's height and width, stood ajar. Schultz passed through the gap, and Hunt followed in time to see him passing a bottle to the gatekeeper. Then they were through, and Hunt could see Schultz striding along the wharf. A quick backward glance showed him the bottle disappearing from sight and the gatekeeper resuming his seat, with his features well hidden under a cloth cap.

Schultz moved confidently through the shadows until the two men stood concealed behind a pile of timber opposite Pier Four. The *Angelique* showed plainly through the haze of the intermittent rain. There seemed no change from when Hunt saw her earlier that day.

"There's a man at the foremast," observed Schultz quietly. "I considered the captain might set a dockside watch. That limits our options."

"I saw him there this morning. They're taking no chances."

Schultz nodded once. A surge of gratefulness for that small approval rushed through Hunt followed by an equally strong sense of self-condemnation that he should be so dependent on Schultz's favor.

."Even so, that's an unusual precaution for a shipment of low grade French lace. If it were brandy or guns I would understand, but why guard cheap lace?"

"How do you know its cheap lace?"

"The three main exports from France to America are brandy, guns and lace," explained Schultz. "The first two require the ship to call at Baltimore or New York for special customs clearance. Consider that the list you took showed the *Angelique* came straight from France and, according to Lachlan, she hasn't yet unloaded. Then look how high she's riding. Lace is a far lighter cargo than guns or liquor."

"You're saying she's carrying lace. How do you know its cheap lace?"

Schultz shrugged. "As far as the quality is concerned I can tell you all the expensive lace goes to the salons of Boston and New York. Washington may be the nation's capital city, but our ladies don't spend as much on finery as the cities further north. It would be a brave man who committed expensive lace to a small ship like this. Far safer to wait for a three-master. Therefore, if she is carrying a regular cargo, it will most likely be cheap lace. Let's get closer."

Schultz led Hunt past the pile of timber to a storeroom opposite the *Angelique*, where, with ten seconds work, he opened the door and led them inside. Hunt couldn't see if Schultz used a key or performed some trick with a lockpick. Either way, Hunt wasn't surprised that Schultz had their vantage point already planned and waiting for them.

The old, poorly constructed shed had seen better days. The planks on the walls were uneven and unfinished beams supported the cobweb coated roof. A single window let in enough of the harbor light for the men to pick their way between packing cases and stacked tools. Matted sawdust lay on the floor of thick planks. Schultz moved to the window, and then stepped aside to let Hunt share the view. The *Angelique* rested quietly at her mooring, rocking with the gentle swell. Hunt sat on a packing case and took the chance to remove his leaking boot and wring out his wet sock.

"All peaceable for the moment," observed Schultz, sitting on a small bench. "We still have ten minutes to wait."

"Then what, dammit?"

Schultz looked at his partner then his eyebrows unfurrowed and his face relaxed. A soft chuckle escaped his lips. "That's a good question, Detective Hunt. That's what we're here to discover."

"Blast it, Schultz! Maybe this is all some game for you, but if this is enemy territory then it's my life on the line also if your rip-roaring idea goes wrong! Now tell me what you're planning here."

Hunt waited. Eager anticipation and damnable frustration battled within his mind. Schultz's crisp voice came straight to the point.

"Hunt, mayhap I owe you an apology - mayhap not. I've been at the Fifth Precinct for years now. I've put up with partners for some of that time, but when Donohue left, I told Price I'd be working on my own from then on. He didn't say no to that. Now you ride into town and I'm supposed to slow myself down to your way of working?"

"Now don't get all-fired up about my words here," continued Schultz. "I'm telling you where I'm at, and you can like it or lump it, but it won't change what I'm thinking."

"Go on."

Schultz's bright eyes shone up at Hunt with a peculiar energy. The depth of his beard hid his mouth and Hunt couldn't see his lips moving. Hunt sought his own anger for reassurance, but it shrunk to a size unable to sustain his fury, pushed aside by his hunger to learn.

"Donohue and I worked well together because he let me do the thinking. He wasn't stupid, but we both knew his limitations. He could only ever see the obvious answer."

"You think I'm the same as Donohue?"

"Keep your voice down!"

"Sorry."

"Alright then, suppose you tell me. Given the events of the last few days, how would you rate your ability to look beyond the obvious answer?"

Hunt caught Schultz's oblique reference to Picard's arrest. He couldn't blame his partner for putting him in the same class as Donohue.

"You're new to this game," continued Schultz. "That's not your fault, but neither is it mine. We're working on a case that may have some deadline, and there's not the time for me to put all of my thoughts down on paper and give you a daily newssheet."

"You're my partner! It's your duty to work with me."

"Don't preach to me, Hunt," snapped Schultz. "I know my duty well enough. It means upholding the law - all of the law - not just the parts I like."

"Murphy said you say that a lot."

"Mayhap I do. I live by that code. You have a problem with it?"

Hunt shook his head. "You're getting me wrong here. I want to be helping you. How can I do that if you won't tell me what you're thinking?"

Schultz waved his hand dismissively.

"Ask me your questions and I'll answer them if I can. You need to remember that detective work is no schoolboy test. Some of your questions may have four or five equally valid answers at this point. What do you want to know?"

Questions crowded Hunt. He didn't know which one would open the logjam of facts and theories stored in Schultz's head. He chose one.

"You wrote "RALLY" on Picard's case notes. What did that mean?"

A noise outside prompted Schultz to stand and look out of the window. He peered left and right along the waterfront then moved away from the window, settled himself back on the wooden crates and rubbed his hands to warm them.

"Picard trapped himself in the storeroom at the Herald by the time the murderers came downstairs. The thick door prevented him from overhearing their entire conversation, but he distinctly heard one of them say that word."

"It makes no sense."

"Not yet. But it would if we knew its context. There is a Copperhead rally planned outside the Capitol this coming Sunday and mayhap some mayhem is in the making for that event."

Shultz paused for a moment, then chuckled. "You'll admit Hunt, that those words were clever now. Mayhap – mayhem - making. Unplanned I'll grant you, but clever none the less. No matter. Let us consider this meeting set for Sunday. Normally the Herald wouldn't cover such red rag news, so I cannot yet see the link."

"And you said something about destroying the evidence," pressed Hunt, eager to hear the older man's theories. "At the Belvedere Hotel, right before Jane - Miss Anderson - joined us."

"Yes, I did! The murderers lit a fire in the front of the office. It scorched the woodwork but didn't burn the building. Ask yourself then, why, in an office storing thousands of pages of newsprint, did the arsonists light their fire next to the safe rather than in the paper store?"

Hunt didn't have the answer, but he knew Shultz did. "Tell me."

"Simplicity itself. They weren't burning the building; they were burning some object, some piece of evidence they came there to destroy. They may have tortured its location out of Anderson and then, when they finally owned the prize, they destroyed it. Could it have been a letter? A daguerreotype image? Forged Bearer Bonds? We may never know. Suppose it had been a document. The document itself possessed no intrinsic value or they would have kept it, but they stole a man's life in order to ensure the destruction of that document. What kind of threat did that document represent? That, I do not yet know."

Hunt shivered and reached over to feel his sock. The cold wet cloth would never dry in this room so close to the river. He took the sock, gave it a final squeeze and pulled it back onto his foot.

"Then why are we here? What links the *Angelique* to Anderson's death?"

Schultz stood and paced the storeroom. The dim moonlight though the window played tricks with Schultz's shadow, making him appear as being immense and then miniscule in turn.

"The cuts on Anderson's arms and face were done with a very sharp knife. Now your average thief may carry a knife, but doesn't endure the weeks of boring watch keeping that are a seaman's lot. Hence, the mariner sharpens his knife on a daily basis while the hoodlum's knife rusts away in its scabbard. Both weapons will do their task, but a finely honed weapon did the work on Anderson. Then I found the smell of tar on Anderson's wrists. Sharp knife and tarred rope tell me the waterfront should be my next stop."

Hunt replaced his sock and boot. The clammy wet wool chafed his toes, but it would be warmer than standing barefoot.

"Why the *Angelique*?"

"Of all the ships arriving within the last week, two showed unusually slow journeys. The *Hill of Grace* came down from New York and, as I found out later, lost her rudder on the way. That would cause her delay. On the other hand, the *Angelique* sailed from Brest, but she left there well over a month ago. That leaves plenty of room for a side trip to meet a blockade-runner out of Charleston or some other southern port."

Schultz stopped by the window and consulted his pocket watch. "Not long to go."

"Not long till what?"

Schultz chuckled lightly. "I'm doing it again aren't I? Let me explain."

He beckoned Hunt to the window and then pointed down the pier.

"The *Angelique* sits there with a port watch guarding her cargo of third-rate lace. We'll allow that master runs a tight ship and it's in his habit to keep such a watch posted. Apart from that, the crew will have turned in or perhaps be drinking brandy over some card game. Are you with me so far?"

All that seemed reasonable. Hunt gave a nod.

"Tell me now," continued Schultz in the tone of a schoolmaster. "If all is quiet on the docks and then a pistol shot is heard what would such a crew do? Mind you, this will be close by – not the sound of a distant barroom brawl getting out of hand. It will be a pistol shot within fifty paces of their ship."

Hunt considered his answer carefully, and then thought about it again before replying. "I suppose the man on watch would investigate."

"Most certainly he would. And perhaps one or two from below would stick their heads up for a look. That's to be expected. Then we can expect after a few minutes of head scratching and shoulder shrugging the crew will settle back down again. On the other hand, a ship with a secret might behave a little differently."

"And if she does?"

"Then we have something worth investigating," pronounced Schultz in a satisfied tone. "We'll be back here in the morning with a warrant, and the *Angelique*'s cargo and crew will be the subject of rather thorough inspection."

Hunt couldn't keep the anger out of his voice. "That's it?"

Schultz's head turned to face Hunt. "Yes, that's it. You asked what we're doing here and I've told you."

Hunt's fury returned in full force. Schultz tracked down their enemy, and now he wanted them to skulk around in the shadows and do nothing. This wasn't Hunt's idea of detective work.

"Damn you Schultz…"

"Keep your voice down!"

"Damn you all the same! You get me down here on the notion you've found the murderers, and now you want to sit here all night and watch them?"

"In the first place Hunt, I never claimed to have found the murderers. In the second place, I suspect this case is more than a simple murder so it is smart to learn all we can before we play our hand. In the third place, we agreed I would be running this case so you'll shut up and do things my way. Now keep your voice down!"

Schultz's acid rebuke stunned Hunt. His fingers retreated from the hilt of his Bowie knife and he sat back on the packing case.

"How old are you Hunt?"

"Thirty-four!"

"You're not thirty-four."

Schultz turned to look out of the window and Hunt felt himself cast out from the senior detective's plans. He had been tensed and ready for a fight, then, once again, Schultz argued him down. Every time in his life he knew what to do, someone would prove him wrong. It had been the same as long as he could remember. It had been the same back at Scott's Ford in June 1863.

Scott's Ford

"Shit." The expletive hissed through the steamy Virginian afternoon as sharply as a minie ball from a musket. Two Confederate soldiers sat in the shade of a tree fifty yards to the front of where Lieutenant Hunt and Sergeant Slater lay concealed in tangled undergrowth. The rebels hadn't been there four hours earlier when Hunt mentally marked that defile as the retreat path for his men.

He flicked a hand to brush away the hovering flies. A distant chorus of crickets strummed their song, presenting their continual sound as a backdrop for the random bird voices of the hot Virginian summer. Slater's voice whispered beside him. "Sir, we could still try the creek bed."

Slater spoke too much. He should be keeping the enlisted men in line, not usurping Hunt's leadership.

"Sir?"

Hunt shook his head. Trying the creek bed meant backtracking for a half mile and then moving down an unknown path. It had been tough getting his six-man patrol through the Confederate lines to determine the enemy strength and Hunt remained resolved to bring his men back along this route. It would be madness to leave the one path they knew. They would risk getting lost in the woods of middle Virginia. "No sergeant. I know this track."

"I could check out the creek."

"You think you know better than me?" hissed Hunt vehemently, snapping his head around to glare at the sergeant. "I'm in charge! You do what I say!"

"Yes, sir."

Hunt scowled at his sergeant for another two seconds before turning back to look at the enemy. He heard Slater move down the hill to check on the men.

Good! Let him do his job!

The two Confederates seemed completely unaware of Hunt. They were facing away from him, but their muskets were within arm's reach, and when he'd move his patrol through the defile, they would see him.

His choices were limited. He could wait for the Confederates to leave, he could retreat and try Slater's creek bed or he could attack the enemy. Many hours remained before sunset, and it would be too risky to delay until then. Another Confederate patrol could stumble over their position while they waited. They needed to keep moving.

Hunt's hand caressed the grip of his Bowie Knife. It had been his father's gift to him on his tenth birthday, and he couldn't remember the last time he dressed without strapping on the weapon. He liked the way his hand had worn the haft smooth over the years. It would take less than a second for him to place his knife anywhere he wanted within twenty paces. Once he got that close, then the first Confederate would die. No question there. How to deal with the other man without firing a shot and betraying their position? None of his other men carried a throwing knife.

Hunt glanced up. A cloudless sky let the full heat of the sun pour down onto the earth. Would the rebels doze off in the warmth of the afternoon air? Hunt couldn't stay around to find out. Moving carefully to avoid dislodging stones or breaking twigs, Hunt made his way down to the trail and continued south to where his men were sheltering.

Sergeant Slater set the four men each looking out along one point of the compass. He had been a career soldier since long before the war started and you'd sooner catch a weasel asleep than trip him up. The fact that Slater never made a mistake made his insubordination that much harder to take. Hunt reached the men and squatted down.

"Small problem ahead, men. Couple of rebels sitting in the sun facing our lines. Easy life for some I'd say." Hunt looked at each of his men in turn but none of them smiled at his joke. He commanded their attention but they gave their loyalty and confidence to the sergeant. Damn Slater! It didn't matter - he'd show them what he could do.

"Johnny Reb has a good view of the trail," he continued. "I'm going to cut through the woods and take care of them. Sergeant, wait here for a count of three minutes and then take the men home along the path. I'll have cleared the way by then."

"Sir, I'd be betting we can get back along the creek bed."

"It'll be quick and clean, sergeant. Two less rebels for us to fight later."

The men needed to know his skill with the knife. They needed to have confidence in him. He flipped his knife out of its sheath and spun it in the air without looking. It fell back into his hand as it had done a thousand times before.

"We're supposed to avoid combat, sir."

"I'm not running away from a couple of rebels, sergeant."

"We don't need to do this, sir."

Hunt slammed the flat blade of the knife into his open palm. Private Hotham jerked back in surprise but Slater's gaze never wavered. Hunt curled his hand around the blade to hide the small cut he gave himself, and forced his voice out hard and even. "I gave you an order, sergeant!"

"Yes sir."

Slater's subservient voice acknowledged Hunt's authority, but the sergeant's

94

eyes never dropped. Dumb insolence, they used to call it.

"Right then. When you move, keep it quiet. Start your count now."

Hunt easily covered the ground from the trail to his previous position. He moved over the boulder, then around the tree and under the vines. The same rock sat in the same position, and on that rock sat one man, whittling on a small stick. Hunt frowned, searching for the other Confederate. Such appalling bad luck that the other man should move away immediately after Hunt set the patrol in motion. He pushed back past the vines, and carefully moved closer to the whittler. Crouching low, he looked across the scrub.

There were still two muskets there next to the remaining Confederate. The other man might be in the bushes taking a dump. Hunt realized he stopped counting. He reached forty-something back when he noticed the absence of the second man. It didn't matter now. The knife handle felt cool in his grip, despite the heat of the day. His fingers held it lightly, continually rebalancing its weight as he moved off the path and up the hill towards his victim. Another half-dozen steps should see him there.

A small scuttling sound in the underbrush far to his right disturbed a bird, sending it screeching into flight. The Confederate paused in his whittling, and looked up at the bird.

Hunt stood frozen in place. If the rebel turned slightly to follow the bird's flight, then he must surely see the danger. Sweat trickled down Hunt's wrist and along his thumb. The confederate scratched his cheek with the half-whittled stick then dropped his gaze and resumed his work. Hunt gave himself a count of five before taking another step.

"Jeb!"

The shout came from his left, further up the hill. Hunt whirled, seeing a man up there tying his belt. The whittler reached for a musket as Hunt swung back to face him. His blade sang through the air, taking the rebel through the side of his throat and pinning him briefly to the tree until the weight of his corpse dragged the metal from the wood. Belt Man scrambled downhill almost reaching the muskets. Hunt's revolver came free from its holster and he squeezed the trigger, shattering the silence and knowing instantly that he missed and now faced an armed enemy. He forced himself to stand still.

The rocks hid the man, but Hunt could see the rocks. Belt Man needed to come out from behind those rocks and into the open before he could shoot at Hunt. Surely Slater would be getting the men through the defile by now? The deafening song of the crickets stopped and only the faint buzz of insects disturbed the silence. Any Confederates for a mile around would have heard the shot. Even now, an enemy patrol might be moving on their position. If Slater could get the men through the defile, then Hunt and his knife could cover the rest of their retreat. He knew his skill could do that. The fallen tree to his left would be good cover if he could reach it without taking his eyes off the rocks that shielded Belt Man.

The heat of the sun soaked through his jacket and his body sweated into the cloth, chafing and distracting him. His breath thundered in and out of his lungs. Belt Man must surely hear it. He made the choice and started a slow move towards the dead rebel. A stick cracked under his boot and he dove for cover; reaching it but losing his view of Belt Man's position and banging his ankle painfully in the process. They were even now, both armed and unsure of the other's position. He'd lost the initiative.

Fear gnawed at him. He would die here, or worse, be captured by a dirty-arsed Confederate private. He jerked up and peered over the fallen tree. The dead Confederate lay directly ahead, sprawled over a rock with a pool of blood growing under him. The handle of Hunt's Bowie knife stood at right angles from the corpse's throat, and a musket lay in the dirt between them. Even now, the enemy might be aiming the other musket at him.

Hunt looked up and down the hill but saw no sign of Belt Man. Perhaps he'd run away. The death of his companion must have shocked him. Hunt lifted himself higher and looked out again. He stayed there for a full minute with only the slowly building sound of the crickets for company. Slater would have the men halfway through the defile by now. There were distant shouts from further down the hill. He needed to leave.

He drew himself carefully to his hands and knees, and crawled cautiously to the dead Confederate. His eyes scanned the rocks while his fingers walked up the corpse to find the knife. It twisted easily out of the wound and Hunt wiped it on the dead man's shirt before returning the weapon to its sheath.

He'd put his revolver on the ground while he cleaned the knife, and he picked it up as he stood. A click of boot on stone gave him warning, and he spun to see Belt Man barely twenty yards away, looking at him over the musket's open muzzle. Their guns sounded together and a bullet crashed into the rock beside him, showering his body with splinters of stone. He jerked away from the pain, stumbling on the uneven, rock-strewn ground and fighting for his balance. The shriek from his adversary told him that his own shot hit home, and by the time he recovered his balance to sight his gun for a second shot Belt Man lay motionless on the ground. Hunt approached the corpse carefully but, like its companion, it would never move on its own legs again.

He stood there and stared down at the corpse until he noticed the feeling of sticky blood flowing down his arm. The fallen tree made a good seat and he sat down, giggling with the shock of the battle and feeling the strength leaking out of both knees. His uniform jacket came off easily enough and he could see where the fragments of stone sliced through it in a dozen places. There were slivers of the rock buried in his arm and a warm tingling in his cheeks and neck. He picked out the pieces he could find in his arm, blinking away the blood from his eyes, and feeling no pain despite the depth of the wounds. Strips of cloth torn from his shirt did well enough for a bandage. The bleeding slowed but did not stop.

The shouts were closer now. It was time to go. Less than ten minutes after the start of the fight, Hunt stumbled down through the defile towards the next valley and the river. There were voices behind him and perhaps some gunshots in the distance, but the noises grew fainter as he pushed his way north towards the river. He didn't catch up with Sergeant Slater and the men. That didn't worry him. He'd see them on the other side.

The Union pickets at Scott's Ford heard Hunt pushing through the undergrowth long before they saw him tottering towards them. The corporal on duty had his head set on right and sent a detail across the river to meet Hunt and carry him back into the perimeter of the sentry post.

"It's OK," muttered Hunt as they laid him on a rough stretcher made from nearby saplings. "I got them. They're not following me."

"Infirmary, boys!" ordered the corporal. "Wilson, run ahead and warn the doc."

"Got both of them," repeated Hunt, as four men lifted the stretcher and set out for the infirmary at a steady pace. The bouncing of the stretcher turned his stomach but at least he couldn't feel the pain in his arm any longer. The world slowed down. A blurred face hovered over him.

"That'll need stitching," said a voice from the bottom of a very deep well. "Take him inside."

Then the taste of leather choked his mouth, and hands held him down as wild beasts chewed at his arm, neck and shoulder. Feeble screams died in his throat, and after the torture they laid him on a bed where he could hear the sound of groaning and somebody sobbing in the distance.

An unknown time later, Hunt came back from the depths. A hand on his good shoulder shook him gently, and a distant voice called his name. It took time before Hunt could force his eyes open. A surgeon stood over him wearing a leather apron splashed with the crusted blood of half a hundred soldiers. His rolled up sleeves and hairy arms contrasted strangely with his neat string tie.

"He's awake, Colonel. Keep it short."

The morning sun shone through the open sides of the hospital tent. Had he slept through the night? Colonel Lukey and Captain Stacey were there, dressed in their finery. Hunt tried to move but the Colonel's upraised hand bade him to stillness.

"Rest easy there, son. Sawbones says you lost a lot of blood."

The Colonel drew up a chair and sat beside Hunt's cot. The man's tall frame dwarfed the wooden chair. "Feeling better, son?"

"Yes." That simple word seemed too difficult to say. The doctor held a cup to his lips. Blessed cool water ran through the wasteland of his mouth.

"Has Lee's army moved? Were there only pickets left?"

"Only pickets," replied Hunt, forcing out the words.

The Colonel leaned back in his chair with a sigh. It seemed to be the news he expected. Captain Lukey spoke from the end of the bed.

"Other scouts reported the same, Hunt. General Lee's on the march. Don't worry about that for now. What happened to your men?"

Hunt answered as best he could. In short sentences he told the story of their patrol, emphasising his difficulty in dealing with Slater and reliving in detail the encounter with the two Confederates sentries. The act of talking gave him strength and the Colonel listened to Hunt's description of the fight.

"You killed them both?"

"Yes."

"By yourself?"

"Yes sir."

"Like in February?"

"Sir?"

"Your patrol last February, when you brought in that prisoner by yourself and told Slater to cover your retreat. Only this time you sent Sergeant Slater and the men back ahead while you stayed to fight those rebels."

"Yes, I knew I could handle a couple of rebels. The second one got a lucky shot at me, that's all."

Colonel Lukey pursed his lips and looked over at Captain Stacey, then stood up, pushing the chair back to the end of the bed from where he'd taken it. Captain Stacey nodded slowly, but his hard eyes forewarned of something disturbing.

"Sergeant Slater and the other men haven't returned yet."

Hunt looked up at his commanding officers. Their faces were serious. They had to be wrong. "But they - they went first. I sent them back first."

"They haven't returned. We've checked with units all along the front."

Hunt sneezed. The sudden effort shot pain up his arm and garbled his thoughts. He struggled to compose himself. "I'll find - got to find them! They were my men."

"They were my men too, Lieutenant."

The Colonel's firm voice closed the issue. The senior officers looked down at him lying helpless on the cot. Hunt saw the condemnation in their eyes, their verdict on an officer who hadn't protected his men and didn't even know where they were.

"Get well Lieutenant," added the Captain as the two officers turned away.

Hunt stared at the roof of the tent. Somewhere in Virginia were five Union soldiers who trusted him to get them home. Now they were prisoners. Or worse.

"You'll be fine soon," broke in the doctor's voice. "A couple of weeks afore you're recovered, but there's no damage to the bone and none of your tendons were cut."

The man held a thin sliver of stone an inch long and almost a quarter inch wide. "Pulled that one out of your shoulder. Another quarter inch and it would have nicked the brachial artery. You'd have bled to death before you could have made it back here."

Hunt took the stone and considered it without emotion. Such a small thing to control the fate of a man. The point of it felt quite sharp. "Thank you," he replied tonelessly.

"Happy to help, Lieutenant. You'll be up and walking tomorrow, and out of here in a few days."

A cry of pain echoed down from the other end of the tent and the surgeon looked towards the noise. "Better see what's happening. You lie there and rest."

Hunt watched the sawbones walk away to deal with the latest emergency. He lay unmoving for a while, hearing the cries from the end of the tent subside. He heard the other noises of a hospital tent rise and fall as the hours went by. An orderly helped him eat a meal. From time to time men on crutches and wrapped in bloody bandages limped past his bed, but that vision of hell wasted itself on the unseeing Hunt.

At some point, he became aware that he still held the splinter of stone that the surgeon gave him. He stared at the stone, and saw Slater's face staring back from its jagged surfaces. Three days later, as Hunt ate his breakfast, the surgeon came to see him.

"There's a letter for you here Lieutenant. Looks official."

Battle on the Docks

The crack of a gunshot bought Hunt back to the present. In an instant, both detectives were at the window peering through the gloom. The *Angelique* floated peacefully before them. Further along the dock a cawing flock of seagulls launched themselves into the night and cast fleeting moonlit shadows across the window.

"Look for movement," instructed Schultz. "I doubt they'll show lights."

Hunt nodded. His eyes darted across the ship looking for shadows that might grow or shrink unnaturally. "There! At the gangway!"

"And by the stern light."

"Somebody on the fore hatch."

Schultz chuckled to himself. "Oh my lovelies, you are a worried lot. See, they have muskets at the bow! What ship carries loaded muskets while moored at the Washington docks?"

The detectives watched as two men with muskets advanced down the gangway and passed out of sight towards the dock gates.

"Tell me, Hunt. Would you take that on with your knife and fists? Far better to return in the morning with a warrant. Now we need to wait for them to return to sleep. I daresay a half-hour will see... What is it?"

Hunt heard it first and cocked his head to determine the source of the noise. Schultz, forewarned by Hunt's expression, heard and then recognized the sound.

"Running men, mayhap a dozen of them."

A second gunshot split the night. The splashing of running feet grew louder. The sailors with muskets raced back into sight, leaping up the gangway and onto the *Angelique* amidst shouts of alarm and snapped orders. Hunt and Schultz peered through the window, each trying to see the new arrivals, while the crew of the *Angelique* swarmed up the ratlines and dropped the sails.

"Damn, she's making sail. That offshore breeze will... God's Blood!"

Hunt saw it also. A loosened sail caught on the door of a locker and spilled its contents for the world to see. Clearly visible amongst the ropes and other gear lay the Stars and Bars flag of the Confederacy. Hunt had fought against that flag on the battlefield. "Rebels!"

"What in the name of Hades are they doing here? This is deeper than I'd thought."

The *Angelique*'s crew cast off lines and retrieved the gangway before the rest of the running men arrived. A convenient current and a downriver breeze pulled the ship out into the Potomac. The pursuers used their rifles. A sailor fell with a shriek from the rigging to the deck. The men on the dock followed the ship downriver as far as they were able, moving along the wharf in formation and sending ragged volleys of bullets in her direction.

"They'll be stopped at the Long Bridge."

"They'll get away," corrected Schultz. "The guards open the drawbridges at night to stop deserters crossing into Virginia."

"Damn!"

"We'd better leave. They may search here."

Schultz's words were prophetic. As they turned from the window, the door behind them opened. The crack of rifle fire drowned the thud of Hunt's flying knife slicing through flesh, and a blue-coated man with a smoking weapon collapsed in the doorway. Hunt's heavy fist put the matter beyond doubt, and he leapt out through the door checking for other searchers. Shouted orders and the continual rattle of gunshots came from further along the docks, but no one stood in sight of the doorway. The sounds of the battle with the *Angelique* would have drowned the noise of a single rifle shot within the storeroom. Hunt's knife slipped from the unconscious man's shoulder. The wound oozed blood but there wasn't the pumping of a severed artery. The man would live. Hunt leaned back into the shed.

"Come on Schultz! Oh God!"

Schultz clutched his thigh where a dark stain spread beneath his hands. Hunt scooped Schultz over his shoulders and maneuvered out of the door. Carelessly stacked crates hid them for twenty yards and then the moonlight revealed the path to the sally port. Two soldiers with rifles stood there.

"Take me back down the waterfront. Past the shed!"

Hunt didn't argue. He moved quickly through the shadows, and followed Schultz's directions. The high walls of the dock hemmed them in all the way along.

"Here is fine. Put me down."

Hunt lowered Schultz beside a crate and eased his cramped shoulders. The stain on Schultz's thigh slowly spread, but Hunt stayed in control, ripping the leggings apart to probe the wound and confirm the bone wasn't broken. "Only a splinter wound. You'll live."

"Thanks - aaaargh - that wasn't a place to stay."

Hunt cut cloth from Schultz's trouser leg to form a field dressing and bandaged the wound. A cannon shot boomed out across the harbor. He turned to see the *Angelique* far down the Potomac, setting her course towards the distant Atlantic. More cannons fired but the splash of their shot stayed far behind their prey. Dark shapes down the river were the silhouettes of moored warships, but they'd need to beat to quarters quickly to catch the fleeing Confederate ship.

Then, coming out of the shadows on their right, Hunt saw two men carrying their rifles at the ready. The detectives didn't have to warn each other. They hunched down behind a crate and watched the men pass across their view.

Hunt turned to Schultz. "We're all on the same side here. I'll flag them down."

"No! Our badges won't protect us from Hobart. They'll search the whole waterfront. We have to keep moving."

"The sally port is guarded and you'll never get over the fence with that leg. We can't get out."

"There's another way. Come on. Help me up."

With his leg bandaged, Schultz could manage a slow hobble, leaning all of the time on Hunt's shoulder. They set off between the dock wall and a stone building until they came to a wooden door. Hunt turned the handle, but the door wouldn't move.

"Bolted on the inside! We can't get in."

Schultz sunk to the ground and examined the door hinges. A scrabble in his pocket produced a long thin piece of rounded iron and he placed it underneath the hinge and pushed upwards. With a short squeak, the pinion slid clear of its housing and clattered to the ground beside him.

"Try the top one," he said, offering up the iron.

Hunt took the iron and duplicated the feat on the top hinge. It took him longer than Schultz, but with less than a minute's effort, the door fell free from its bolts and hinges. A second minute saw the door reassembled with them secure inside the room. Hunt dropped to the floor beside his partner. He found himself grinning irrepressibly as the tension leached from his body. "I shouldn't have asked for more action. You certainly provided that."

Schultz shook his head. "Not me. I purchased only a single pistol shot and our man on the gate had instructions to tell any curious visitors that the sound came from inland. Mayhap a patrol chose to walk past the gate right at that time. On the other hand, could be that someone else planned to raid the *Angelique* tonight and our little trick forced their hand. Now the ship is gone they'll be mad as peeled rattlers and looking for someone else to lynch."

"We're safe here."

"Mayhap, but we'll be safer still when we're back in town. When they find your wounded friend and my fresh blood they'll have the hounds after us."

"We need to talk to them, Schultz. You need a doctor!"

"Can't do it Hunt. The Port Authority is loyal to Hobart. If they catch me here then not even Superintendent Webb could save me."

"Damn your job! I'm worried about saving your leg!"

"I'm worried about saving our lives. The leg will be fine for now. It's only a flesh wound."

"Is there another way off the waterfront?"

"There is, but you won't like it."

"Try me."

With a grimace of pain, Schultz pushed himself to his feet and led Hunt deeper into the moonlit room. He opened a door and entered a low hallway, holding the door ajar until Hunt joined him. Hunt could see only a few yards into the corridor before the door shut, leaving them in complete darkness.

"Keep your hand on the left wall. Go slowly."

Schultz's irregular footsteps echoed across the floorboards. Hunt turned his head left and right but found no light anywhere. The sound of dripping water lay ahead, and he pushed out his left arm until he could feel a rough wooden wall. A splashing footfall ahead of Hunt marked Schultz's steady progress. The wall changed from wood to brick before Hunt stopped walking. No sound pierced the darkness, except their breathing and the muted roar of the river beneath them.

"Take another few steps," advised Schultz from further down the corridor. "Feel for the iron bar on the left." Three steps later Hunt's hand found a rusted vertical bar attached to the wall.

"Hold onto that bar," instructed Schultz's disembodied voice. "Remember that, should you ever come this way again." The screeching of iron scraping on iron assaulted Hunt's ears for a moment and he could hear the rushing sound of the Potomac.

"You're mad, Schultz! The river will be freezing. We'll die down there!"

"I'll take that chance. If Hobart's men catch us here, they'll throw us down there with our hands tied and a hundredweight of lead in our pockets. It's our only chance. Come on now - I'll be waiting at the bottom. Cover the hatch when you're through."

The cacophony of the waters were silenced for a second, as Schultz's body briefly blocked the opening and then came Hunt's turn for the descent. He took off his buckskin coat and knotted it high around his neck. If they made it out of the river alive, he would need the dry coat to keep out the chill of the wind.

His feet found the ladder easily enough and he could reach up to slide the round iron cover back over their escape hole. Nine iron rungs downward Hunt met the freezing waters of the Potomac. His knees and thighs and even his waist passed into the liquid ice before his searching boots found the foul bottom. The vicious current tore at him, splashing daggers of iced water around the new obstacle in its path.

They were down between the stone wall marking the riverbank and the piles that supported the wharf. Slimy wooden towers festooned with seaweed rose from the dark river and stood motionless against the steady push of the water. The current flowed inexorably around each pillar, creating a continuous pressure, which threatened to push them off balance. In the dim starlight that reached them from the edge of the dock, Hunt could see Schultz's pointing arm directing upstream.

Gripping a rusted metal rung Hunt stretched for, but could not reach, the next pillar. He pushed off and staggered into the waters; only achieving his destination as the current pulled his legs from under him. His grasping fingers tore themselves on rough wood and barnacles, but his hold stayed secure. The stench of raw sewage flowing under the wharf rose to his nostrils and he gagged.

Breathing through his mouth, Hunt pushed against the current to maneuver upstream of the pillar until the flow of the river could press him against the pile. The icy water beat at his legs, stiffening their movements and forcing him off balance. Hunt stretched out his arm back towards the dark shadow waiting at the downstream pillar and found a hand stretched out in reply. Schultz's wounded leg could not compete against the strength of the current, and Hunt had a tough haul to get both of them securely upstream of the slimy wooden pillar.

Hunt's eyes were growing accustomed to their surroundings. Starlight reflected on the water in the center of the river, and a hint of stronger light showed a hundred yards upstream. Another leap into the current and another pillar reached before leaning back for Schultz's hand. This time Schultz slipped, losing his hat to the current and falling neck deep into the flood before Hunt's strong arm dragged him to the safety of the next pillar.

"Can you hang on?"

Schultz's words came in short gasps. "Keep going. No way back. We've got to keep going."

Another step. Another pillar. Two minutes. Five minutes. Hunt lost track of time. Twice he stumbled over unseen rocks and almost fell headlong into the river before his scrabbling fingers gained a fresh purchase on the slippery pillars. The frigid water sapped the feeling from his legs and cramps chewed at his calves. The light ahead grew, and perhaps the current weakened a little. They passed another pillar, and the water level dropped to their knees. They reached the last pillar and the blessed stars shone down on them. The shadow of a drainage canal leading away from the river showed less than twenty yards distant.

They still had a struggle to reach firm land. The canal's current weakened, but the mud felt thicker than on the riverbed under the wharf. The moldering corpse of some animal floated near Hunt's legs, twirling in the eddy of his passing. The stench here smelled worse than that of the swiftly flowing Potomac, and set Hunt's stomach turning.

The steps in the canal wall were little more than toeholds, but they gave the detectives a way out. Hunt pulled himself to the top, and leant back to give Schultz a hand. The older man seemed smaller now, wizened by his ordeal, and showed no power in his legs to push himself up the canal wall. Hunt dragged Schultz over the lip of the canal and rolled him away from the edge.

The sharp wind cut through their wet clothes, numbing their limbs. Hunt's teeth chattered uncontrollably. Despite the rough treatment of his wounded limb, Schultz barely made a sound. Hunt knew it wasn't bravado. The effect of the leg wound and the escape through the freezing water would be sending Schultz into shock. He could hear Schultz's breathing changing to the rapid in-out pattern of a man losing his battle with the elements. The escape had been tough enough for the young detective but for the older man with a wounded leg it would be traumatic, even life threatening.

A horse trough stood fifty paces from where they emerged from the canal, and Hunt carried the semi-conscious Schultz to rest in the lee of that small structure. The freezing water in the trough stung his hands, but it served well enough to wash off some of the slime and muck.

"Schultz! Stay awake!" shouted Hunt. "Can you talk?"

"Talk? Yes," said Schultz in a staccato whisper. A spasm shook him and his hands trembled rapidly in the brisk breeze of the freezing night air. If the wind dropped, it would be the weather for snow. A soft rain returned, too light to wash off the canal sludge, but too heavy to ignore.

"We've got to get under cover," said Hunt through his barely functioning lips. "Time to stand up and... wait!"

Voices were approaching. The movement of shadows revealed men coming up the road from the docks, but the lack of light prevented Hunt from identifying them. They could be as regular Union soldiers or they might be Councilman Hobart's guards from the Port Authority, and after Schultz's warning, Hunt didn't feel inclined to take a chance in asking them for help.

Hunt pushed Schultz closer to the horse trough and burrowed after him. If one of those men walked a dozen paces to look into the canal, he couldn't fail to see the detectives. Hunt dared not look. The troops were too close. Rapid footsteps clattered on the duckboards. One set grew louder, too loud for comfort. They stopped on the other side of the horse trough and Hunt felt his hand sliding towards his knife. With an effort, he stopped the movement. He couldn't fight a dozen armed soldiers. Besides that, they were supposedly on his side. It would be tough enough explaining wounding the soldier in the shed. He silently damned Schultz for getting them into this mess.

A sudden splashing from the other side of the water trough told Hunt the nature of the soldier's mission and an involuntary smile stilled his trembling lips for a few seconds. The sound seemed to go on forever. Schultz's body twitched with an occasional shiver showing life hadn't left him. At length the soldier finished his task, and moved off to catch up with his comrades. Hunt forced himself to count to ten after the last of the footsteps faded before he nudged Schultz.

"Come on now. They've gone."

Schultz tried to get up, but that simple task was beyond his faded strength. Hunt untied his coat from around his neck and pushed Schultz's unresisting limbs into the garment, then hoisted the older man evenly across his shoulders and set off towards the city. There would be a house or a hotel or something somewhere in the next mile or so. He'd settle for anyone who wasn't the Port Authority. Only his tattered longjohns and a thin shirt protected Hunt's torso from the elements.

"Turn... that track there," said Schultz through chattering teeth. "Shack... behind those trees."

Hunt followed Schultz's directions, eager to find the closest available aid. The hut stood where Schultz indicated. It was a single room shanty with a poorly thatched roof, but it had a chimney and an inviting pillar of smoke issued from the flue. Hunt kept Schultz over his shoulder and knocked on the rough door. A sudden barking started and a coarse voice answered instantly.

"Be off! I'll set the dogs on you!"

Hunt felt Schultz shake himself to work some life back into his body. His weak voice croaked some words. "Sebastian! It's Schultz! Let me in."

The words produced a scraping sound from within and the door opened a crack. The cautious face staring out at them changed in an instant when it saw Schultz.

"Bejesus man! What've y'done? Come inside."

Hunt carried Schultz into the hovel and set him down by the hearth. The dying embers of the fire cast welcome warmth. Two brown dogs of indeterminate parentage paced back and forth behind Sebastian, but their master's friendship towards the newcomers seemed to keep them satisfied. Hunt stripped off Schultz's filthy coat and pants, and Sebastian stoked the fire as Hunt worked. The absence of the biting wind and the promise of a rebuilt fire filled Hunt with renewed energy. "He's been shot – splinter wound. Have you got antiseptics? Liquor'll do if it's hard spirits."

"Aye. I've got that."

Their ancient host had a leathery face framed by dank, gray hair. His clothes were poor quality, and the fixings of the hovel betrayed his life as one of the thousands who scratched out an existence at the edges of society. The scroungers, the scavengers, the menials who worked by day and starved by night. He rummaged behind a wooden box and retrieved an unlabeled bottle. Hunt guessed it contained moonshine whiskey, but it would be better than washing Schultz's leg in whatever muck passed for water in this neighborhood.

"God's Blood, I'm cold!" whispered Schultz through chattering teeth. His limbs were cold and clammy to Hunt's touch.

"Steady on Schultz! We'll get you warm."

With their host's help, Hunt finished stripping Schultz's wet clothes from the unresisting limbs and wrapped him in a threadbare blanket. The fire threw its warmth at them, and Hunt knew they would be all right. The important thing now would be to thoroughly clean Schultz's wound. All forms of foulness would have soaked into the open flesh during their time in the Potomac. A bloody hole indicated where the shard of wood passed into the leg. Hunt splashed the wounds with the neat spirits, then worked the splinter out of the wound, glad to hear Schultz's hissed intake of breath indicate he hadn't lost all feeling. The lack of blood surprized Hunt. The splinter must have missed the blood vessels, and the freezing water restricted circulation better than a tourniquet.

"I can't tell if part of the wood, or even some pantaloon fabric, is still in the wound," said Hunt. "If that bullet hit the bone you'd have lost the leg. You're darned lucky you only took a splinter."

 "Doesn't - aaaargh - feel lucky, Hunt."

The abysmal light in the room hampered Hunt's work. He probed the wound to clean it thoroughly, with his actions accompanied by Schultz's irregular grunts of pain. At length Hunt wrapped the wounded leg in a makeshift bandage, and help Schultz move closer to the fire. "It needs a proper doctor. I've seen legs lost because wounds weren't cleaned properly."

"It will do until tomorrow," replied Schultz, with a little more strength in his voice. "I know a surgeon. He'll fix it."

Hunt stripped off his own sodden clothing and washed himself using a pail of water provided by their host.

"I'll see t' these," said Sebastian, gathering up their befouled pants and mud-crusted stockings before going outside. A wooden shutter darkened the single window and the only light came from the fireplace. Hunt could hear the rain dripping off the roof and splashing into the puddles alongside the hut. Even Burnside's mud march in '63 hadn't been this miserable. At length Sebastian returned with their poorly washed clothes and began draping them around the room.

"They'll not dry outside," he explained.

"I owe you for this," said Schultz. His breathing had returned to near normal from the shuddering gasps that marked him when they were climbing out of the canal.

"That y'do. A few quarts will square it. Your friend there poured my last bottle on your leg."

"This is Detective Hunt," said Schultz with a shiver. "Hunt, meet Sebastian Cole."

The two men nodded to each other in the awkward manner of strangers to whom an introduction feels unnecessary.

"We're working together on a case," explained Schultz. "It got a little out of control."

"I didna think y'were out fishing. Don' ask, don' tell, that's my motto. You two stay there t'night if y'want."

The rising hammer of the rain on the roof made the offer irresistible. "There's sacks in t'corner. Can't offer y'more than that for blankets. Got some tack if you're hungry."

The detectives shook their head in unison.

"All right then, stoke t'fire a bit if y'want. I'll be gettin' back t'sleep. Privy's behind t'shed out back."

Sebastian lay on the bedding to one side of the hearth and Hunt tended the fire. Plenty of dry wood stood ready to feed the fire, and at length Hunt's labor produced a roaring flame. The sacks Sebastian indicated were coarse and grimy, but they made a better bed than the bare earth. Hunt finished his tasks then lay down, and silence descended for a time broken only by Sebastian's snoring. The scent of the dogs lay heavy in the air.

Schultz spoke first. "There's still some whiskey in this bottle."

Hunt answered with an outstretched arm. After a while, Schultz held out his hand, and Hunt returned the bottle. For the next few minutes, only the periodic sloshing of the bottle and the hammer of the rain on the roof disturbed the silence. The bottle passed frequently between the men, growing lighter after each journey.

"You're handy with that knife, Hunt."

"Handy enough."

"I daresay the man you hit will have his own friends. They'll be up all night looking for us. We'll stay here for now. I couldn't have come much further anyhow."

Hunt took another drink. He'd been through a war, and he knew that the real fears began only after the battle, when the realization of a narrowly-missed death came back to haunt the survivors. Best to drown those fears in their infancy.

"You think we're still in danger?"

"Ben Ackroyd sat at the dock gate tonight. A bottle of rum bought us entry there, and another bottle would buy that information back from him. Ackroyd has no loyalty. We stumbled into a hornet's nest, and I need time to consider what happened."

"Ackroyd fired that first shot?"

"No. Albert Lachlan did that. He owes me a few favors and agreed to fire a pistol shot at a time I requested."

"Then tell me what happened there. Why all the soldiers?"

"I wish I knew. Those customs officers..."

"Those weren't customs officers," interrupted Hunt. "I know an infantry tunic when I see one, and I've not seen step-through volleys like that fired outside of the battlefield. Those were army men."

"Army men then, and that makes even less sense. I'll talk to Lachlan tomorrow. There's not much happens on the docks he doesn't see. He'll know who let those troops in and what they were after."

Hunt felt the hard liquor moving through him, and his thoughts began traveling in circles. Maybe Donohue had the right idea after all, and he should be content to let Schultz do the thinking. He upended the bottle and took a long swallow. Schultz moved his wounded leg, triggering a sharp intake of breath. Hunt passed across the crude anesthetic and heard the other man take a double mouthful.

"They were after the *Angelique*," prompted Hunt.

"It appears so. She left that dock and made sail down the Potomac like greased lightning. Why would a Confederate ship sneak up the Potomac and moor in Washington port under a false flag? They have few enough ships to risk one on such a mission."

"You're sure it was a Confederate ship?"

"Innocent ships don't run away, which means either smugglers or rebels, and smugglers wouldn't come into a public berth like these docks. A quiet creek or fishing village is better for them. Then you saw the flag fall on the deck. They were rebels for sure. But why risk a ship?"

"A ship gives a fast getaway."

"A ship is too easily blocked in her berth. If this had been daylight, she'd have been caught at the Long Bridge. Sending a ship up the Potomac is madness."

"What if she needed to transport something too big for a man or beast to carry? Something that required a ship?"

Schultz shook his head. "Albert said that she hadn't unloaded anything in all the time since she docked. I'd venture she slipped through the blockade, collected southern agents somewhere along the Confederate coast, and needed to get them to Washington in a hurry."

"You said you didn't guess."

"I don't. A guess is an assumption of fact. A hypothesis is subject to investigation and confirmation."

"We still don't know why Johnny Reb wanted to kill Anderson."

"Why indeed? Whatever evidence they destroyed on the floor of the Herald must be more important than I realized. I considered some businessman or politician was afeared of what Anderson planned to publish, and sought to stop it. Now it appears we're dealing with the Confederacy instead, and I'm hard pressed to see what Anderson could have written about the South that hadn't already been said a dozen times by The Intelligencer and the Star, and every other newspaper in this Union."

"Maybe he overheard something? Some Confederate battle plan or the like?"

"Perhaps. Or perhaps someone told him something in confidence, and then became concerned that Anderson would spread the secret further. Tomorrow you'll go back to the Herald and see if they have a correspondence book. There'll be nothing from the south of course, but a letter could be sent via England or France."

"Fine. I'll check at the Herald for letters."

The bottle sloshed again, and more liquor slid down Hunt's throat.

"We must also investigate Anderson's house. If the Confederates have beaten us there, then so be it. There's nothing we can do about that now."

Hunt stifled a whiskey-laden belch. "Check Anderson's house also."

"That still doesn't explain the attack on the *Angelique*. It's too much of a coincidence that soldiers should be planning to seize that ship the very night we're looking for Anderson's murderer on her."

"Yep. That can't be a coincidence."

Schultz's voice became firmer. "I don't yet see why they were still moored at the dockside two days after they killed Anderson. I can't understand what they were waiting for."

"Beats me Schultz. When we catch them, we'll ask them."

"We'll do that," promised Schultz before lapsing into silence.

The fire flickered and the room felt warmer now. It had been a full evening. Eventually Hunt spoke. He couldn't leave the emotional wound alone. "Did Colonel Lukey really say I was intelligent?"

The long pause before an answer indicated that the response would not be a good one. Hunt should have said something then, told Schultz to forget it, made some other comment. He felt like a jackrabbit caught in the light of the oncoming locomotive, waiting for the crushing impact that would flatten him, but unable to move out of the way. He stared at the fire, waiting for the blow.

"Intelligent? Yes, he said that. He also said you were impulsive."

"Impulsive?"

"That's what he said."

"But he did say intelligent?"

"The officer has the necessary intelligence and combat skills to perform well on the battlefield, but lacks the ability to lead troops," quoted Schultz. "He is impulsive in his response to tactical situations and shows a preference for using his own abilities rather than coordinating the talents of the troops under his command."

To Schultz's credit, he sounded like he didn't want to say those things. Oddly enough, Hunt realized that he expected to hear those kinds of words in Lukey's report. Deep down he knew that he could never be a leader of men. The alcohol numbed his brain sufficiently, so the slur on his abilities didn't matter.

"That's the army. It's different here. You handled that fight on the docks pretty well tonight."

With that point noted, both men fell silent. Hunt felt strangely at peace. Despite his earlier mistakes, he'd come through tonight and proved himself a worthy partner for Schultz. The old man might have the right theories, but when the chips were down and the bullets were flying, it had been Hunt's knife that saved them. Schultz couldn't deny that.

Maybe he should tell Schultz his real age. Perhaps Schultz would understand why he took advantage of his mature features to put his age up when he joined the army. The thought that most underage youths would pass themselves off as the minimum enlistment age of eighteen prompted him to add on another few years. And it worked! The recruiting sergeant hadn't seemed to care what age Hunt wrote down - probably didn't even bother to read it.

The extra years helped Hunt gain his battlefield commission, and then his job with the Metropolitan Police. Nevertheless, such secrets cried out to be shared. Would Schultz keep the secret, or would it cost Hunt his job? Thinning clouds permitted the moonlight to wash intermittently through the cracks in the shuttered window and over the dirt floor.

At length, only the regular breathing of the two dogs and the three sleeping men disturbed the silence of the room. On the ground between Shultz and Hunt lay an empty bottle, mute witness to a comradeship neither man yet fully welcomed.

The morning after

Shafts of cold daylight were streaming through cracks in the shutters when Hunt opened his eyes. His tongue needed water, his head needed darkness, and his bladder needed relief. His bladder won the battle. The clothes draped around the room from the previous night's washing were still clammy to the touch, but he pulled them on regardless, and with flapping bootlaces and undone buttons set out in search of the privy. When he returned, he found Schultz sitting up, examining his unwrapped wound.

"I count myself fortunate that I only took a splinter of wood instead of a musket ball, but hellfire and darnation this leg hurts."

"You'll see a surgeon today?"

"First thing," promised Schultz, rebandaging his leg. "Come on, help me up."

With the help of Hunt, Schultz got to his feet and managed a limping walk to the door. "It won't do. I can't come in to the station like this. If Hobart follows up on last night's riverside shindig with the Superintendent, then Price will call me in for a talk. One look at this leg and the whole story will come out. Hobart knows I'm on his case about the fraud with the city council, and he might suspect that I hosted last night's party, sniffing about for more evidence. Right suspect. Wrong reason."

"I'll lay low for a while. If anyone at the station asks after me, then tell them … tell them I've gone to Pittsburgh for three days. Say it's about the Spaulding matter. I've done that sort of thing before. They won't find it unusual."

Hunt nodded his agreement and helped Schultz with his clothes. Hearing Schultz acknowledge his oversight gave Hunt a good feeling. If the Thinking Machine could admit to his own failings, then perhaps he would be more understanding of similar lapses in others. In that case, Hunt could find a way to be his partner.

Sebastian and his dogs had already left for the day's activities without waking their uninvited guests. Hunt felt some shame over finishing the man's liquor, but his guilt vanished when Schultz rolled up a currency note and pushed it halfway into the neck of the empty bottle. "He'll buy a few gallons with that," said Schultz. "Let's get to town."

They moved out of the hovel into the glare of cold sunshine, where Hunt's knife carved Schultz a crude crutch from the limb of a nearby tree. The wet smell of the ice on the earth gave a welcome change from the suffocating stench of the hut.

"Hunt …" said Schultz, then paused.

The younger detective looked at Schultz.

"Hunt, I need to … I want to … thank you for last night. I couldn't have got out of there without you."

Hunt didn't know what to say, so he said nothing. The moment passed, and Schultz started issuing orders again.

"For today, I need you to go back to the Herald. Check what headlines Anderson planned for the coming week. I should have checked that on Monday. Let's go."

The sky's unexpected brightness provided a welcome change from the rain of the last few days, and the two men made steady progress back to the main road. A hundred yards along the road, the driver of an eastbound buckboard laden with vegetables answered their hail, and for a couple of thin dimes agreed to give them a ride the city. They parted company on New York Avenue with Hunt jumping off to allow the deliveryman to take Schultz to the surgeon. "You'll lie low for three days?" queried Hunt. "How will I contact you if I find anything?"

"Ask for Gregory at McRae's Hotel. He'll find me. If I need you, I'll send word to the station using the name 'Thompson'. Wouldn't do to run the risk of the captain figuring out I'm still in town. Friday should see me walking much better than now. You know what you have to do?"

"I check at the Herald for recent parcels and then look in on Miss Anderson."

"Search Anderson's house also. Check his personal papers and see if he's had any recent visitors and ... darn this leg!"

"Don't worry, Schultz. I'll search it all. You go see the surgeon."

Schultz raised a hand to the driver. A chuck of the whip and the cart drew out into the road between a plodding carthorse and an almost empty omnibus.

Hunt started walking. The cool morning wind bit through his damp clothes, but at least the skies were clearer than they had been for the last few days. With luck, there would be no rain today. Hunt needed a change of clothes, but the geography of his situation dictated a large dogleg back to his boarding house to achieve that. He decided to visit the Herald first to ask for the Anderson's home address, and then go home for a shave and new shirt before visiting Jane.

Hunt knew that his legs could find their way to the Herald without conscious effort, so he let them do the walking while his mind struggled with the issues of the case. He still owned too many unanswered questions. Why did Schultz release Picard? How did the murderers gained access to the Herald's offices? What could be the significance of the Illuminati lapel pin on the bedroom floor? Thoughts churned inside his head as he strode along the sidewalk towards Eleventh Street.

The walk warmed him up. There were shops selling breakfasts at the side of the road, and the smell of eggs and sausages tempted him more than once. The exertions of the previous night gave him a raging appetite but, for the moment, his mind set itself on reaching the Herald office. He would visit there first, and eat later. This time, he had only a simple task to perform. Get the headlines for the coming week. A simple task, he told himself. How many of those had he failed in his life?

He pushed the negative thoughts from his head. He would be a success as a detective. Anyone else could have made the same unfortunate mistake with Picard. Anyone except... No, dammit! Schultz wasn't perfect. Last night he hadn't known the answers when those army troops arrived to battle the *Angelique*. His high and mighty, smarter-than-thou attitude hadn't seen that little circus coming. Perhaps the passing of time would solve the problem. If Hunt applied himself, then surely he would reach the level of Schultz before long.

Cheered by that thought, he turned the last corner before the offices of the Herald. Yesterday's crowds were missing, and the death of John Anderson was now literally yesterday's news. Only Anderson's friends and family would remember his passing.

Squeezing his way past two plump matrons standing on the sidewalk, Hunt entered the offices of the Washington Herald, then abruptly stopped. Jane Anderson stood in the office, talking with Hackett.

Hunt struggled with this predicament. The last time he had been here, Hackett and the others saw him triumphantly arresting Adam Picard. Now he needed to admit in front of Jane that he had been wrong, and to anger himself even further, he recalled he hadn't yet received a straight answer from Schultz about why he lied to Price about keeping Picard in the cells. He looked down at his damp and filthy clothing. Better to go home now and clean up.

"Detective Hunt!"

Hackett saw him. He couldn't leave now. He discretely checked the buttons on his fly and lifted a hand in reply. Never run away from these situations, he reminded himself. Tugging his shirt into shape, Hunt advanced into the office.

122

"Mister Hackett!" he called out in reply, intently scanning Jane's face for a welcoming smile. "Hello, Miss Anderson. This is a pleasant surprise."

Despite the sombre clothes she wore, Jane Anderson shone with a radiant beauty. She curtseyed, and held out her hand. With a thrill in his stomach, Hunt took her hand and in flamboyant slow motion, pressed it to his lips. A tiny smile played on her face, sending a thrill up his spine. His dreams were made of moments like this.

Then he saw his own hands, grubby and torn, ingrained with whatever foulness he had dredged from the depths of the Potomac, and hadn't managed to remove in the dingy light of Sebastian's hovel. He dropped her hand abruptly, before she could see his fingernails.

"I hoped to see you later today," he continued with a calmness he didn't feel. "Pardon my clothes. I've been doing some underground … undercover work."

"I thought to get an early start on father's affairs. Mister Hackett has been telling me about how the paper operates. I'm afraid I didn't take much notice of it in years past when my father… when…"

Her face stiffened and she stopped talking. Hunt longed to stroke her cheek and enfold her in his arms, but such familiarity would be impossible here. Hunt could see Bessie fussing around down at the back of the office, while Tom attended to one of the hand presses. If only Hackett would leave, then he could have a private conversation with Jane.

It must be difficult for her to accustom herself to her father's death. A young lady like her, suddenly thrust into the world of business, would be struggling to come to terms with some harsh realities. He had no doubt that she would be glad of his compassionate ear. He cleared his throat. "Miss Anderson, I need to talk with you, but I see now isn't the time. May I call on you again?"

The words were too harsh. He wanted to have said something softer. It didn't seem to matter, though. Jane smiled at him through her tears.

"Tomorrow would be good. I will be at father's house in Georgetown.

"Would ten o'clock be fine for you?"

"Yes. I'll look forward to it. We can talk more then. You will find me at Braemear in College Street"

"It's as well you're here," said Hackett, spoiling the moment. "We discovered something else which may be related to the robbery. The Thursday file is missing."

Hackett looked expectantly at Hunt.

"And what is the Thursday file?" prompted Hunt.

"Sorry there," apologized Hackett. "We publish twice a week. We keep two files, one each for the Tuesday and the Thursday editions. When you were here on Monday, we checked the Tuesday file since we needed that immediately, but we neglected to look at the Thursday file. We didn't notice its absence until after you'd gone. Perhaps we should have sent a message, but we've been too busy rewriting it for tomorrow's print run."

That should be significant. Hunt felt some gratification Schultz hadn't picked up the point about the missing file. "That must have been what the intruders burnt on the floor."

"We thought that also. By then, of course, Bessie'd cleared away the rubbish, and we had no way of checking it. Not that it would have mattered. The fire destroyed everything there."

"At least that gives us a motive for the crime. What breaking news did you have in the folder?"

Hackett's crestfallen face gave Hunt the answer even before the tall man spoke.

"Mister Anderson kept that pretty much to himself. We have the regular columns, shipping reports and such. I helped him with those, but he wrote the editorial and most of the articles himself. Tom would get the folder the day before press day. Then we'd do the layout ready to do the pressing that night. I don't know what he wrote for tomorrow's edition."

"Weren't there any notes or drafts? Was everything in the one folder?"

Hackett's unhappy look provided the answer.

"Then we're no further ahead," shouted Hunt in frustration, then, embarrassed at his public display of anger, he turned to apologize. "I'm sorry, Miss Anderson. I want to catch these murderers as much as you do."

"What about that fellow you arrested on Monday?" asked Hackett. "Wasn't he the man?"

The embarrassment returned. Hunt knew he had to brave it out.

"He turned into a potato who fell into a hot stew," replied Hunt, badly paraphrasing Schultz. "We're still searching for the motive. Whatever that Thursday file contained might have given us a fresh line of inquiry."

Jane's face tightened on hearing that news, and Hunt's stomach churned. A fine display of professional policing he'd given her. "We're looking at other leads," he offered. "Do you keep a correspondence book? Did any unusual mail arrive in the last week for Mister Anderson?"

"I can't tell you about any personal mail to his home," replied Hackett. "Miss Anderson would have to help you with that. I check the mail that comes in here. There's been nothing out of the ordinary."

"Nothing from Europe or Canada?"

"Nothing apart from the regular packet from England. I opened it myself. Last month's European newspapers, the new London Almanac, a half-dozen woodcuts we ordered in October. Nothing we didn't expect."

"I see," said Hunt confidently, before realizing his slumping shoulders and lack of further questions provided clear evidence that he saw nothing.

"We can't tell you much more at this point. If we realize anything else is missing, we'll send a runner to the station. In the meantime, we'll print whatever news we have. It'll be stretched a bit this week, but we'll make our deadline all right. There's always some war news we can use to fill the columns, like the naval skirmish on the Potomac last night."

Hunt smiled to himself. The *Angelique* hadn't made such an easy escape after all. Perhaps it would be best not to show too much knowledge of that event. "Do tell."

"A runner brought us the news half an hour ago. A battle on the docks. Gunfire and soldiers and such, but the ship escaped and fell in with some navy gunboats near Alexandria."

"That gives you something to write about."

"Normally we wouldn't bother with that sort of news, but right now we're battling to fill all of the pages. The ship went aground, and the patrols are still looking for the crew. If they catch anyone today, then it'll be more fresh news for our Thursday edition."

"Went aground? Where?"

"Somewhere past Berry Point. Went aground on the north bank and burned somewhat they said. Ho there! Where are you going?"

Hunt raced out the door and sprinted for the stationhouse. If the *Angelique* grounded on the north side of the Potomac he still had a chance to catch the crew. Someone on that ship held the key to Anderson's death and a few minutes wasted now might mean the difference between their escape and capture. Two blocks later, a cab came into view and Hunt hauled himself into it without giving the driver a chance to object. "Fifth Precinct stationhouse cabby! Faster now! This is police business."

The cabby whipped the horse, and the carriage picked up speed, sliding from side to side on the slippery roads. Hunt caught his breath and tried to force his thoughts into order. He needed to find out where the *Angelique* grounded and he needed to be there with sufficient authority to take charge of any prisoners. This now moved beyond his limited police experience. When the cab reached the Fifth Precinct he spotted a familiar shape walking up the steps into the stationhouse.

"Sloan!" shouted Hunt, fumbling in his pockets for coins to give the cabbie. The shape stopped and turned.

"Sloan, I need a hand. I need to get down river as fast as possible. Berry

126

Point."

"Down river? A police matter?"

"Most definitely. A suspect in the Anderson case. I think he's on that ship that grounded at Berry Point last night."

Sloan shook his head. "That's outside our area. We can go there, but we've no authority."

"What's the quickest way?"

"Police boat at the navy yard. Where's Schultz?"

"Gone to Pittsburgh for three days."

"Tell you what. I'll come with you." The cabbie still sat there waiting for his fare. Sloan and Hunt climbed aboard, and seconds later the cab rejoined the traffic and plowed through the flooded streets towards the Navy yard.

Hunt and Sloan at the Navy Yard

Congress established the Washington Navy Yard on October 2, 1799 as the principal establishment for the US Navy, and it remained as the custodian of that role until the occupation of Washington by victorious British troops on August 24, 1814. This event prompted the commandant, Commodore Thomas Tingey, to order its destruction by fire rather than see it fall intact into the hands of the enemy. After the war, the Yard never regained its function as a shipbuilder; other yards possessing better deepwater berths usurped that role.

Sloan and Hunt left their cab at the Latrobe Gate and the two men walked through the Yard to the docks. A single boiler boat sat there with two men standing by the sternpost. Hunt had never been on a steam-powered boat before.

"Detectives Sloan and Hunt," said Sloan. "We need to go down river."

One of the men held a steaming mug of coffee. He nodded genially. "No problem. You know how to fill out the book?"

Sloan moved across to a desk and picked up a nib. Hunt stepped onto the boat next to the coffee-drinker.

"You fellows in a hurry now?"

"There's a boat aground downriver with a murder suspect on board," replied Hunt. "He doesn't know we're coming."

"The *Angelique*?"

"That's her!". You know where she is?"

"Don't know about the actual boat," conceded the boatman. "But the navy brought up a couple of prisoners this morning. They're still in the guardhouse, far as I know."

"Here? The prisoners are here?"

"Right in that stone building on the end there. One fellow came in a bit poorly I heard, but the other seemed fine."

"Reckon we'll leave you here then," said Sloan. "Thanks."

The coffee drinker raised his free hand in a half salute and paid them no more attention. Hunt scrambled back up onto the pier next to Sloan and joined him in a rapid walk to the guardhouse.

"That's luck for you," said Sloan. "Course we might have a bit of trouble getting hold of the prisoners. The navy can be a bit sticky at times. Bit too fond of their paperwork for my liking."

The guardhouse occupied a squat stone fort with gun slits for windows and a thick wooden double door as an entryway. The solitary marine standing at ease outside the doorway ignored them as they walked into the building where an aging petty officer sat behind an old wooden desk.

"Detectives Sloan and Hunt from the Fifth Precinct police," said Sloan by way of introduction. "You're holding prisoners off the *Angelique*?"

The petty officer looked at them. "You men have badges? Let's see them."

Hunt and Sloan dropped their badges on the desk and the petty officer scrutinized them carefully. At length he seemed satisfied, and turned to look down the corridor behind him. "Benson! Front and center!" he yelled.

A clatter of boot heels on flagstones foreshadowed Benson's arrival. A lad barely old enough to shave stumbled to a halt at the petty officer's desk; all elbows and thumbs, and looking ill-suited to his seaman's uniform.

"Get the Lieutenant, Benson. There's a couple of patrolmen here to see him about a prisoner."

Benson responded with a poorly co-ordinated salute and disappeared at a frenzied pace down the corridor. The petty officer shook his head sadly as the echo of the youth's heels faded in the distance, then turned back to the detectives. "Lieutenant Westaway will be here in a few minutes."

"Thanks," replied Hunt.

Sloan and Hunt retrieved their badges, then stepped away from the desk and back into the doorway. The cold wind blew strongly here, and blown white peaks crested the waves on the water at the end of the dock. Salt spray from the Chesapeake rode high with the winter winds, and flavored the pine tar and manila rope smells of the dockyard.

Enthusiasm bubbled inside Hunt. This break could crack the case wide open. To have a prisoner who could explain the link between Anderson's murder and the *Angelique* seemed too good to be true. Once they knew why the intruders killed Anderson, then the rest of the pieces should fall into place.

Measured paces grew in volume behind them, and the detectives turned towards the corridor. A lieutenant appeared, smart and clean-shaven, wearing a uniform pressed to knife-edge creases. He introduced himself. "Lieutenant Westaway. How can I help you?"

Hunt felt himself to be in his element with this conversation. He worked with men like this during his time in the army. "Detectives Hunt and Sloan from the Fifth Precinct. I understand you've picked up some men from the wreck of the *Angelique*?"

"That's right. One didn't make it, but the other had nothing worse than a bang on the head. Sawbones looked at him and said he's fine. The rest of the crew scattered into the countryside. The army's put patrols out looking for them."

"Who did you pick up?" asked Hunt, keeping his voice sharp and leading the Lieutenant in a pattern of rapid question and automatic answer.

"Jimmy Owens, but he's not talking much."

Hunt clapped his hands together in a gesture of satisfaction. "That's the man! We want him for the murder of John Anderson last Sunday night. We'd be glad to take him off your hands."

The Lieutenant looked at Hunt warily. His careful tone showed that he wasn't going to agree automatically with that request. "That explains some things," he said. "Not everything though. Murder, you say?"

Hunt nodded. "There's a gang of them came into town on that ship. We almost caught them at the docks last night, but they slipped out ahead of our patrols."

Hunt knew that he took a risk in assuming that Lieutenant Westaway didn't know the full story of what happened on the docks. The shambling bureaucracy that ran the armed services of the United States did not communicate effectively between its different branches. Under normal circumstances, it could take weeks before the Lieutenant could expect a reply from the Washington garrison regarding what happened to make the *Angelique* leave port so suspiciously. Hunt bet the Lieutenant would jump at the idea of having the problem removed from his jurisdiction, but he needed to play his cards carefully. Westaway didn't seem completely convinced yet.

"Of course, I could get my captain to come down here and talk to your captain. Though I'm guessing neither of them would be too pleased with that idea."

The pause lengthened while Hunt's words hung in the air. Even at the best of times, no military man wanted his senior officer disturbed with an issue that could have been resolved lower down the line.

"You're probably right," demurred the Lieutenant. "Tell you what. I'll reclassify him as an escaped felon rather than a prisoner of war. Give me a receipt for him and he's yours."

"Easy enough," agreed Hunt. "Then we both can get about our business."

"Wandsworth!" said the Lieutenant to the petty officer. "Make out a receipt for the prisoner. If you gentlemen wait here, I'll have him brought down."

Hunt clasped his hands behind his back and strode to the door. This kind of police work thrilled him. Dealing face to face with a criminal had much more appeal than puzzling over strangely shaped lapel pins. Sloan came up beside him.

"Is he the man you want?" he asked in a low voice. Hunt grinned, and replied to Sloan quietly.

"Tell you the truth, Sloan, we don't know who on that boat did the murder, but if Owens is all they've captured so far, then we'll start with him and see where that leads."

Sloan nodded agreement, and began the rhythmic process of cracking his knuckles. "Seems a good idea. I'll get a wagon to carry the prisoner. There's one at the boatshed. You stay here and finish the paperwork. You carrying any wrist irons?"

Hunt admitted he hadn't bought cuffs with him. Sloan passed across a pair.

"Handy things to have. Wristirons, badge and revolver. I don't leave the station without them."

Sloan stepped out into the roadway, and strode back towards the boatshed. Hunt stayed in the doorway, impulsively bouncing up and down on his toes and struggling to keep a professional demeanor. He'd learned a few things since the arrest of Picard, and now he felt more comfortable with the procedure. Jimmy Owens mightn't be the actual murderer, but he'd have a good idea who did the crime. Hunt took some comfort Sloan wasn't objecting to this approach.

"Sir, we'll need you to sign this release."

The petty officer held a sheet of paper. Hunt stepped to the desk and read a receipt detailing that Detectives Hunte and Slone accepted responsibility for prisoner #812. Hunt smiled at the misspelling of their names, but decided it wasn't worth correcting. He didn't care what the navy called him as long as they signed over the prisoner. He added his signature to the bottom of the document and thrust it back. It would be as well to get the paperwork out of the way now. The petty officer took the paper and resumed his seat.

Hunt needed to pace. He stepped out past the sentry at the door and strode up and down the front of the guardhouse. Twelve paces up. Twelve paces back. Hands clasped behind his back with tension riding high on his shoulders. Should he wait for Schultz to return before interrogating the prisoner? Schultz needed time to recover so he could appear back at the station without enduring embarrassing questions about his wounded leg. Hunt would have to do the interrogation.

Very well. He could manage that. He'd start by composing a list of questions. He needed to find out why the *Angelique* had come to Washington. Who murdered John Anderson? What evidence did they burn on the floor of the Washington Herald? The questions tumbled over themselves faster and faster in his mind, and he longed for paper to write them down. Benson called him from the doorway. Hunt realized that Benson had already called three or four times. Muttering an expletive against his own preoccupation, he broke off his pacing and looked at Benson.

"Sir, your prisoner's ready."

Hunt couldn't see Sloan anywhere, so he followed Benson back into the guardhouse, trading the crisp scent of the sea for the cold damp smell of stone. Lieutenant Westaway stood there in front of three men. The two on the outside wore regulation navy uniforms, but their limping walks betrayed old wounds. After three years of war, the Union needed all able-bodied men on the front line. Those whose fighting days were over did the rear echelon work.

Between the sailors stood a sallow youth, barely twenty years of age and dressed in faded denim pantaloons and a simple blue shirt. Minor cuts and bruises on his face could have been from the battle on the river, or from rough handling in the guardhouse cells.

"Jimmy Owens," he pronounced gravely. "There are questions we need to ask you."

Owens looked up sullenly, and tossed his lanky hair away from his face. His demeanor echoed that of a new recruit challenging the parade sergeant to a duel of wills. Hunt could live with that for now.

"You want to put him in irons?" asked the Lieutenant.

Hunt, grateful for Sloan's forethought, pulled the cuffs from his pocket. One of the sailors held Owens by the collar while the other removed the navy irons from his wrists and allowed Hunt to replace them with his own pair. As he straightened from the operation, Hunt heard the clip clopping of a horse and the clanking of a wagon. By the time the sailors escorted Owens to the door, Sloan arrived with an enclosed police carriage.

"That's the boy? Let's get him in then."

Sloan took the lead now, and Hunt had no problem with that. They pushed Owens into the carriage through the single rear-facing door. The padlock clicked shut and the two detectives swung onto the front bench seat on either side of the whipper, a mustachioed German who reeked of sauerkraut and mumbled foreign sounding songs to himself for the whole trip.

Neither the duty sergeant at his desk nor the turnkey in the cells paid them any attention as Sloan helped Hunt move Owens into a single cell away from the other prisoners. The damp cell contained only three sturdy chairs, and smelled like a sewer.

The detectives pushed an unresisting Owens into one of the chairs and Sloan recuffed his prisoner's hands behind him. Irregular dark stains covered parts of the floor. Hunt didn't need to guess what they were.

A mossy strip ran down one wall where water trickled down in a slow stream. The walls were free of the words and crude pictures that the more literate prisoners might have etched there as they whiled their time away. The lack of a bunk or chamber pot suggested this cell's sole function

134

centered around interrogation of prisoners. Sloan looked down at the seated prisoner. The prisoner stared back.

"I ain't saying nothing. You don' scare me."

"Let's start with your name then," suggested Sloan pleasantly.

"Jimmy Owens an' that's all you get from me."

"We're not in a hurry here Owens. We can take as long as we need to get answers from you."

Owens set his mouth and looked at the floor.

"Where'd the ship come from?"

No answer.

"Tell me the captain's name."

No answer. Sloan looked at the ceiling of the cell for a moment, then launched an enormous backhand blow that knocked Owens and his chair onto their side. Sloan shook his hand a couple of times to lessen the sting, then dragged Owens and the chair upright. Hunt understood the need to get rough with a prisoner who wouldn't talk, but it felt more intense to be bashing prisoners in these cells than questioning a captive out on a battlefield. Down here, the contest had no honor.

Blood smears marred the prisoner's face. Sloan moved out into the corridor and motioned for Hunt to join him. Hunt stepped out of the cell.

"Tell Ridley we need Private Pemberton," said Sloan quietly.

"Pemberton?"

"He'll understand," smiled Sloan with a knowing wink before going back into the cell. Hunt repeated the instructions to himself as confirmation, then went in search of Ridley. He found the one-armed gofer talking to the duty sergeant and, as Sloan foretold, Ridley had no problem with the instructions.

"Pemberton'll be there right smartly," he said with a chuckle. "You get back to the prisoner, Mister Hunt. I'll look after Pemberton."

Mystified, Hunt returned to the cell and listened to Sloan string together cuss words in new and inventive ways. The prisoner sat bloodied but unbowed, and showed no sign of co-operating. Unsure as to whom Private Pemberton might be, Hunt moved to the back of the cell and leaned against the cold wall to watch Sloan berating the prisoner. A few minutes later Hunt heard a noise. A scraping sound from the corridor that grew in volume, and then Ridley appeared at the door to the cell.

Ridley wore a tattered Confederate uniform and sat on a battered wooden cart, which he maneuvered by digging a short stick into the potholed floor and using the leverage from that to push his cart forwards. It seemed an awkward and most inefficient way to travel, but Ridley kept it up until his trolley advanced into the cell. He stopped beside the prisoner's chair. Ridley's ankles were manacled and wrapped in rags, and on his lap sat a collection of scrubbing brushes in a bucket of water. A pair of bent eyeglasses with one cracked lens sat on his nose.

Sloan interrupted his invective to glare at Ridley. "What you want, boy?"

"Capt'n told me to clean the cells, suh," replied Ridley in a deferential southern drawl. "He says to clean all of them suh, begging yore pardon Mister Detective suh."

"I'm busy, Pemberton. Git yore ass outta here."

"Suh, the capt'n told me…" Ridley's voice trailed off.

Sloan straightened up and walked over to where Ridley sat on his trolley. His voice sounded dangerously smooth. "How long you been here now, Pemberton?"

"Don't rightly know, suh."

Sloan's boot lashed out, catching Ridley in the ribs and sending the bucket and brushes clattering and splashing against the cell wall. Hunt could see Sloan held his foot limply so the impact on Ridley would be no worse than catching a twelve-pound bag of coffee, but to Jimmy Owens it would all be terribly real. Ridley tumbled off the trolley in a smooth, maneuver, slapping his one hand noisily against the floor as he rolled up against the wall behind Owens. When he rolled out of the prisoner's sight the cringing demeanor stopped, but the whining continued.

"Don' hit me, suh. I don' know what day it is in here, suh. The Union is winning, suh! God bless President Lincoln! Don' hit me, suh!"

"You clean the cells when I'm finished with them, you piece of southern shit! Talk back to me again an' I'll cut off your other arm!"

"Yes, suh! Don hit me, suh!"

Sloan walked back to the front of the prisoner and put his left foot on the prisoner's lap. He dug his boot into the prisoner's groin, and leaned forward on that leg until his nose almost touched the young Confederate's forehead, and his mouth sat less than an inch from the youth's eyes. His voice calmed to an almost conversational tone.

"Pemberton here's been living down in the cells for a few years now. Some of our cavalry boys chewed up them rebel Fairfax Rifles at Frayser's Farm back in '62 and they picked up Pemberton in the rubble. Wouldn't you know it, his name never made it onto the roll of prisoners. Haw! Haw! We paid a barrel of beer for him, an' he's been cleaning latrines down here ever since. Maybe one day we'll let him see sunlight again. Maybe not."

Sloan picked a speck of dirt out from under one fingernail and flicked it into the prisoner's face. The pain of Sloan's foot digging into his lap would be difficult to endure, and the boy's demeanor changed from nervous defiance to plain nervousness. Behind the prisoner, Ridley closed one eye in a slow wink to Hunt then grabbed one of the brushes and scraped it back and forth across the cell floor.

"I's cleaning the cell sir, like capt'n told me."

Sloan and Ridley had obviously been through this routine before, and Hunt found himself hard put to keep a straight face. He moved another pace to place himself directly behind Owens, lest an unplanned grin give the game away.

Sloan continued his one-sided conversation with Owens in a flat unemotional voice. As he talked, Sloan resumed his open-handed hitting of the prisoner's face. His blows were not gentle.

"You see boy…" SLAP!

"Pemberton here got an infection a few months back…" SLAP!

"an' the surgeon took off his arm." SLAP!

"Gangrene and all that…" SLAP!

"from working in them there sewers." SLAP!

"Lost me a whole five dollars betting he wouldn't make it…" SLAP!

"but the old coot pulled through." SLAP!

Sloan paused and looked at his fist, then back up at the prisoner. "Damn you Owens! Now you've gotten blood all over my hand!"

Sloan straightened to stretch his back, then hawked and spat over the prisoner in Ridley's general direction. Ridley continued his deferential whimpering, but he put down his brush and gave a mock salute to Sloan.

"Thank you for that suh. God bless you suh."

Hunt clenched his fist in his mouth to stop laughing as Ridley mumbled softly to himself in his southern drawl. Sloan twisted his lip contemptuously at Ridley, then looked down at the prisoner.

"Now you've given me an idea, boy. Maybe we need an apprentice to help Pemberton here with cleaning out the cells. Of course, we'd have to break your ankles like we did with Pemberton to stop you running away, but don't you worry, we'd feed you every day or so. And if we ever caught you complaining to another prisoner and asking for help, we'd cut off your balls. Pemberton here lost one afore he learned his lesson, but now he don't talk to anyone 'less we say so. Haw! Haw! Haw!"

Sloan's laugh carried a sinister and most believable note. Ridley's aimless brushing resumed, and the effect of that combination of sounds showed in

138

the spasmodic clenching and unclenching of the prisoners bound hands. Ridley began whistling a pathetic rendition of "The Star-Spangled Banner" as Sloan moved in for the kill.

"What you think, Detective Hunt? Should we get the sledgehammer now? Best take off your boots boy, so I can aim better. I'd hate to have to hit your ankles more than once each."

"Don't recall doing any paperwork for this prisoner," Hunt added helpfully. He wanted to say more, but needed to bite his tongue instead to swallow a laugh.

"Well now, that's right," said Sloan. "There ain't no paperwork for this boy. Looks like you'll be listed as 'Missing' when they call the roll back home. Course, we'll know where you are, but don't you worry about that. We can keep a secret."

"You cain't do that," interjected Owens weakly.

"Ain't that funny," chortled Sloan. "Them's the same words old Pemberton used when we brought him in here two years ago, and he ain't been outside ever since. After the first year, he stopped calling for his mammy. You don' want your mammy, do you Pemberton?"

"No. suh," came Ridley's cringing reply over the sound of his scrubbing. "Youse my mammy, suh."

"An' when you going home, Pemberton?"

Ridley stopped his scrubbing and dropped his voice to a whisper. The sound of tears washed through his answer, though Hunt could see Ridley's eyes were quite dry. "I ain't never going home, suh. I's gunna… gunna… I's gunna die in here."

Ridley gave out a few sobs, then absentmindedly used the brush to scratch his leg. Sloan nodded and looked back at the prisoner. "You see? He's got it all figured out. Now how'd you like to keep Pemberton here company for the rest of your life?"

"Uh … I … ah…"

139

"What's that boy? I can't hear you."

The prisoner's mouth gaped, but no further sounds came out.

"Pemberton! Go get the hammer and 'nother set of leg irons. You've got an apprentice to teach how to clean the sewers."

"Yes, suh" sniffed Ridley, dragging himself back to his trolley and arranging his limp legs on the tortured old cart. "God bless you, suh! God bless President Lincoln!"

Ridley noisily poled himself out through the cell door and down the hallway. Sloan stood back from the prisoner, then sat on a chair facing him.

"Course we could start by explaining to you 'bout your other duties." Sloan's hand rubbed his crotch. "Me and the boys get a bit lonely here sometimes, and I'll bet a nice fresh country lad like you could help us out. Pemberton's getting a bit old…"

That did it. The prisoner strained upwards in his chair against the bonds, then collapsed in a heap.

"I'll tell you. I'll tell you. Don' keep me here. Gawd sakes, please don' keep me here!" he cried pitifully.

"Well maybe we do and maybe we don't," concluded Sloan. "That depends how good you answer some questions now." He looked over at Hunt and raised one eyebrow. Hunt picked up his cue and walked over to the prisoner.

"What's your name, boy?"

"Jimmy Owens, suh. I told you that afore. I ain't lying."

"And where did you get on the boat?"

"I been on her for three years. Since afore the war. When things started, we sailed to Brest … that's in France … and got new papers for her. We was the *Mary Therese* after the Capt'n's mother, then last year we become the *Angelique* after a girl he met in France."

"Who's the people you brought into Washington?"

"They was some men. Three of them. They was 'bout thirty, forty years old. They keeps to themselves and don' tell us their names. God's truth I'm telling you. We picked them off the Carolina coast two weeks ago. They don' keep mess with us. They ate separate and stayed by themselves. When we gets into Washington, we's confined to ship and those three go ashore."

Owens's words were tumbling over themselves in the prisoner's desire to tell everything.

"After they killed Anderson, why didn't you leave port?"

"I don' know who they kill or don' kill and that's the truth. They goes ashore on Saturday night an' come back on Monday morning, and we sits there waiting and playing cards till all hell breaks loose and we goes to sea. Then we meets that Yankee warship down river an' we lose the battle an' I don' remember any more."

"You were playing cards?"

"We was waiting."

"Waiting for what?"

"For President Lincoln. He was coming back south with us."

An impossible plan

The silence lasted for a beat. Hunt saw right into the prisoner at that point. The overwhelming fear of the hideous future Sloan painted crushed the youth, and his broken voice showed a pathetic eagerness to be believed. Mingled sweat and blood trickled down the side of his face. The secured hands lay limp in abject surrender. Hunt knew the boy told the truth.

Sloan broke the silence. With a curse, he pushed himself out of his chair and rained blows on the prisoner. "You rebel slime! You think I'm buying that?"

Hunt dragged Sloan away from the prisoner. The youth hadn't resisted Sloan's blows. He seemed utterly spent. Continued beatings wouldn't help.

"You were going to kidnap President Lincoln?" asked Hunt softly.

It took some time for Owens to respond. "Not me. Mebbe someone else would, but Jimbo would say ... he's the capt'n ... Jimbo would say how he'd sail into Charleston with Scarecrow Lincoln tied to the foremast to frighten off them Yankee warships."

"Who was going to do the kidnapping?"

"Don' know that, so help me God," sniffled Owens. "Jimbo would say that Mister Lincoln wouldn't sound so cocky sitting in a jail cell in Charleston."

"Was there anyone in Washington who would help you?"

"I heard them fellas talking about some big bug called Creeley or the like. But he weren't involved. It was like he'd be watching."

Sloan leaned forward. "Greeley? Horace Greeley?"

"That's him! I dunno what he's doing with it all, but they spoke about him a couple of times."

"Anyone else?"

"Mister Pearson also. He had some paper or something."

"Pearson? You mean Anderson?"

"No, not Anderson. It was Pearson and he had a paper."

"A newspaper? Was he an editor like Anderson and Greeley?"

"I don' know. I don' know any more!" cried Owens. "I tol' you everything."

The prisoner's sobs slurred his answers into gibberish. Sloan caught Hunt's eye and jerked his head towards the door. Hunt nodded, and the detectives moved into the corridor out of earshot of the prisoner. Sloan rubbed his hand on his jaw as an expression of his concern. "You think he's talking straight?"

"I can't say, but I reckon he believes what he's saying."

"Kidnapping the President? I don't accept it!"

Hunt shrugged. "Maybe they're planning to drug Lincoln. Fill him full of opium or something."

"They'd need to grab him first. You telling me that three broken down rebels were going to take on the whole United States army, drug the President and then sail him south to Charleston?"

"I know it sounds crazy, Sloan, but sounds like that's exactly what Owens thinks they were going to do."

Sloan waved his hand dismissively. "It's too far-fetched for my liking. Horace Greeley … you know Greeley?"

"I've heard the name. Some newspaper fellow."

"That's the one. Editor for the New York Tribune. Maybe that's your link with the Washington Herald. Greeley's never been keen on the war, but I'd not have taken him for a traitor."

"We've only the prisoner's word for that. I'd say Owens believes what he's saying, but that don't make it gospel."

"I never heard of this Pearson fellow though. Hell, there's a thousand newspapers in the country. It'd take months to check them all."

"Maybe it will," conceded Hunt. "But that's two leads we've got now. Greeley and Pearson. That's better than what we had yesterday."

Sloan sucked his bottom lip.

"Anything involving the President we need to tell Captain Price."

"Let me talk to Schultz first," temporized Hunt, holding up one hand. "We can tell the captain tomorrow."

"Schultz back from Pittsburgh already?"

Hunt opened his mouth to give some excuse, any excuse, but Sloan wore a grin.

"Makes no nevermind for me, Hunt. If Schultz says he's in Pittsburgh, then he's in Pittsburgh."

"You think there's anything else we can get from Owens?"

"Maybe, but I can't stay with this. I've got my own cases to worry about. Captain's all over me about those missing soldiers at the hospital. Tell you what. I'll put young Jefferson Davis here back in the cells with some leg irons to keep him warm, and you go catch up with Schultz. First thing tomorrow morning, you and I speak to Captain Price. Now I can't do fairer than that."

"It's a done deal, Sloan. I'll hold you to it."

Hunt strode through the cellblock corridor and out of the stationhouse. The complications of this case were more than Hunt could comprehend. One newspaper editor dead and two others somehow involved in a plot to kidnap the President.

It took only a few minutes to walk to McRae's Hotel where the man at the reception desk owned to being Gregory.

"I need to talk with Detective Schultz," said Hunt. "Where can I find him?"

"No Schultz here," said the man in a clipped New York voice.

"Probably not. But do you know where he lives?"

"Never heard of him."

Hunt remembered Schultz's confident assertion that Gregory held the key to contacting him, and decided to try another tack. He reached into his wallet and pulled out a greenback. It seemed wrong to be desecrating one of the new government currency notes and he didn't have many notes to his name, but what Hunt had in mind wouldn't work with coins. No other option presented itself. He would need to rely on the man's greed.

Tearing the note in half he stuck one portion onto the message spike at the side of the desk. "Look Gregory, I know that you know how to find Schultz. Tell him that Timmins … no, Tonkin … dammit, tell him Detective Hunt needs to talk to him immediately. If he gets the message within the hour, then the rest of this money is yours. I'll be at the Jefferson Saloon till closing time."

"Never heard of him," repeated Gregory, but he made no effort to give back his half of the note. Hunt walked to the Jefferson Saloon and passed through the front door into the smoke-filled, dingy interior. He found a corner table with a wall at his back and bought a tankard of beer to keep him company. The strong smell of stale beer and sweaty clothes worked together with the laughter of intoxicated patrons to keep Hunt from getting much thinking done.

Time passed slowly, and Hunt went through alternating periods of excitement and despondency. It still lacked quarter of eight when he saw Schultz's potbellied frame moving towards him. Not surprisingly, Schultz leaned on a stick as he walked. He sank into a chair beside Hunt, laid his stick on his lap and massaged his leg.

"The surgeon said to exercise the leg. I've certainly done that today."

"Probably good advice. It'll hurt for a while."

"That's the truth," agreed Schultz. He pulled a half note out of his pocket and passed it across to Hunt.

"I settled with Gregory. You showed good thinking with that idea. Price has a fund for these sorts of things. I'll fix it up with him when I officially get back from Pittsburgh. What's been happening?"

It took Hunt a full ten minutes to explain the events of the day to Schultz. The older man listened and wrote comments in his small notebook as Hunt spoke.

"Ridley pulled the Private Pemberton routine? He's good at that. He gets a bonus for every performance, although he's so enthusiastic about it that I'd venture he'd do it for free."

"It started the prisoner talking. He said they were there to kidnap Lincoln."

Schultz's expression didn't change. Hunt realized he hoped for a stronger reaction. "Do you think that's what they're planning?"

"I wasn't there. What I think isn't relevant at this point. Far more important to consider what Owens thought."

"Owens seemed sure it would happen."

"Even allowing for Pemberton's little routine, Owens had no reason to tell you the truth. If I accept what he said, it's because I don't think he had the time to invent that story. Did Sloan believe him?"

"Enough to want to report it to Captain Price when the finches fart tomorrow."

146

"He believed it then. When you get back to the station, tell Sloan that Marybelle knows more about the missing pocket watches than she's telling him."

"Marybelle?"

"It's a case he's working on. One good turn and all that."

"Fine, fine. What do we do about the President in the meantime?"

Schultz massaged his leg again.

"Tell Captain Price like Sloan suggested. This case has a few more miles to go before we're through, and at this point your duty is clear."

Hunt sniffed disapprovingly. "I thought you didn't like my idea of duty."

"We're not talking about the army now. You're a Washington detective and your duty is to keep the peace. The sooner we arrest these Confederates, the sooner Washington will be a safe place for Abraham Lincoln. Besides being our president, he's a resident of Washington, and entitled to our protection."

"There's two names we got out of Owens. Greeley and Pearson. Owens said Pearson owned a paper, and Sloan guessed Greeley as the editor of the New York Tribune."

"I know of Greeley, but I haven't heard of Pearson. Seems there's some newspaper thread running through this whole matter."

Hunt leaned back on his bench. "This case doesn't make sense."

"Oh it makes sense all right. The trick is to look at all of the facts from the right angle."

"And which angle is that?" shot back Hunt. "We've got a dead newspaperman and a harebrained plot to kidnap Abraham Lincoln."

"Haven't quite found that angle yet myself. But rest assured it's out there somewhere. We've got our teeth well into this one and the answer is coming. Trouble is, I feel there's a deadline we don't know about, and that concerns me."

Hunt took a pull at his ale. He'd made good headway on this beer, his second one for the night, but he considered that as fairly restrained for the hours he'd been waiting.

"You want a drink, Schultz?"

Schultz shook his head.

"Last night's moonshine should do me for a while. I need a clear head over the next few days. Did you check the correspondence book at the Herald?"

"I did. Nothing unexpected. Some packages from England, but Hackett could account for them. Last month's newspapers and an encyclopaedia or the like."

"At least we've checked that now. Bully for you. There's still the chance a letter went to his home address."

"Miss Anderson has moved there from the Belvedere. She invited me … us … around there to talk further, but if you're supposed to be in Pittsburgh…"

Hunt's voice trailed off.

"That's fine Hunt," laughed Schultz. "I'm not completely blind. You go there and talk to her, but try to make conversation about the case from time to time."

Hunt felt himself blushing, and buried his face in his beer. Damn Schultz for his insights! No one had any secrets with that man in the room. Hunt put down his ale and looked at Schultz intently. "You're a strange one, Schultz," he said at last. "I'm not sure whether to like you or hate you."

"That's your choice. So long as you do what I say, then we'll get along fine."

Hunt felt a smile growing on his face. If only Schultz wasn't so egotistical then Hunt knew he could genuinely like the man. If Hunt admitted the truth, then he should say that Schultz let him off easy with the mistaken murder charge against Picard.

"You let Picard go," he exclaimed, grateful for the thought that crossed his mind. "After you told Captain Price you wanted Picard locked up for a week, you released him."

"I did that. I had my reasons."

"Reasons to release Picard or reasons to lie to Price?"

Schultz laughed again. "An important distinction there. All right. I lied to Price, and not for the first time either. The short answer is that our Captain Price likes to believe all cases are but a few days away from an arrest and a happy ending. Having Picard in the cells gives Price a good feeling, so I let him stay there."

"What about when he realizes Picard isn't there?"

"Hopefully I'll have solved the case by then."

Hunt noted Schultz's use of the singular but decided not to comment. Schultz set the investigation on the right track after Hunt's disastrous start, and always seemed two or three moves ahead of his partner's thinking. Surely they could share the credit for this case? Hunt pushed that thought to the back of his mind. He needed to focus on finding Anderson's killers.

A clatter and rising clamor behind them claimed their attention for a moment. From the inner rooms came a man, retreating before a hail of pots and bread and curses. A woman followed close behind, stopping in the doorway to hurl abuse and other objects at the man before her. He retreated behind a bar from where his voice came forth with an occasional ineffectual sally. The woman had the best of the exchange, and at length the man gave up the unequal struggle and just glared at his tormentor.

Then came a moment where she drew breath, and in that instant a spontaneous cheer and scattered applause arose from the assembled patrons. Suddenly aware of her audience, the woman hissed one last insult at the man behind the bar and retreated to her kitchen.

"Quite a show," observed Hunt with a chuckle.

"Martin and Alice have been married these twenty-three years," replied

Schultz. "They only thing they hate worse than each other's company is the thought of being separated."

"You know them?"

"I know them. I had occasion to help them with a minor matter a few years ago. It seems their marriage hasn't improved any since then."

"That's their mistake for not understanding each other," declared Hunt. "I figure I'll take the time to understand a woman before I wed her."

"With that kind of thinking I'd say you'll never be married then. In my experience, a man only knows small parts of the woman he marries, and he soon finds out he is wrong about those."

"You'll need to pick your wife carefully," explained Hunt wisely. "You need to take your time."

"I did pick my wife carefully. That's how I figure I can make these comments."

"Your wife?" Hunt could feel the ale sliding around the edge of his mind and fuddling his senses. He felt annoyed with himself. He needed to start thinking before talking.

"Yes, my wife. I think mayhap I'll have that ale after all. Barkeep!"

The next minute kept them busy procuring a tankard of ale for Schultz and a refill for Hunt. Eventually the drinks arrived and Hunt found his words.

"Look Schultz, I'm sorry. I didn't realize you were married. No reason for you not to be..."

Schultz put up his hand to stop Hunt. "Save your apologies. We're not together now. We had differences. It ended a few years back."

"Where ... how long were you married?"

"We were together some three years. Things got difficult, so I decided to leave."

"Difficult?"

Schultz toyed with his tankard, pushing the handle around one way then the other. It seemed that he wasn't altogether comfortable with this discussion.

"There's a difference between men and women, Hunt. Some say one or the other is right or wrong, but that's not my point. Folk get married and expect their partner will become like them. I thought Louisa would drop her ways and settle down to my ways of doing things. Trouble is, she thought the same about me."

Schultz pushed his ale away and leaned back. His hand reached down to massage his wounded leg.

"After a couple of years we were only talking when we had to, and those times were few and far between. She had her feelings, I had my thinking, and it seemed the two different ways would never meet. Young Roger had come along by then, and I couldn't see how things would ever get better. In the end, the house wasn't big enough for both Louisa and me. I came home one day and found her with someone else."

The chasm of Schultz's pain opened up before Hunt. He could see the wounded pride, the betrayed trust, the fear of similar undiscovered episodes.

"The bastard," breathed Hunt.

"I called both of them worse than that at first. I made some plans, then I thought about it and decided a life in jail wasn't for me, so I packed my things and left."

"That must have been hard. Having a child and all."

"It wasn't easy. Louisa carried on with her caterwauling, and saying we could work things out, but to my mind this way made the best outcome for all. I send her regular money to help with Roger, and mayhap there's someone else there permanent for her now."

"Do you ever go back? I mean, to see your son."

Schultz shook his head. "A clean break. Those two don't need me rolling back into town every couple of years to stir things up, and then disappear again for God knows how long."

Hunt didn't know how to proceed. His partner, a tower of logic and precision, now admitted a massive failure in his life. The tensions and scars from that time would be intense, but Schultz carried on through the story as if describing a building on the corner of the street.

Schultz sat upright and looked at Hunt. His calm voice carried an air of finality. "They're better off without me, Hunt. I know that."

"You don't know that! Hell Schultz, you're a fine man. Your boy would be proud to have you as a father! You get yourself back home, and I'll wager he'll tell the town about you."

The air of melancholy around Schultz quickly swallowed the wry smile that briefly crinkled his eyes. He retrieved his beer and resumed turning the tankard around itself. "You've never been married, Hunt?"

"No, but I know what a young boy wants."

Schultz's tankard described another slow revolution on the table.

"Mayhap you do. Sometimes marriage all seems to make so much sense a man asks himself why he would ever think of doing anything else. I saw Louisa like that. If you'd asked me before the wedding, I'd have bet my bottom dollar we found happiness. I'd reckon she'd have said the same."

Hunt could feel the shame in the man as he described his failed life. Hunt would do this for his partner. If Schultz had the need to talk right now, then he would find a receptive ear in Hunt.

"I tell you, Hunt, after young Roger came along I could see things were getting harder. I tried to make things better, but the war wouldn't end."

"Did it have to be war? Surely you both wanted it to work?"

Schultz looked up and glared at Hunt. He seemed angry with himself for talking too much. Then he broke out in a short laugh, shattering the connection the two men shared. His hand found the tankard again and raised it to his lips.

"Come on now, Hunt," he said after the drink. "You've got me off the topic here. We're supposed to be talking about Anderson. You know they call this town "The City of Magnificent Intentions? Seems I could say the same about how we're handling this case."

Hunt nodded, trying to burn the previous conversation into his memory. He didn't think Schultz would be that talkative again in a hurry. "I'd say Greeley is our next point of investigation."

"I'll go along with that," agreed Schultz. "He's in New York and that's a fair trip. I'll get an appointment set up and get word to you at the stationhouse."

"Anything else I should be asking our prisoner?"

"Nothing right now. We've got to find out how Greeley fits into this picture first and then we might need to talk with your sailor friend again. We need to make sure Sloan tells the duty sergeant to keep Owens by himself in the cells. Keep him lonely, and mayhap he'll want to talk to you some more."

"I'll do that," retorted Hunt abruptly, then, repentant for his terseness, softened his remarks. "I mean there's no need to bother Sloan. He's helped us enough."

"Good. We'll see if Greeley knows this Pearson fellow. There's some work to do in that area." The tone of the conversation became crisper as Schultz plowed straight on with his next point. "I've found the troops who raided the *Angelique*. They were a detachment from the Washington garrison."

"You worked fast," replied Hunt in astonishment.

"Not really. They made no secret about it. Most soldiers are happy enough to talk when someone buys them a drink."

"Even with your leg like that? You've been going from saloon to saloon talking to soldiers?"

"Certainly not! After my visit to a surgeon friend, I've spent most of the day at home. Fortunately, I have some associates who are willing to ask such questions for me. They take their payment in my professional advice and such other services as I can offer them."

"You're amazing, Schultz."

"Be that as it may, the answers get us no further ahead in this case," replied Schultz dismissively. "That wasn't a planned raid on the *Angelique*. Those soldiers were a regular patrol of military police returning from breaking up a brawl at the Good Luck Grocery. They were only a hundred paces away when Albert fired his gun, so they went onto the docks to investigate and they ran into the crew from the *Angelique*. I don't know who shot first after that, but it doesn't matter. You know the rest."

"It happened by accident?"

"You could describe it like that. Washington's a city under siege. Any gunshot would bring soldiers running. I should have thought of that."

Hunt felt satisfaction in hearing Schultz acknowledge his failure to plan for that encounter. Schultz certainly owned a king-sized ego, however most of the time he showed the talent to match that ego. "What about the soldier I wounded?"

"No mention of him. My guess is he's in the infirmary listed for a medical discharge."

Hunt didn't feel guilty about that. The soldier shot at Schultz without warning, and then received as good as he gave. There had been no time for pleasantries.

"Tomorrow you'd best talk to Miss Anderson and look at her father's effects," instructed Schultz.

"I'll need to see Captain Price first. Someone's got to stop this plot to kidnap the President."

The words sounded ludicrous and melodramatic, and Hunt looked around to see if he'd been overheard, but the other patrons were all lost in their own conversations.

"It's getting complicated," agreed Schultz. "All right then, I'll get a message to Sloan about how to handle the threat to Lincoln. You go and see Miss Anderson. Then on Friday get down to the *Angelique* and see what you can find in the wreck. We've probably left it too late. The navy will have taken anything of value, but they might let you check the inventory. I can't tell you what to look for there."

"I'll have a good look," promised Hunt. "You can count on it."

A spy revealed

Three blocks south of the Jefferson Saloon stood Mrs Brown's Tea Rooms, a rough and tumble house that hadn't served tea to its customers since the war started. In a city visited by hundreds of thousands of soldiers, higher profits came by providing other services. It presented as a two-storied wooden building with perpetually closed curtains on the upper floor windows, not that the customers cared, because they didn't come there for the view anyway. Wide duckboards led from the sidewalk to the front steps where a weathered sign on the porch forlornly implored customers to "Wipe Your Feet".

A constant stream of visitors passed through the doors on this night despite the weather. The working girls managing their time as best they could, leaving their departing customers with a smile and an invitation to return the following week. Ridley stood to one side of the front door to let a party of soldiers leave the house. He pushed through the door and nodded politely to the mountain of a man sitting in the foyer cleaning his nails. Ridley had seen that man escorting troublesome visitors off the premises before and he had no desire to leave the same way. He walked into the front room where the Lady of the House welcomed him. "Hello dearie. Feel like some company? You're in the right place."

Ridley smiled. Women didn't talk to him that often, and Ridley enjoyed the moment, despite the Madam's hard-as-nails eyes.

"Is Mandy in? I usually talk with her."

"Mandy will be down shortly, love. Sit and have a drink. She won't be long."

Ridley moved into the bar area, and bought a small beer for twice the price charged at a regular saloon. He had been coming to this House twice a week for quite a while now, and knew the bar quite well. A piano man played cheerful tunes, and two sailors arm wrestled on one of the tables cheered on by their mates. Three girls draped in the laps of their comrades joined in the cheering. In the corner, a well-dressed dude stared into his drink and mumbled to himself while Ridley sat and waited.

It took ten minutes for Mandy to appear. She caught Ridley's eye, and he finished his drink with one swallow before following her out of the room and up the stairs. An oil light on the wall cast dim light over the threadbare staircase carpet and into the first floor corridor. Mandy led him into a bedroom, then closed and latched the door behind them. Ridley parked himself in a chair and watched Mandy sit on the bed and light a cigarette. She'd reached her late twenties, with the full figure that men liked and a twinkle in her eye that Ridley saw her turn off and on at will.

"How's business?" he asked.

"Cut the talk. What have you got?"

"Where's the money?"

Mandy slipped a currency note out of a pocket in her bodice and laid it on the bed.

"I should charge you more."

"Suit yourself," replied Mandy. "You're not the only cop looking for money. You're not even a cop. Maybe I should pay you less."

Ridley shrugged and took the money. Mandy wore the same perfume as the Madam. In a House like this, the girl's perfume needed to be strong enough to cover the smell of the sweaty sheets, and of the unemptied chamberpot, and Mandy's cologne did the job.

"Schultz is in Pittsburgh. Hunt caught some Confederate spy off a ship, and he sung like a kettle on a campfire. Reckons they were going to snatch President Lincoln."

Mandy glared at him. "You making this stuff up? The people I talk with don't want fairy stories."

Ridley scratched himself. Maybe he'd spend some money later tonight. Not with Mandy though.

"You wanted to know about Schultz and Hunt. I'm telling you what I heard. Hunt tried shaking down this rebel prisoner, Jimmy Owens he was, and he starts squalling about this plan to grab Lincoln."

"A rebel you say. How'd he get to Washington?"

"Off some ship. I told you that."

"What are they doing about it?"

"Gonna talk to the capt'n I guess. I don' hear everything in there."

Mandy considered what the old man said. She met Ridley some ten months previously after her arrest for plying her trade. He had been cleaning the cells, and a casual conversation grew into a mutually profitable arrangement. She knew that some of her customers would pay for knowledge of what the police were doing, and she set up the old cripple as her spy in the Fifth Precinct station. Normally she passed along information about planned raids on gunrunners and the like, in return for some dollars into her savings fund. Twice she passed word to the Madam here about planned visits by sanitary inspectors, and each of those tipoffs earned her a satisfactory bonus.

Some of the Washington criminal fraternity were aware of Mandy's back door into the doings of the local police, and occasionally she received requests for specific information. The current assignment to report on the detectives working the Anderson case arrived as a surprise to her, but the offer came from a man she respected, and the job offered a pleasing number of dollars. It didn't make sense, but that didn't worry her. She'd worked the game in a number of cities, and set herself a goal of saving a thousand dollars, then going to Canada and from there to England. A thousand dollars would get her out of the trade and set up in a small shop. Maybe then, she could even find a man who hadn't seen her working here.

"You say Schultz is in Pittsburgh?"

"Gone for a few days I heard. Some case up north maybe."

Mandy needed to keep the old man talking for a bit longer. Even a man of his age should take more than a few minutes in a room with her. "Tell me about the rat-catchers. When are they coming back this way?"

Ridley spoke for a while longer and when he left, Mandy repeated the information back to herself. A harebrained story about a plot to kidnap a president didn't seem worth the money she'd paid the old man. She shrugged and decided to pass it on anyway. That way her benefactor would know that she'd been working.

Time alone with Jane

In 1751, the Maryland Assembly approved the creation of a new town on the banks of the Potomac River, to be named George Town in honor of George Augustus, more commonly known as George II, the then reigning King of England. Tobacco farming and shipping gave a good economic base for this fledgling community, and for its first century of life it outshone its neighbors, including the upstart District of Columbia. People worked in Washington DC, but Georgetown remained the fashionable place to live.

Geographical proximity linked Georgetown and Washington, but beyond that, they shared very little. Brash and powerful Washington served as the seat of government for a mighty nation. Georgetown stayed quiet and well-mannered as befitted the home of polite society. It had no desire to house the machinery of government, and remained a refuge for the high and mighty when they tired of their labors. There were suggestions that the city of Washington would eventually reassert its social primacy by annexing its pretentious neighbor, but that problem belonged to a future generation.

Hunt knew about Georgetown's reputation for sophisticated living, and on this morning he took pains to scrub himself up well enough to pass muster in that refined neighborhood. He shaved carefully, honing his razor to a fine edge and slowly scraping the stubble from his face. His best shirt suffered only the one wearing from when they called at the Belvedere Hotel on

Tuesday, and fortunately he'd changed into older clothes before the adventure under the docks. His primitive efforts at laundering seemed to have removed most of the Potomac mud from his pantaloons, but at length he decided to wear his woolen breeches. It seemed right to wear his Sunday best for this opportunity to talk with Jane.

Tying his buckskin coat around his neck before their time in the Potomac kept it mostly clean. Yesterday's street mud still clogged his boots, but even if he polished them, they would be just as filthy after ten paces through the streets of Washington.

Hunt picked up his hat and left his diggings at nine in the morning to set out for the Anderson house. The sun periodically fought its way through the black pregnant clouds, only to be swallowed up again less than five minutes later. Rain had been coming and going all week, and today's weather looked no different. Water lay puddled across the sidewalks, and the muddy rivers that made up Washington streets were no firmer than yesterday. It took a few blocks of walking before a cabbie answered his hail. Gratefully he climbed into the shelter of the cab and gave his destination to the whipper. The cab driver claimed he knew his way to College Street, so Hunt relaxed and enjoyed the rainswept view.

Going to see Jane felt like traveling to another world. The road to Georgetown ran along Pennsylvania Avenue past the Executive Mansion and continued for another dozen blocks before reaching Rock Creek. Georgetown began on the other side of that narrow stretch of water. The roads were no better maintained than those in Washington, but the traffic thinned noticeably and the stench of the boggy roads and inevitable horse turds intruded less on the senses.

A thin gleam of sunlight broke through the clouds during the journey, and its faint warmth, together with the rocking of the cab, combined to lull Hunt into a daydream. Jane proudly introduced him to their neighbors, while her pet spaniels sniffed playfully around his boots. Mason Island and the Aqueduct Bridge were visible from their gazebo where they sat sharing a genteel conversation. He belonged here, with her. Work belonged to another world. It could never be as as important as their life together. Jane told him their address twice, then three times. Her voice became more and more insistent until it changed into the harsh tones of the cab driver.

"College Street I said sir, an' there's the house you wanted."

The dream dissolved, and the humidity of the day stuck his collar to his neck. Far above, the sun disappeared behind leaden clouds. He stumbled out of the seat, fumbling in his pocket for the fare. The cab acknowledged the tip with a salute and then left, his cab wheels slopping through the mud back towards Washington.

Hunt looked at Jane's house. A white wooden house with a manicured garden and a picket fence. The name 'Braemear' in gold cursive script on a small wooden nameplate adorned the gate. The gate opened at his touch and he walked up the path. Wet gravel crunched like musket shots beneath his boots to announce his presence to the neighborhood. The wooden porch beckoned. Green and lilac decorated the trimmings of the balustrade around that little sanctuary. Soft cushions scattered across a swinging bench down the end of the porch offered a haven where two people might spend an hour or two in conversation. Plans of sweet romance flowed in Hunt's head. The two steps from the path to the porch were his stairway to heaven.

Hunt strode forward and grasped the bell pull. The sound of a chime deep within the house rewarded his solid tug on the cord. Frosted glass panes on the front door provided a pleasant pattern of blues and greens with their intricate leadlighting. Hunt brushed down his coat, and stood at Parade Rest, waiting for his inspection by the beautiful Lady of the House. The interminable wait made him nervous, but at last he heard the sound of movement and saw a shape with flowing skirts approaching along the hall. The blurred glass made identification difficult, but Hunt could see it wasn't Jane. A matron with the black blouse and starched apron of a resident housekeeper opened the door. She looked well over fifty, with the dour expression of someone who knows the arrival of visitors means that more cleaning must be done afterwards.

"Detective Harrison Hunt to see Miss Anderson. She's expecting me."

The matron sniffed, as if passing judgment on the questionable social decisions of her mistress.

162

"Wait here," she ordered gruffly, closing the door.

Hunt stood on the step, angry with himself for making a poor impression on the housekeeper. Would Jane be led by the matron's opinion? Perhaps the matron had once been Jane's nanny and even now held a treasured place in her heart. He dismissed the thought. What that matron thought didn't matter; he only cared about Jane's reactions.

He tried to concentrate on the case at hand. He needed to search through John Anderson's personal effects. Jane said she would help with their investigations so he should have no problem with that task. Perhaps they would have a brief chat and exchange pleasantries first. Should he interview the staff? Schultz would do that. Therefore, he would do so also.

After that, they would sit on that swing seat and talk of more pleasant things. Slowly, softly, the conversation would change from the details of her father's affairs into a talk about her own life, and perhaps she would share her dreams with him. Any neighbor walking on the road would have an uncluttered view of the swing, so there would be no need for a chaperone. Would it be appropriate to ask her out for dinner, or should he leave it until they met together a few more times? The sudden opening of the front door, and the return of the matron startled him.

"Miss Anderson will see you now."

"Thank you. Thank you, ma'am," replied Hunt. He felt embarrassed as if he had been caught rearranging his clothing in public. A flush burned his cheeks, and he felt grateful for the darkness of the hallway. The matron led him through the corridor to a sunroom at the back of the house where Jane sat at a table. The air lay heavy with humidity and Hunt could see beads of moisture on the inside of the windows. Ledgers and folders sat stacked on the table in front of Jane.

"Detective Hunt," announced the matron, with the enthusiasm of an elderly grandmother proclaiming that the spring-loaded rattrap in the cellar had found a victim.

"Miss Anderson, thank you for meeting me."

"My pleasure, Detective Hunt," responded Jane sweetly. "I've been hoping to see you again."

Was that true? Hunt swallowed, and decided not to press the point. "Are these your father's affairs?" he asked, indicating the books and papers on the table.

"They are. I started to work my way through his papers. Mister Hackett and Tom have indicated they can keep the Herald going for the next few weeks. Indeed, I suspect Mister Hackett sees this as an opportunity to prove himself. He knows the newspaper business almost as well as father did..."

A tear appeared at her eye and she looked away. Hunt stepped forwards to offer her his kerchief, but the matron arrived there before him with her own linen, fussing about and glaring at Hunt as if he personally created all of the misfortune.

"Don't you fluster yourself so, Miss Jane. I'll fetch a cup of tea. I don't know why you treat yourself like this. It's not right you should go through all of this."

Hunt wanted to be the one to comfort her. The urge to cast the matron through the window ran through him, but he bit down on his temper and stopped himself. Jane came to his rescue, and his temper faded under the calming balm of her words. "You mustn't fuss so, Emily. It's not the fault of Detective Hunt. He's helping to find the people responsible for all of this."

The reassuring words of her mistress calmed Emily, but Hunt knew the matron still saw him as a disruptive influence on the peace and harmony of this household.

"Do you have any news, Detective Hunt?" asked Jane softly. The tears staining her eyes were acid on Hunt's heart. "When you left the office so quickly yesterday I felt sure you were on to something important."

Hunt chewed his lip and cast a glance at Emily. Jane saw his look and took the cue.

"That will be all for now, Emily."

Emily looked back and forth between Hunt and Jane, clearly scandalized at the thought of leaving Jane alone in a room in the company of an unknown male.

"You may leave the door open," offered Jane as a compromise. "Detective Hunt and I need to talk."

In the face of a direct instruction from her mistress, Emily's only possible response had to be obedience, albeit provided with a disapproving exhalation of breath.

"Yes miss," she said, dropping in an automatic curtsy before leaving the room. Her footsteps faded down the corridor. Hunt waited a few seconds before cocking an ear. He could hear no sound of Emily coming back.

"She won't listen to us. She has been with my family for many years, and my father trusted her completely. So do I, for that matter."

"Then I will do likewise," declared Hunt gallantly. He moved to the table and took a chair opposite Jane.

"It is good to talk with you again, Miss Anderson. May I call you Jane?"

There. He had taken the first step towards a closer relationship. Her response came swiftly.

"Of course you may, Detective Hunt," she replied without batting an eyelid. "If we are to work together then it is as well to trust each other."

That wasn't quite the response he hoped for, but it would do for the present.

"And you must call me Harrison. Let me tell you where our inquiries have taken us."

Jane sat with her hands folded in her lap and looked up at him. Today she wore a cream dress with a burgundy sash around her waist. There would be no need for black mourning clothes if she stayed in the house all day. Delicate lace trimmed the collar and sleeves. She wore no jewelry. Hunt searched his memory, wondering whether she wore jewelry on the two previous occasions he met her. He couldn't be sure. Once again, her dress flowed down over her ankles, and Hunt could almost imagine her stockings.

"Harrison?"

He realized with a start that Jane had called his name twice, and he had been standing there for heavens knows how long looking at her. A flush tickled his neck and he fought to keep it off his face. "Ah, sorry. I needed to arrange my thoughts. So much has happened."

He busied himself taking out some notepaper from his pocket. He intended to write down some questions before arriving, but that never happened. Now he needed to take this interview at the gallop and without a battle plan.

"The ship on the Potomac," he began.

"The battle Mr. Hackett mentioned?"

"It meant something to our inquiries. We thought the ship managed to escape, but the news that it foundered meant we might capture some of the crew."

"Oh?"

"We did catch one of the crew," he announced grandly. "I questioned him thoroughly, and there are some clues; definite leads I would call them. Nothing conclusive yet, mind you, but we have a stronger path to follow. I've sent Schultz to follow up on some points, and I need to ask you some questions now, if you don't mind."

Jane looked at him, waiting for his questions.

"Do you know Horace Greeley?"

"Of course. He owns the New York Tribune. I met him a few times when I accompanied my father to social events in New York. Father and he did business from time to time, but I couldn't tell you what it was."

"And what about an editor named Pearson?"

166

"That name isn't familiar to me. Is he in Washington? I haven't lived here for a while now."

"We don't know where he lives," admitted Hunt. "He is a focus of our investigation for the moment."

"Perhaps father's papers might have some information," said Jane, indicating the piles of books and documents on the table in front of her.

Hunt surveyed the mountain of reading. "Is this where your father worked?"

"Oh no. These are the papers from the office that I had sent here. I need to understand what to do with the Herald, and I wanted to look at the accounts. Father's study is at the front of the house.

"Perhaps I should look at your father's study? You seem to have a good beginning on this side of the business. I might do better searching though other information."

"Of course," replied Jane, standing up and smoothing out her dress. "Please come with me." Hunt enjoyed following Jane down the hall. He took the opportunity to admire the way she glided across the rugs, and especially the way her hips swayed beneath her dress. Emily's absence suited him fine. At the front of the house, Jane opened a door on the left of the hall and stepped back to allow him to enter.

"This is father's study. It always has been, as long as I can remember. I never went in here without him. Even now..."

Hunt turned to her in time to see her lips tighten and her eyes moisten. His hand caught her arm and held it gently.

"Jane."

She bit her lip.

"Jane, I'm sorry you're going through this."

She nodded, then her arm moved free of his hand and she fumbled with the small handkerchief Emily had given her. Had he offended Jane by taking her arm? It had been a forward thing to do. He couldn't blame her for feeling affronted.

"I'm fine," she said at length. "Please look at what you need to. I'll be in the sunroom."

Then she walked back down the corridor, one hand dabbing her eyes with the piece of fragrant linen. Hunt watched until she went into the sunroom. It had been going so well. Now she sat alone, and in tears. With a snort of self-disgust, he stepped into the study.

Heavy bookcases lined the walls, except where the doorway, a window and a fireplace occupied their own space. A massive desk with a gilt-edged leather top occupied the center of the room, and a heavy wooden chair stood behind the desk. The study had only that single seat. Either Anderson never met with guests in this room, or the visitors stood throughout the entire conversation.

A pen, inkwell, and paper knife sat alone on the desk. Hunt expected the easy mess of a working desk, covered with letters and papers and open files, and he felt discomfited by the unexpected neatness.

He stepped further into the room. Through the window, he could see the rain returning, and the heavy clouds showed the storms would be around for the rest of the day. Hunt had no idea how he could get back to Washington through the rain, but he pushed that thought out of his mind for the moment.

The chair slid easily from out under the desk and he settled himself into the seat, closing his eyes and let the sense of power wash over him. He could be an editor like Anderson. People waited for his weekly words of wisdom while businessmen and presidents alike clamored for his ear. Gossip and news reached him before the rest of Washington heard the story. At the end of the day, his coach and pair carried him home to a house like this, where a servant helped him off with his expensive boots, and a matron like Emily had a mug of ale waiting and his dinner prepared. Jane would be there to talk with him.

"Would you like tea?"

His eyes flew open. Emily in the doorway, looking down her nose at his foolish flights of fancy. His hands gripped the arms of the chair.

"I was thinking!" he began defensively. "Thinking! I was thinking … wondering if Mister Anderson built a safe here. A strongbox perhaps, with important papers."

Emily stood back a little. Her eyes focused somewhere in the distance as she considered the matter.

"A strongbox? You'd have to ask Miss Jane."

Hunt recovered somewhat. He swore at himself for his wandering mind, and determined to complete the rest of the visit on a professional note. "There is a safe at the office. Hackett and Tom looked through that. I thought your employer might have a safe in this house."

"I really don't know," she sniffed. "Miss Jane asked if you wanted tea."

"That would be wonderful. I shouldn't be too long here."

Emily gave a small nod and retreated down the hall. Hunt looked at the desk. Each side housed three drawers. It seemed wrong to place his fingers on this beautifully piece of woodwork, but he reminded himself that he had Jane's permission, and searching through the desk might reveal the clue to the identity of Anderson's murderer. No one watched him, yet guilt still sat on his shoulders.

Silently wishing a plague on his uncooperative emotions, he stood up and stepped to the window. He had never been in a house like this before. His hand traced across the window ledge and up the line of the bookcase. Beautiful woodwork. The books were works of art. Leather bindings with embossed titles arranged across the shelves. He lifted out a volume of the Encyclopaedia Britannica and leafed through the pages. Soft paper with colored plates and intricate maps held the knowledge of the world. Shipping these books from England would not be cheap. The books in this room might cost more than his yearly wage.

Suddenly afraid of damaging the expensive book, Hunt carefully closed it and slipped it back into the shelf. Books on history, economics, philosophy and half a hundred other subjects lined the walls of this small room. Hunt couldn't fathom why a person would want to spend so much time reading. This household of newspapers and politics belonged to a world about which he knew very little. He shuddered at the strangeness of it all.

Books didn't matter. Right now he needed to finish his search, so he could have tea with Jane. With that pleasant thought to spur him on, Hunt sat once more at the desk. He started on the left side and worked his way down.

Blank notepaper and other writing paraphernalia took up the first two drawers. The bottom drawer held unsorted household accounts. Perhaps Anderson stored up his personal accounts in one drawer, and pulled them all out for a grand reconciliation once or twice a year. They hardly mattered now.

The right hand side of the desk produced better fruit. A diary and a bundle of letters tied up with string sat in the top drawer. Hunt put the diary aside for a later, and closer, examination. The bundle of letters looked more interesting. The ribbon undid readily and the faint smell of jasmine reached his nose. The first letter started with the words 'My Darling John' and concluded with 'Your affectionate Beatrice'.

Hunt stopped, and thought carefully. The contents of these letters would contain private and personal thoughts. Schultz said Anderson saw Beatrice on the weekend he died. These notes would be personal, but hidden inside them might be the clue that solved the mystery of Pearson's identity. His duty required him to read the letters, regardless of the potential embarrassment to the dead man. There might even be mention of Jane and discussion of the things that were important to her. He began again; reading each letter in turn and trying to maintain a detachment that would let him forget the information as soon as he read it. He told himself that only if he found something pertinent to the case would he stop and reread the information. Beatrice wrote with happy references to past excursions, and her words gave evidence of her growing relationship with John Anderson.

Some parts of the letters were unmistakable evidence of an association that would have scandalized the more sedate sections of Washington society. Such complications didn't matter to Hunt. He'd experienced a few amorous adventures in his past, and he didn't look down on Anderson for the man's romantic escapades, though it wouldn't do to let Jane see these letters.

At the thought of Jane, he looked at the doorway. She wasn't there. He hurried through the rest of the letters, but nothing there shed light on the identity of Pearson or on Anderson's business dealings with Greeley. He retied the letters in their string, and thrust the package into his pocket. After a moments reflection he stored Anderson's diary in his other coat pocket.

The second drawer held three folded documents wrapped in red ribbon. Five minutes of reading complicated legal phrases left him no wiser except for the observation that each document referred to a court case from the start of the century. There seemed something familiar about the sound of *United States v. Burr*, but *Ex Parte Bollman* and *Ex Parte Dorr* meant nothing to him.

He scanned the documents briefly, struggling to see the significance in them. There were other legal documents stored along two shelves of the bookcase in front of him. Why were these three documents been stored separately? The documents joined the diary in his pocket. Schultz could work out their meaning later.

The bottom drawer wouldn't open.

A closer examination revealed a small keyhole near the top of the drawer. Between the top lip of the drawer and the crossbar of the desk frame Hunt could see the tongue of metal locking the drawer. His Bowie knife explored the metal. He knew the strength of his weapon, and did not push the blade beyond its limit. After a few minutes of probing, a satisfying click rewarded his efforts, and he could lean on his knife to push the lock open. The drawer held a well-made metal case with a simple latch. Opening the lid revealed an inlay of velvet surrounding a folded apron and a set of cuffs. The same eye enclosed within the triangle that adorned the lapel pin Schultz showed him, stared at him from the embroidery sewn into each of those items. Even Hunt could understand the meaning of his find. John Anderson had been a member of the Illuminati.

"Your tea is ready."

Emily's sharp voice jerked Hunt out of his thoughts. He looked over the desk at her, standing in the doorway with her arms crossed.

"Fine," he replied.

"Miss Jane" - could there be the slightest emphasis on the title? - "asked if you would take tea with her in the sunroom."

"Yes, that would be good."

He stared at Emily, but she didn't seem inclined to move.

"I will be there presently," he said firmly.

With that comment, she turned down her lip and left. Her sulky manner reeked of defiance, and he needed to find a way around that attitude before he questioned her. Hunt couldn't see why she showed him so much hostility. Perhaps she was just a loveless old maid, who took her frustration out on any male with whom she came in contact.

He refolded the regalia, replacing it in the case and sliding the drawer shut, before standing up and walking out of the study. He had learned some things today, but he had no idea how they all fitted together. Anderson's membership of the Illuminati didn't explain why he would be tortured and killed by Pearson or Greeley, or anyone else for that matter.

Jane waited for him in the sunroom. The clouds outside mocked at the room's designation, and flicked cold raindrops against the windowpanes. A fire in the grate shared its warmth with the air, providing a comfortable sanctuary for the two young people. A tray with tea for two sat on the table in front of Jane.

"How did you fare with your search? Did you find anything?"

"Only more questions," he admitted, settling himself in a chair at the table next to her. "What about the accounts?"

172

"They aren't good. Circulation has been dropping for many months. Father's views about the war were never popular. The paper won't last beyond the end of this year under the current circumstances."

"You are clever with these things. Not many women could do what you are doing."

Jane smiled her acceptance of his compliment. "Father made sure my education went beyond needlepoint and sewing.

"Have you thought what to do with the Herald? Will you sell it?"

Her eyes clouded over for a moment, but she swiftly recovered. "I don't know. Father started the paper. He was devoted to it, but he always spoke his mind, and that didn't sell newspapers. It seems a betrayal to let it pass out of the family, but what are my choices? I can read a balance sheet, but to be a newspaper editor? I wouldn't know what to do."

The moment appeared again, inviting him to embrace it and to respond with the words Jane needed. His tongue grew in his mouth like a swollen ball of cotton and his hands were great hams. He swallowed, but the words weren't there.

"I'd like tea," he managed to say, knowing instantly the words were safe, but wrong. Sure enough, the moment disappeared, and Jane looked at him from a distance.

"Of course. How thoughtless of me."

She turned to the teatray and busied herself with the cups and saucers. Hunt screamed silently at himself for his rudeness, but he could see no way to reclaim his words. He could feel himself doing it again; tearing down a relationship that might have been reaching out for him.

"You look nice today," he said clumsily.

"Thank you," she replied evenly. "Cream and sugar?"

"No sugar, black is fine. Thank you."

She stood up to pass him the tea. His hand reached out and awkwardly grasped the cup and saucer. Jane moved across the room to sit in the window seat. The tea tasted pleasant, but he felt alone in the room with only that liquid for company. He tried again.

"Could you get Hackett to run the paper for you?"

She looked out into the rain. "Perhaps."

The single word answer told him nothing. He needed to say something. Needed to keep the conversation moving. "Did your father have a strongbox in the house?"

Jane turned back to him. "If there wasn't one in the study, then I don't know where he would keep it. It wouldn't be in this room. This is where I did my work when I lived here."

A new chance for conversation! "Your work?"

Jane smiled at him. "I'm an artist, Harrison. Painting is my life, and my father indulged me. He paid for me to study art in Baltimore at the Maryland Institute, and since I graduated I have built my business doing portraits for the ladies of the city."

"You have your own business?"

"Is that so strange? I do my work and run my own accounts. My advertising is mainly word of mouth from my satisfied clients, but that keeps me busy enough. On the wall behind you is a portrait of my father that I painted as my major work in my final year."

Hunt turned and looked at the picture. It showed a handsome man standing in a formal pose. Her talent shone through the texture, the brushstrokes, the hints of light and shade skillfully worked into the portrait. Jane painted her father with fine detail, and Hunt could see her suggestions of the man's transition from the prime of life into older years.

"That's well done."

"Thank you. I'm trying to organize an exhibition, but it's so difficult for a woman to be taken seriously as an artist. It would be easier if I had been

174

born a man."

"I'm glad you're not."

Jane looked at him coolly, and Hunt realized that once again he had made the wrong remark. He couldn't see any problem with letting Jane know that he appreciated her beauty. "I mean, compared to other women, you're quite a picture. If I could paint, then I'd like to paint you … I mean a picture of you."

It was all going wrong. He stopped talking, and waited for Jane to say something.

"Painting isn't an easy profession, Harrison. It can take many days to do a portrait correctly, and there is always the chance that your customer will take an unreasoning dislike to the finished product."

"That's a shame. To do all of that work, and then they don't appreciate you. Sometimes I feel like that with my job. Maybe we've got that in common?"

Her paintings. His work. The weather. The strongbox. What else could he talk about? He knew nothing about politics, and even less about religion.

"Does painting portraits pay well?"

"It pays well enough, thank you. Did you have any more questions about my father's business?"

This conversation was dying a painful death. The dark skies outside reflected how Hunt felt about himself. Perhaps the right words could have been said even then, but Hunt didn't know them. He put down his tea, and looked at the china cup and saucer in front of him. It seemed so delicate, so fragile, and so easy to destroy with one sweep of his arrogant, incompetent, self-serving arm. Time to end the agony.

"I need to talk with Emily."

Jane replaced her cup on the saucer, walked across to the doorway and pulled on a bell cord Hunt hadn't even seen. Schultz would have seen it. A minute passed. Jane stood there, looking into the hallway for the whole time. At last, footsteps approached.

"The detective needs to talk with you," said Jane to Emily. "Please answer his questions as best you can."

Emily looked disdainfully at Hunt. It seemed that the prospect of potentially disclosing family secrets did not appeal to her. Jane moved into the doorway and turned to face them.

"I will be in the parlor," she announced, then walked away.

Jane left him with his cup of tea and Emily.

"Please sit down Emily," he began. She sat and folded her hands primly in her lap. Her abrupt movements and fixed expression told Hunt that she didn't want to talk with him. Hunt determined to reach Emily, to understand her feelings, before asking her any questions. That might work better than just demanding answers.

"Emily, I know you're upset with Mister Anderson's death. It's my job to find out who did this."

"Ask your questions then," she flared. "I've got work to do."

She wasn't to be appeased. Her status as a domestic servant might be the only thing keeping her tongue in check. Hunt longed to be back on the battlefield, alone with his revolver, and away from this house. "Do you live here Emily?"

"I have a room. I've worked for the Andersons since before Master William was born."

The answer dawned on Hunt. She had no ring on her finger. Emily devoted her life to the Anderson family, possibly passing up the opportunity for her own marriage and family because of her service to the Andersons. Now, with the mother long buried, the son dead in the war, the father murdered and the daughter living in another city, this week saw the end of the world as she knew it. No wonder she could not be comforted. She would want to shriek her anger at the world, and Hunt remained as the closest target. There would be no consoling her. Perhaps the oblique approach would get him the answers he desired. "Are there any other staff here?"

 "There's only me. I keep the house in order, and there's a boy lives local who looks after the yard and chops the wood."

"Did Mister Anderson have any visitors these last two weeks?"

Emily looked at him as if battling her better judgment, but then, perhaps in response to her mistress's instructions, she answered the question. "Only on Wednesdays, like every week. That's his card night."

"He played cards on Wednesday? Here?"

"Here," she confirmed. "There's four or five of them arrive about eight after I've finished for the night."

"Five of them you say?"

"Four or five. I never met them so don't bother asking. Mister Anderson lets them in and sees them out."

"They played cards? In this room?"

"On that table there. I'd set up the cards and leave the coffee things there and fill the kettle, and Mister Anderson would boil the water himself."

A cast iron crane with kettle hung over the fireplace. The sturdy sunroom table could be covered with a cloth, and they could play their cards with plenty of room for all.

"What did they play? Faro? Draw poker?"

"I couldn't say," answered Emily with disdain in her voice. Obviously no respectable woman could be expected to know how to play cards. "He kept the cards on that bookshelf there in that brown box."

Hunt stood and walked to the bookshelf. The wooden box measured about six inches by three, It stood less than two inches tall deep, with Indian carvings around the edge of it. Curious to know what card game a man of Anderson's ilk would enjoy, Hunt lifted the box and opened it. The lid came away easily enough. Inside the box were two decks of used playing cards.

Their mottled surface and well-thumbed corners were evidence of previous use, but Hunt found a more interesting fact in the fine layer of mold covering both the cards and the inside of the box.

Hunt considered the furry cards. Mold grew wherever things got damp and a stack of cardboard moistened by sweaty fingers and loosely sealed in a wooden box provided ideal acreage for the rot to spread. The growth in the box could not have developed in less than three months. Whatever Anderson and his friends were doing on Wednesday nights, it wasn't playing cards.

Hunt replaced the lid on the box and put it back on the bookshelf.

"Today is Thursday," he observed. "Did anyone turn up to play cards last night?"

"No," said Emily, with sudden realization. "They must have heard."

"I expect so. Did you ever see these people? Did Mister Anderson ever mention any names?"

Emily paused for a moment in thought then, with a purposeful shake of the head, ended that line of enquiry. Hunt kept the conversation going with more questions about Anderson's habits, but there seemed little Emily could, or would, describe beyond the man's domestic preferences. At length Hunt dismissed her.

He would love to spend the hours and search this house from top to bottom for clues, but he had no idea for what he would be searching. Perhaps the answer lay in the mountain of papers and journals sitting on the table. Hunt picked up a sheet. Something about advertising receipts and monthly totals. He put the sheet back. He knew a bit about accounts, but knew nothing about the world of newspapers. He needed to talk with Schultz.

The echo of his footsteps followed him up the hall and he found Jane sitting in the parlor as she promised.

"I need to leave now."

He lied. He needed to stay, but he didn't know how to do that. Jane rose to her feet in one graceful movement. Their communication remained as strained as it had been when she left the sunroom.

"I'll see you out," she said. Her voice still held warmth, but he didn't know how to respond to that warmth. He followed her to the front door. "I hope today has been helpful."

"It has," he replied, wishing he could start their meeting again. "Thank you for seeing me."

Jane opened the door and viewed the clouds. "We don't have a carriage. Will you be all right with the weather?"

"I'll be fine. It's a good chance for me to walk and think."

The door closed behind him, and he stood alone on the porch. From five yards away, the empty swing seat mocked him. All of his plans for an afternoon of pleasant conversation destroyed by his foolish words. The gusting wind blew splashes of the returning rain across the porch to wet the seat cushions. They couldn't have sat there anyway.

With a muttered expletive, Hunt walked down the steps and strode over the wet gravel to the white gate. The drops of rain sought him out, then called for their friends. A deep roll of thunder met him at the end of the path and he slammed the gate shut behind him, turned south and hoped to remember the way back to Washington. By the time he reached the end of College Street, his clothes were completely saturated. Water streamed down his neck and slashing rain stung his eyes. He kept moving, looking for a place to hide from the storm's fury.

Ten minutes of fast walking brought him to the River Inn and he gratefully stepped inside its doors. A roaring fire in one corner and the breath of the half dozen inhabitants fed a comfortable fug in the room. He pushed forwards until he fronted the bar and ordered a beer.

No comfortable chairs were available near the fire, but a solitary stool stood near a window ledge. Hunt moved there, and perched himself on it. The rain beat solidly at the windows. He would be there for a while.

The River Inn took in a view of the Chesapeake and Ohio Canal and of the

Potomac, but the ever-changing curtain of rain made it difficult to see across the river. Glimpses of Virginia came and went with the varying intensity of the storm. Hunt sipped his ale and watched the rain squalls intermittently hide, and then reveal, the Confederate lands across the river.

Anderson. Bankruptcy. Illuminati. Pearson. There must be a link.

Perhaps Pearson wrote his paper as an almanac of the rites and rituals of the Illuminati? As a member of the Illuminati, Anderson would know all of their ceremonies and he could have accidentally let slip that he planned to publish these secrets. It would be a betrayal of their group, but the threat of bankruptcy could drive a man to desperate measures.

The international brotherhood might then have sent the three Confederates into Washington to kill Anderson. If all went well, the Confederates would return south and the Washington Police would be powerless to track the murderers and solve the crime. All this talk about Lincoln could be a decoy to throw them off the trail.

Lightning blazed its way across the sky, landing somewhere in the Virginia countryside. The brief flash lit up the Potomac illuminated a person scurrying north across the Aqueduct Bridge. The bass notes of the thunder rolled across the river adding grandeur and majesty to the storm's power. The person and the bridge vanished in the renewed downpour.

Hunt saw an image of his own life there. The perpetual search for a haven. It appeared as if he wouldn't be finding it with Jane Anderson. Hunt scowled at himself, and determined to try again. This very afternoon he would send her a telegram suggesting that they meet again tomorrow.

It took another hour for the weather to moderate sufficiently for him to attempt the walk back to the stationhouse. He trudged along the sodden roads of Georgetown under heavy skies, passing an abandoned wagon laden with goods. The unhitched horse stood forlornly under the shelter of a nearby tree. Water ran off the wagon's oilcloth-covered contents and joined the muddy stream reaching halfway to the wheel hubs.

Hunt found a cab a few dozen yards before Water Street crossed Rock Creek, and he climbed inside its shelter. He rode eastward, stopping briefly at a post house to send a message to Jane. It took some minutes to find the right words. At length he jotted a few lines inviting her to join him on the trip down the Potomac to inspect the wreck of the *Angelique*. Perhaps a ride down past Alexandria on a police launch might impress her. At least they would be together, and away from the disapproving scowl of Emily.

A faint ray of sunlight broke through the clouds during his trip back into Washington. It seemed a good omen.

Schultz and Hunt compare notes

A message from 'Thompson' waited for Hunt when he arrived back at the stationhouse. He took the time to find Sloan and pass on Schultz's tip about Marybelle's watches before setting out for the meeting.

The thunderclouds were massing to repeat their earlier performance. Slurry from the sodden roads remained stuck to his boots, and Hunt could feel the cold slimy touch of mud once again worming its way into his left boot. Shortly he sat opposite Schultz in a small coffee house near McRae's Hotel.

"Had lunch yet?" asked Schultz.

Hunt nodded. A serving of beef stew helped pass the time at the River Inn. At least, they called it beef. He didn't feel hungry now. "Coffee would help."

"Always does," agreed Schultz, turning to the counter and indicating the need for an additional cup of coffee. "How did you fare at the Anderson house?"

"Good. I found some things. Anderson had some clothes with that eye-in-a-triangle sign on it."

With that news, Schultz set down his coffee and leaned back in his chair. His left hand stroked his beard.

182

"Interesting."

"I found it in a metal box locked in his desk. I thought it best to leave it there. We can get it later if we need it."

"Perhaps."

"Does that mean he's a member of that lodge thing? Could it be that badge you found at his office belonged to him? He could have been dropped on the floor accidentally."

"Anderson might well be a member of the Illuminati. I considered that idea, but thought it unlikely that Anderson would leave his insignia on a desk waiting to be knocked to the floor. Mayhap I made a mistake there. What else did you find?"

"Anderson's paper is going poorly. Jane thinks it will be out of business in a year. She's not a bookkeeper, but she seems smart enough."

"She is smart. Perhaps too smart for her own good. Go on."

Hunt wasn't sure how to take that last comment. "There's an old housekeeper called Emily. Hardnosed woman. Didn't talk much, but she told me Anderson has a regular Wednesday meeting at his house with four or five men. They're supposed to be playing cards, but they're not."

Hunt debated whether to share the fact of the moldy card box with Schultz, but decided to leave his statement as it was. Schultz taunted him previously by providing conclusions without sharing the evidence behind them. Now Schultz could take a turn on the other end of the pointy stick. "Last night should have been their card night, but no one turned up. I'd say they all knew Anderson wouldn't be there."

The lack of knowledge about the cards didn't appear to worry Schultz. He slowly tapped a spoon on the table. When Hunt stopped talking, Schultz replaced the spoon near its companions and started caressing his thumbs in his palms. These random mindless mannerisms annoyed Hunt and he keenly felt the need for the self-discipline to ignore them.

"Anderson's death has been in the papers," replied Schultz. "Though perhaps some of his friends had advance knowledge of the event. If he hosted members of the Illuminati at those card evenings, I'd lay odds I could name half of Anderson's guests."

"I also have his diary. And love letters from some Beatrice woman. The letters seem nothing important, and I haven't looked at the diary."

"Show them to me."

Hunt passed across his trophy, and watched his partner spend the next few minutes flipping through its pages.

"Interesting," said Schultz at last. "He writes full names in some places and uses initials in others."

"I'd say he wants to hide the names of some people."

"So it would seem. His tactic gives away more information than it conceals. We might focus our attention on the initials. Here is a JL and an MC. I expected those. Who is PJ? There is our HG, but that is a few months ago. I will need to study this."

"For my third trick," announced Hunt grandly. "I found some court documents stored in the desk along with the diary and the letters. There were other court documents stacked in his bookshelf, but I figured there must be something special about these because they were in his desk."

With a grunt of satisfaction, Schultz leaned over to take the documents. Hunt never before noticed his partner's fingers were so short and thick. He drank his coffee while Schultz untied the documents and flipped through the pages. As he watched Schultz reading, Hunt realized how much the man's directness of action contributed to his overwhelming presence. Schultz always remained focused completely on the task at hand, and easily dominated the conversation when talking with Hunt. When Schultz directed his attention at something other than talking, he appeared as just a short balding man with a potbelly. He could be the neighborhood grocer.

Hunt grinned at the thought. It took Schultz a while to finish his reading of the cases. He re-tied them, then sat back in his chair and tapped his fingers on the table. "Interesting set of cases," he said at length. "Two are federal issues and one is a state matter. All of them deal with treason."

"Treason against a state? Isn't treason a federal crime?"

"Not according to these documents. The Rhode Island Supreme Court convicted Thomas Dorr of treason in 1844. Then the Federal Supreme Court acknowledged that judgment in *Ex Parte Dorr* four years later."

"Pearson! Did any of them mention Pearson? Owens mentioned Greeley and Pearson."

"No Pearson anywhere in those cases. The summary of the judgments is no help. *United States v. Burr* says that conspiracy to commit treason is, by itself, not a crime. However once that treason has been committed, then *Ex Parte Bollman* declares anyone involved with the planning of it is as guilty as the actual offenders. I don't pretend to understand it all, but what I read here sheds no light on our case at all."

"Then if these Illuminati were planning to kidnap President Lincoln, they'd all be guilty of treason?"

"Only when they attempted the kidnapping from what I read. I'm not pretending to understand all the law on this, but it seems they could plot the kidnapping without committing treason. The crime occurs when they set the plan in motion. However, kidnapping Abraham Lincoln is not treason. It's certainly a crime, but it's not treason."

Hunt wasn't surprised that Schultz distilled the essence of those rulings in a single reading. He felt a pang of jealousy at the man's brilliance, but he pushed away that feeling.

"Then why would Anderson be reading about it?"

Schultz raised a warning finger. "Don't presume that this plot is limited to abducting Lincoln. There may be associated activities involving other countries and that could involve treason. Remember that the Illuminati work without regard for national borders. There's also the possibility that these particular documents were sitting in Anderson's desk for some other reason, and have nothing to do with this case. You might also consider that Owens could have given you wrong information, deliberately or otherwise."

Hunt felt frustrated. His search of Anderson's house hadn't moved their investigation that much further ahead. The President remained in danger and they were no closer to finding Anderson's killers. He needed to know what Schultz discovered. "That's all I've got. How did you fare?"

"It turns out Horace Greeley isn't in New York after all," said Schultz, placing Anderson's diary and the court documents in his coat pocket. "He's away on business, and I'll give you one guess which town he's visiting."

Hunt knew that Schultz enjoyed his little dramas. Prolonging the suspense and maintaining center stage seemed to be one of his primary interests in life. If only he wasn't so good at his job then Hunt might have some comeback.

"Not Pittsburgh, I'd say," he responded cautiously. He learned it didn't pay to give Schultz the obvious answers.

"That's correct at any rate," continued Schultz, unperturbed by Hunt's evasive reply. "The esteemed editor of the New York Tribune is staying in Washington this week, and is attending the president's charity ball on Friday."

Hunt's drank more of his coffee to give himself time to absorb the news. Owens hadn't said that Greeley actually belonged to the group who planned to kidnap the President, but it seemed too much of a coincidence that the editor would be meeting the President later that week. Hunt wondered how much evidence he needed before he could justify suspecting Greeley. Schultz's next words helped him.

"We'll talk to Greeley. The editor of the New York Tribune is a powerful man and doubtless a regular correspondent with the President. I can't see why he would be involved with a plot to kidnap Lincoln, but since I don't know his private thoughts he remains to be proven as a friend."

"Where is he now?" asked Hunt, sure that Schultz knew the answer.

"Willard Hotel, up on Pennsylvania Avenue. You know it?"

"I've seen it. Never been in there."

"Today you will be. I've sent Greeley a message telling him to expect us at four o'clock."

"You think he'll agree?"

"He'll agree. He'll talk to us long enough to make sure his name isn't dragged in the mud. That's fine by me, as long as we get our questions answered."

Hunt finished his coffee. This would be another day of following in Schultz's footsteps. So be it. Perhaps he could learn something. Fortunately, a cab stood waiting at the side of the road as Hunt and Schultz came out of the café, and the detectives gratefully climbed aboard.

Differences in social status as well as miles measured the distance from the coffee house to the Willard Hotel. Where McRae's Hotel provided a refuge for anyone who could scrape together a few lean dollars, the Willard Hotel stood as the defining stamp of Washington society. The detective's cab ran up onto the ramp and stopped opposite the covered walkway leading into the hotel. A footman opened the cab door, holding an umbrella to shield the new arrivals from the rain. The wind snatched at his umbrella as he greeted them. "Welcome to the Willard Hotel, gentlemen. Any luggage I can help you with?"

In all of his time in Washington, Hunt had never been to this grand establishment. A protective canopy stretching from the hotel doorway across to the edge of the pavement. Hunt felt obliged to tip the footman, but he needed to be careful with his cash and, in this area of town, a tip would probably start at a dollar. He solved the problem by striding rapidly for the doors, leaving Schultz to follow on as best he could. It seemed a crime to leave fingermarks on the freshly polished brass handrails, but fortunately, a gloved and uniformed youth opened the door for him.

Hunt walked straight past the boy, not stopping until he reached the interior of the lobby. Mahogany paneled walls adorned by polished brass gave an air of luxury to the foyer. Hunt felt too intimidated to sit on the plump armchairs. A concierge tipped his hat, and Hunt pretended not to see him. He avoided the man's gaze, and hoped Schultz would soon arrive. He gazed at a portrait of George Washington, and wished he'd scraped the undersides of his boots more carefully on the mat before walking on the carpet.

"We're a trifle early. I've heard Greeley is a stickler for punctuality. Let's put that theory to the test."

Schultz's voice at his side reassured Hunt, and he followed his limping partner to the reception desk. The attendant smiled at them. "You have Mister Greeley of New York staying here," declared Schultz.

The attendant adopted a pleasant look. "I couldn't comment on that, sir," he replied. "The Willard Hotel..."

"Yes! Yes! I know," interrupted Schultz loudly. "Privacy of your guests and all of that. Horace Greeley is expecting us. Detectives Schultz and Hunt of the Metropolitan Police Department, Fifth Precinct."

The expression in the attendant's eyes changed, and, with a look of alarm, he guided the detectives down to the other end of the counter, away from the other guests. "I'll see if Mister Greeley is available. If you gentlemen could wait here..."

The attendant's wave brought a bellboy to the counter at a run, and Schultz wandered away to let instructions be passed in peace. Hunt followed Schultz to the armchairs, but he didn't sit down. Schultz smiled at Hunt. "People like Greeley often travel under assumed names. It could have been a real problem making them admit that Greeley checked in here. Fortunately, no hotel likes having a detective ask after one of their guests. It raises all sorts of ugly possibilities in the minds of their other visitors. The Willard is no different in that respect, so they are eager to solve the problem and help us depart."

"It's a beautiful hotel. There's a painting of Lincoln. Looks like they're quite dedicated to the Union cause."

Schultz snorted. "In this lobby they are. Go around the other entrance, and you'll see everything Confederate except the Stars and Bars, and I'm not sure they don't have that hidden under the counter. The Willard wouldn't let politics get in the way of selling a room for the night."

"Confederate? In Washington?"

"They've toned it down in recent years. But come in off F Street, and I guarantee you won't see a single Union flag. The Willard put on quite a balancing act before the war to make sure they kept politicians of all colors happy."

Hunt shook his head in wonder and decided to say no more. It seemed in this police business every word owned two meanings and every person a half-dozen agendas. He looked around at the lobby, and lost himself in appreciating the ornate furnishings while Schultz subsided into a chair. Fully twenty minutes passed while they waited. The wall clock behind the lobby desk indicated four o'clock before the receptionist walked over from the booking desk accompanied by a keen looking youth wearing a crisp, starched uniform. "Mister Greeley will see you now. Alistair will take you upstairs."

Schultz levered himself out of the armchair and followed the youth. Hunt walked behind. The Willard's main staircase provided a physical tribute to the woodworker's art, and Hunt took the opportunity to admire the intricate scrollwork as he waited for Schultz to labor his way up the stairs. Greeley occupied a suite on the second floor, and Hunt could see sweat on Schultz's face by the time he reached the landing. Hunt respected the older man's pluck. Wounds like the one that Schultz suffered could keep lesser men in their beds for weeks.

The décor of the corridor matched that of the lobby. Crystal oil lights hung in a row from the ceiling, casting an excellent illumination right along the hall. They followed the youth along until he stopped. He indicated a door, then immediately retired, as if not wishing to be associated with whatever perils might lie ahead in this meeting. Hunt considered the uncharitable thought that the boy might be more interested in meeting guests who might be freer with their tips than two metropolitan detectives. Schultz raised his cane and rapped smartly on the door.

Interviewing Greeley

Greeley expected the request for an interview. He debated with the temptation to refuse the meeting, but that would have been inappropriate. The whore's report gave him good information about the upcoming discussion, but he could not predict the results. Perhaps the detectives planned to accuse him of personally plotting to abduct the President? Greeley nodded to his secretary, who rose and opened the door.

Two men stood there, one of them leaning on a cane.

"I'm Detective Schultz," said the man with the cane. "This is Detective Hunt. We're here to see Mister Greeley."

The secretary moved back to allow the men to enter, and then left, closing the door behind him. The two detectives walked across to where Greeley sat at his desk. Greeley neither stood nor offered to shake hands, and his fingers stayed steepled together in front of him. "I'm Horace Greeley," he said pleasantly. "Please take a seat. How can I help you?"

"We're investigating the death of John Anderson of Washington," began Schultz, sinking into one of the chairs. "You had recent dealings with him."

"Probably. I have dealings with most of the newspaper editors in America."

"That would be reasonable for a man in your position. Have you ever dealt with a newspaper editor named Pearson?"

That question surprised Greeley. The detectives didn't seem to know much about the circumstances that led to Anderson's death. Greeley chose to change his manner from a welcoming politeness into an aggressive defensiveness. "No! I don't know an editor called Pearson."

He hoped that would get a response, and the younger man obliged him.

"That was quick. You're sure you don't know him?"

Excellent!

"You ask me if I know an editor called Pearson and I tell you I don't," replied Greeley tartly. "Don't you believe me?"

Greeley caught the quiet glare that Schultz gave to Hunt.

The young one is impatient. I can bait him into getting angry and then refuse to answer him. The older one will be more difficult.

"We appreciate you thinking about your answers, Mister Greeley," continued Schultz. "I'm sure you want us to catch the people who murdered your colleague."

"Humph, maybe you should think more about your questions then. What else do you want to know?"

"I've read some of your editorials, Mister Greeley. Tell me your politics."

"Detective Schultz, I'm a newspaper man. A New York mob torched my offices last year, and that's not good for business, regardless of whether or not it sells a couple of extra newspapers. The sooner this war is finished, and we get back to a business as usual, then the better my life will be I'd say. Regardless of that, the question of how I vote this year is a matter for my conscience, not for your notebook."

Schultz took the rebuff without anger. "Did you write to John Anderson recently?"

"I wrote to Anderson about many things. They were all related to business."

"Any particular business?"

"Nothing out of the ordinary. Territories, sales, future plans. The sort of conversations that I have with editors in many cities."

"You were in Washington the night John Anderson died."

Schultz held his notebook in his hand, as if ready to check Greeley's response against information written there. The detectives were well off course in their investigation and Greeley did not intend to help them find the right track. He pursed his lips and looked at Schultz.

"I get to Washington quite often. In case you haven't noticed, that's where the president lives and congress meets. Lots of newspaper folk come here."

"Indeed they do. You're going to the White House charity ball on Friday?"

Why did he ask about the charity ball? What does he know? He doesn't understand about Pearson, but where did he hear the name? I must be careful.

Greeley waved a dismissive hand. "One of the costs of being in business. These events are a nuisance at times, but there is the occasional chance to do business there."

"Did you plan to meet John Anderson there?"

"Not especially. I didn't know he would be there."

"How about James Singleton?"

"Who?"

"James Singleton, the Banker."

"Never heard of him."

"Fergus Wallace?"

"Wallace is in Boston. Doesn't travel much now."

"Albert Pike?"

"He won't be there," replied Greeley.

"You know him?"

"Not personally."

Keep calm. They know nothing. They are fishing.

"What about Pearson?"

Schultz's ruse didn't work. Greeley looked up, then placed his hands, palm down, on the desk in front of him. "Look here, Detective Schultz. I've told you I don't know any editor called Pearson."

"But you know Albert Pike?"

Greeley abruptly stood, letting the tension he felt come out in a quivering of his body.

If he could put them onto the wrong trail for another forty-eight hours!

"You are becoming offensive, Detective Schultz. I suggest you confine your questions to the matter of John Anderson's death."

"I am doing that, Mister Greeley," replied Schultz in an affable voice. "Up until this point, you and Mister Pearson are the best leads we have."

"I can't help you any further. I regret John Anderson's death, but it came as a complete surprise to me. As far as Pearson's Paper is concerned, I know nothing about it."

Greeley strode to the door and flung it open. "This interview is over. If you have further questions, then address them to my lawyers."

Schultz looked at Greeley for a second, then stood and limped out into the corridor. Hunt fell into step beside him, and Greeley slammed the door shut the instant the two men left the room. A smile grew on his face.

Success!

Hunt struggles for answers

The two detectives spoke no words until they reached the pavement outside the hotel, and were wading through the rain back to the stationhouse. Schultz took the initiative before Hunt could ask the inevitable question. "You'll be wanting to know about Fergus Wallace and Albert Pike."

"You hadn't mentioned them before. How do they fit into this case?"

"Wallace is an editor in Boston. I mentioned him to get Greeley into the flow of answering questions. That's also why I mentioned Singleton. Damn, I need a cab! My leg isn't up to all of this walking."

They spent the next few minutes hailing and boarding a carriage, and then Schultz resumed his explanation.

"Singleton and Wallace don't concern me at the moment, but our General Pike is a different matter. He's a little more dangerous, and I'm not surprised Greeley knew him. If this affair does involve an Illuminati plot against Lincoln, then General Pike would be involved."

"General Pike? I don't recall the name," admitted Hunt. "Is he a Regular or Volunteer?"

"He is, or was, a Confederate General," explained Schultz. "At the start of the war he commanded their Indian Territory out west. In late '62 he fell out of favor with Richmond, and resigned his post. He's now in Texas, and devotes his energies to a voluminous correspondence with people on all sides of politics."

"So why would Greeley know him?"

Schultz grimaced as the cab ran over a pothole. "Albert Pike ranks quite highly in the hierarchy of the American Illuminati, and Greeley is the very model of a man who would be a member of that society. Rich, powerful, politically well-connected and most of all, possessing a burning desire for power. Judging by Greeley's reaction to my question about his connection with Pike, I was right on the money."

"It wasn't a guess though, was it?"

Schultz looked hard at Hunt, and then broke out in laughter. "You're getting to know me too well, Detective Hunt. All right, it wasn't a guess. Secret societies are a special interest of mine, and my studies in that field have proved useful more often than I originally expected. I've been observing the Illuminati penetration into government circles for some years, and I have long suspected that particular connection. Since Greeley recognized Pike's name, it adds evidence to confirm Greeley's active membership of the Illuminati. If so, then we have another connection between Anderson and Greeley."

"You're not making things any clearer. Why would Greeley murder a fellow lodge member?"

Schultz shook his head. "Mayhap I'm straining at gnats here. Greeley admitted doing business with Anderson, but that is quite reasonable given their respective positions. It could be that Anderson told Greeley something, and that information made its way through to Anderson's Illuminati brethren. There's no question in my mind that Greeley knows more about Pearson than he is prepared to admit, but this whole thing could still be a local lodge matter."

"I thought he'd broken their lodge laws. That he wanted to publish their rituals to sell more papers."

"No. The Illuminati creed spells out the consequences of betrayal, and the killers didn't follow that particular ritual in this case. The intruders used the torture to extract information from Anderson, not to serve as a warning to other lodge members"

"But why else would Anderson's lodge members have wanted to kill their leader?"

"We don't know who served as leader of that lodge. Meeting at Anderson's house may have been geographically convenient."

Schultz looked down at his hands, turning them over as if looking for a weakness in them. "I don't know how much the Illuminati are involved in this murder," he continued. "There's the evidence of the lapel pin on the floor of the bedroom. Openly wearing such a pin, by the way, is quite against the rules of their lodge. I considered the pin belonged to either Anderson, or the murderers, or been planted there to confuse the issue. Finding the lodge regalia at Anderson's house answered that question for us. It appears the pin belonged to Anderson after all. The evidence isn't completely clear on the matter, but I am more and more convinced that the criminals did not intend to kill Anderson."

Schultz shook his head slowly. "I mistrust my own theory," he said at length. "It sounds fine, but the evidence doesn't fully support it. Let us put aside the Illuminati for the minute, and look at other matters."

Hunt raised his finger to make a point. "There's one thing which seemed quite strange. Greeley said he didn't know any editor called Pearson, but he sure got upset when you mentioned that name a second time."

"I noticed that. He used the phrase 'Pearson's Paper' as if it had some special meaning. How did Owens describe Pearson?"

"He didn't. Owens spoke of Pearson and his Paper. He didn't say it was a newspaper, but he spoke as if Pearson owned it, whatever it was. Maybe Pearson owns part of Greeley's paper, and Greeley's being smart with us?"

"Too easy for us to check. In that case, I'd expect that Greeley would tell us that fact, but pretend confusion as to how they affected this particular case.

I'm thinking this Pearson will be someone Greeley knows only through a particular set of circumstances. Someone of whom he could deny an intimate connection."

"Could it be a bank paper or some money thing then? Security over a loan perhaps. Lincoln might owe Pearson some money and now Pearson is calling in the debt."

"That wouldn't make the President run south. If it's a southern bank, then Lincoln could ignore the debt until the war is over. If it's a northern bank, then Lincoln could turn a few favors for the bankers to work out a deal. There's no need to leave the country. Moreover, why go south? He could run to Canada or England if he'd a mind to skip out on his debts."

"Some letter Lincoln wrote then. Maybe he's being blackmailed by Pearson?"

Schultz dismissed that idea with a flip of his hand. "Pinkerton's would fix that sort of problem inside a week. I'd say it's something more complicated than that."

"All right then, it's a newspaper," conceded Hunt. "We're back where we started from. How do we find this Pearson fellow?"

"Don't give up so easily," cautioned Schultz. "That's a good idea saying it mightn't be a newspaper. Greeley's reaction suggests Pearson's Paper is important to this case. We know Anderson needed to boost the Herald's circulation, and publishing Pearson's Paper, whatever it is, may have been his plan to fix that problem. If the other Illuminati objected to Anderson's plan, they would first try to talk him out of it, and failing that, adopt stronger measures to prevent the publication. Suppose Pearson's Paper is a document and someone wanted it. Would they commit murder for it?"

"The Thursday folder! They stole it from Anderson's office."

"That makes sense. Mayhap Anderson owned some document that he referred to as Pearson's paper. If he planned to publish it in his Thursday edition, it would be natural for him to sell the story to the papers in other cities also. Greeley would be his first contact to reach the New York market.

Once the story gained the Tribune's approval, it would be easier to sell it to papers elsewhere. Therefore, Greeley would be one of the first to learn of the Paper."

"Then why burn the contents of the folder on the floor of the Herald's offices? All of Anderson's research disappeared in that fire."

"That's what makes me doubt Greeley organized the burglary," replied Schultz. "If he had been involved, then he'd have taken the information for publication in his own newspaper. Greeley knows more than he's saying, but I don't suspect him of murder."

"So it wasn't Greeley, then who would destroy the Paper?"

"If it proved evidence of a personal bank debt, then Lincoln might want it destroyed. A word to Allan Pinkerton, and the job would be done. However, I don't see Lincoln condoning murder for personal gain. He is a man of strong political beliefs, but I have heard no word against his personal honesty."

"Not Greeley! Not Lincoln! Not the Illuminati!" cried Hunt in exasperation. "Then who is behind all of this?"

"Who indeed?" echoed Schultz. "That is the question."

They reached the stationhouse. Captain Price and Sloan were having an animated discussion when Hunt and Schultz walked into the detective's room.

"You're sure of this now?" asked Price. "Last week you were telling me that this case couldn't be solved."

"I found the booty and Marybelle confessed," replied Sloan. "She hid them under her bed all this time. Quite a collection she stored there."

Hunt smiled to himself, then ignored the rest of that conversation. Schultz hadn't been to the station since the affair at the docks. Not surprisingly, there were many messages and other minor tasks that needed to be addressed before he could return to the Anderson case. During that time, Hunt busied himself writing a summary of the events. He found it focussed his mind, and by the time Schultz cleared his backlog, Hunt felt ready for him.

"Listen here for a moment Schultz; this is what I'm thinking. I'm still going with the idea that Pearson's Paper is some Illuminati pamphlet listing all of their rituals and secret signs and so forth. Anderson's a member of that lodge so he writes it all up, and plans to publish it in this coming Thursday's edition. Lots of headlines. Lots of money to save his newspaper. He tries to sell the story to the Tribune, and Greeley betrays him to the rest of these Illuminati. They send these Confederate agents to stop the publication, and Anderson dies while they're questioning him. These Confederates don't have time for all those rituals so they don't do it the right way. They're more interested in destroying the headlines. They burn the stuff then hide out on the ship until it's safe to leave."

Schultz eyed Hunt, and tapped a pencil on the desk. "The truth may lie somewhere between our two answers," he replied diplomatically. "I can tell you that the penalty of death is a very real threat for Illuminati who betray their order. There have been two such executions in the last fifty years, and John Anderson would have no hope of escaping such a sentence. Publishing the Illuminati rituals might save his newspaper, but it would be his personal death warrant. I'd be more inclined to go along with your bank bill idea for the moment, but you still need to explain why that would persuade President Lincoln to go south."

"I haven't got all the answers yet. Maybe Owens lied. Maybe these killers were having a joke with him."

"Perhaps."

His own theory seemed sound enough, but as far as Hunt could see, it brought them no closer to finding the murderers. He sat and chewed a pencil end as he reviewed his scribbling. At last, he turned back to Schultz. "I'd say that we need to talk to these Illuminati people."

"When you find them, let me know. They are notorious for concealing the names of their members."

"Don't you have some contacts? Hell Schultz, the way you carry on, you know half the people in Washington."

"Mayhap I do," replied Schultz, clearly unimpressed by the compliment. "However, in recent years the Illuminati have gone very much to ground. They were there at the start of the war but something happened to stay their hand. My guess is that Lincoln's fought this war better than they planned. The South is losing and that's not what they intended."

"Wait a minute," interrupted Hunt. "You're telling me these Illuminati people started this war?"

"Not exactly. I don't claim they started the war, but I'll stake a huckleberry to a persimmon they saw it coming and set themselves up to benefit from it."

"How would they do that?"

"Not my concern. I'm a detective, not a congressman. I'm interested in maintaining the peace in Washington. My job here is to uphold the law, all of the law, not just the parts I like. When the Illuminati violate the laws of Washington, then I set myself against their activities. Apart from that, whoever wins this war is of little concern to me."

Hunt stared at Schultz. The man's words were clear enough. Hunt walked himself through the sentence again, but the meaning didn't change, couldn't change. Schultz didn't care who won the war. Hunt looked at Schultz with new eyes. All of his admiration for this man disappeared with that sentence. Schultz looked back at him without anger or passion.

"You're a Copperhead," Hunt said heavily.

"Don't be too quick to label people, Hunt. I think this war is pointless, but that doesn't make me a Copperhead."

"At least I volunteered! Where were you in '61?"

Schultz seemed taken aback by the question, and Hunt felt reassured that he could still score some points.

"Where was I in '61?" mused Schultz. "I spent a few weeks investigating the enlistments for Schaeffer's National Volunteers with Colonel Stone, but most of the time I was doing my job right here in the Fifth Precinct. The military life never held any attraction for me."

"Too many bullets, hey?"

Hunt regretted the comment the moment he spoke it, but he couldn't reclaim the words. Schultz pursed his lips and tapped his thumbs together. He waited a full five seconds before he replied. "There are enough bullets on the streets of Washington. I recall meeting one of them a few nights ago."

"I'm sorry. I didn't mean..."

Schultz's raised hand stifled Hunt's apology. "Wait now, Hunt. I don't need to defend myself to you, but I'm going to explain something." He shifted in his chair, scowling with the pain of his wound. "Did you ever read history, Hunt?"

"History? The revolution and all that? Only what they told me in school."

"You missed out on quite a bit then. History fascinated me in my early years. The rise and fall of nations, and the reigns of Kings and Queens. I could never get enough of it. I thought of teaching history as my career. I thought it possible for me to do that. I enrolled at college, and progressed well on my way to graduation."

Hunt could see the light in Schultz's eyes as the older man described his passion. It would never have struck Hunt that Schultz would be content with a living burial in some schoolhouse.

"So why didn't you do that?"

"The usual excuse for these things, I guess. Life got in the way. I met a man, a Union volunteer as you once were; only he had no hands and life reduced him to begging on the streets to survive."

"No hands?"

"He lost them in the Mexican War. A shell landed on his gunpit, and all of the crew, save himself, died. He took months in hospital to recover, and then the army he served discharged him without a pension."

"That's tragic," conceded Hunt. "War makes widows."

"Yes, and countries make wars. It made me start wondering how could there be glory in the acts of a nation that left men crippled and children orphaned. Then I started re-reading my history books, and discovered the Kings and Queens I admired the most were those that fought the most battles. Lord alone knows how many lives were ruined by their glorious wars."

"So you gave up teaching?"

"Never started it. I gave my schoolbooks away, and wandered from town to town for many months until I drifted into police work. These days, my efforts go into making this city safer for those who live here. I'll risk my life for that, but I won't risk my life, or anyone else's, to keep a government in power."

"That's quite a change."

"Quite a change indeed. Not as much as the change Alex endured of course. We went to the same school many years before. He showed some talent for working with wood in those days."

"You went to school with him?"

"Life has a habit of bringing the past back into our lives. Yes, I knew Alex at school. Before he turned to carpentry as a trade. Before he joined the army. He's gone now. Starved to death in some alley perhaps. I can't be everywhere."

Schultz straightened himself in his chair and looked at Hunt. His fingers started a slow, regular tapping on the table. He obviously felt some responsibility for his friend's unknown fate. The silence between them grew, and Hunt knew he'd blundered badly by accusing Schultz of cowardice.

"So you volunteered in '61?" asked Schultz.

202

"Day after the President called for volunteers."

"Then you left the Army with the job half finished."

"They wouldn't let me fight. Hell, I told you that."

"Would you have died for your country?"

"I killed two Confederates in man-to-man combat. They could have killed me. Yes, I'd have died for my country if I had to."

"You'd give your life in battle for your country. That's admirable. So tell me, why should it be too much for you to spend that same life serving the country where it needed you the most? You'd die for your country, but then you refuse to accept an anonymous posting behind the lines passing up the ammunition for other soldiers. I'd say it's not the country you care about, that's a handy cloak to cover your craving for personal glory in battle. Think about that the next time you want to judge others."

Hunt felt his beliefs rearranging themselves under the acid brush of Schultz's words. Would he give his life for the Union now? He still needed somewhere to belong, and a code to live by. Hunt deliberated what to say next. It seemed safest to return to the case at hand. "Tell me then, where do we go from here?"

"I'll follow up the Illuminati. Tomorrow, you'd best get downriver and see if there's anything left of the trail of those Confederates from the ship. Ask for Colonel Welling at Fort Foote if you need some help there. He knows my name and owes a favor. In the meantime, I have another case to consider. You'll excuse me."

Hunt nodded, suddenly eager to be gone from this place. He left Schultz at his desk, gathered his coat and went out into the leaden skies and cold streets of Washington. Schultz could juggle multiple cases, and doubtless make headway in all of them while Hunt felt lost and rudderless in dealing only with Anderson's murder. Maybe the job became easier after a few years, but right now, he found it all too confusing.

For the moment, he needed a good night's sleep.

The wreck of the *Angelique*

No message from Jane waited at the stationhouse when Hunt arrived there early on Friday morning. His work clothes were still damp from their unscheduled mid-week washing, and he disliked wearing his Sunday Best during the week. His old army uniform remained the only choice. Perhaps the fact that he'd once been a commissioned officer would impress Jane.

He delayed his departure from the station for almost an hour, hoping a message would appear. When Schultz arrived in the office, and made a few pointed comments about the *Angelique*, Hunt set off by himself. The police boat crew at the navy yard helped Hunt fill out the paperwork.

The icy wind off the water numbed his face, and Hunt buried himself deep into his buckskin coat as the steam launch puttered its way south. Piscataway Point came and went, then Alexandria appeared on the right. Eventually the wreck of the *Angelique* came into view. Hunt had never been down the Potomac on a boat before, but the riverbank scenery could not hold his interest. His thoughts revolved around Jane, and his mind told him everything he should have said to her. She had been nice to him. He could see her interest in him, and he needed to find a way to help that interest grow.

Round and round the thoughts went, until the police launch tied up next to the *Angelique*, and he found a Lieutenant supervising the salvage crew.

"Detective Hunt," he said showing the slim, fair-haired man his badge. "Fifth Precinct."

"Lieutenant Collins."

Like the rest of his detail, Collins stripped off his heavy coat and worked up a fair sweat trying to refloat the ship. Grimy sailors manhandled the goods from the wreck of the *Angelique* to a barge moored alongside.

"I'm investigating the death of John Anderson. We suspect his killers were on this boat."

"They're not here now. You're welcome to look, but I can't let you take anything. It's all been inventoried."

"That's OK by me." Hunt stepped aboard the *Angelique*. Her foremast had gone in the battle and a fire raged along her foredeck. Where to start?

"Did you want to see the inventory? We've moved most items to the barge except for the cargo. That's only cheap lace."

Of course it was. Schultz had already determined that. "Inventory? Yes. That would help."

Collins led Hunt to pilothouse on the barge, and gave him a fistful of paper. "Here's the Certificate of Capture. It's our only copy. Take care with it."

Hunt nodded his assent as Collins returned to his work. A deck-mounted horn cleat provided a handy seat, and Hunt sat there to read the paperwork. Seconds later, a hard splat announced the landing of a passing seabird's excrement on the deck beside him. He looked to the sky, fearful of a second shot, but the miscreant flew on. Oddly, he detected no smell, or perhaps the steady wind dispersed the aroma before it could reach his nose. If Jane accompanied him today, she might have been standing there.

He must have been mad. How could he think that an educated woman like Jane would want to accompany him on a work boat sent to inspect a wreck? She lived for her family and her work. Maybe she would like the chance to tell him things about how to make art. He should take her to an art place. Art gallery? Art hall? Schultz would know the word. There must be one of those places in Washington. He'd ask Schultz when he returned to the station.

For now, he needed to get to work. The barely readable writing on the inventory sheets listed the possessions of seafaring men; tack, scrimshaw, slop chests. Nothing of special interest.

He flicked through the pages with less care than he knew he should give them. The crew of his launch chatted with each other on the other side of the *Angelique*. What problems could they have compared to his? He checked himself. This attitude led him into making mistakes on previous occasions. He forced his attention back to the sheets, and carefully read each item. Cooking utensils, spare ropes, sail mending tools. The list seemed meaningless, but he forced himself to read every item.

On the third page, he found what he looked for. The list showed three formal suits complete with clawhammer coats and top hats. Those items had no business on a trading ship. He worked his way through the other pages, but the rest of the inventory held no surprises. Hunt left the papers in the pilothouse and returned to the *Angelique*. According to Schultz, three men murdered Anderson. Three suits of formal wear were stored aboard the murderer's ship. Why would the murderers need formal wear when calling on Anderson? Top hats and clawhammer coats were worn only at the best society banquets.

He looked at the ship and decided the work crew would have found, or trampled, anything else of importance. He needed to get back to the stationhouse. Maybe Jane sent a message after all. Hunt thanked the Lieutenant for his help, and headed back to Washington. The launch made heavy going against the run of the river. The rain held off for the trip, enabling Hunt to sit alone in the bow of the boat and think.

Late afternoon arrived before Hunt could get back to the detectives room. Osborne and Sloan discussed the details of an upcoming court hearing and Schultz sat writing at his desk. Hunt dropped into the chair next to Schultz, and recounted his achievements of the morning. Schultz took it all in, grunting once when Hunt mentioned the three sets of formal wear. After Hunt finished, Schultz picked a folded sheet of paper from the desk and passed it across to him. "This arrived for you from Miss Anderson. I've read it."

Schultz didn't seem embarrassed by owning to reading the mail from Jane. Then again, why should he? As far as he knew, it would be police business. Hunt turned the letter over in his hand. He wanted to smell it, to know her perfume again. He could do that later. The letter unfolded in his hands and he saw her smooth writing.

.

Detective Hunt,

Thank you for your note of this afternoon. Owing to my father's funeral set down for tomorrow morning, I must regretfully decline your invitation.

Your servant,

Jane Anderson

.

A spasm grabbed his stomach. He hadn't thought to ask about her father's interment. Instead of being at her side during her father's burial, he proposed they enjoy a ride on the river. Of all the ignorant, selfish, stupid, plain thoughtless ideas he ever suggested to a woman, this one beat them all. He read her words again, seeing his dreams disengage themselves from reality and float away. He knew those dreams would return on future sleepless nights to torment him with proof of his own inadequacy.

Schultz continued writing in a folder. His partner must know what this meant for Hunt. It took a minute for Hunt to compose himself. He thrust the paper in his pocket. The time now arrived for him to become a stronger man.

"I don't think she can help us further," he managed to say.

"Probably not."

Hunt retrieved her letter and read it again. It still said the same words that he read before. He returned it to his pocket, and resolved to throw it away later that night. "So what are our plans?"

Schultz laid down the nib and blotted the paper. He spoke without looking at Hunt. "I have some leads on the Illuminati. Get downstairs and find a cab. I'll be there presently."

Hunt followed instructions. That would be easier than wrestling with his thoughts. Within minutes, Schultz joined him on the pavement and they boarded a cab. The rain still came down, but not with the intensity that scoured Washington earlier in the day.

"Seventeenth Street Northwest, cabbie," said Schultz. "A whisker past Massachusetts Avenue."

The two men settled in the cab for the ride. "I'll tell you what we're doing now," said Schultz. "So you don't think I'm leading you around by the nose again."

Hunt appreciated the conversation. Right now, he would appreciate anything that stopped him thinking of Jane.

"I've been through Anderson's diary. His two most frequent contacts are JL and MC. My guess is those initials represent Jonathan Lombard and Morgan Carlisle. Both of them are prominent in the Washington lodge hierarchy, and they're a good starting point for our inquiries."

Hunt nodded and let Schultz talk for another five minutes before the conversation tapered off. Hunt had nothing to say. That simple note from Jane somehow allowed him to see things from a different perspective. He knew that he had been infatuated with Jane Anderson and, truth be told, he still was. He could see that weakness now, and, if he could see it, then he could control it. He could also see how he tried to use his job to impress her. That would stop from this point. His job must come first.

The first stop, at the house of Jonathan Lombard, did not help their cause. A gardener and a neighbor conversing at Lombard's front gate confirmed that Lombard went to Canada a month ago on business, and would return in a fortnight. Fortunately, their cabbie hadn't left yet owing to a tedious, yet necessary, adjustment of the horse harness. A few minutes later the pair sat once again in the same cab, pushing their way through the mud to the Carlisle residence.

"Morgan Carlisle is a member of a lodge in Washington, called the Ancient Order of Societas Gotha," began Schultz.

"Gothas? I thought we were looking for the Illuminati."

"Lodge members sometimes have overlapping memberships. Some two hundred years ago, Johannas Dixon published an excellent work on the membership connections between lodges. Read that book if you want to understand more about it. For the moment, take my word that Carlisle is a man we need to see. The Gothas practise a variation of the Swedenborg rite and have some links with the Illuminati. Carlisle is an accountant who works from home. We should find him there."

Schultz scowled as a bump in the ride jolted his leg. He adjusted himself before continuing. "If Carlisle had been one of Anderson's Wednesday night guests then he will be a little sensitive right now, regardless of whether he had anything to do with the murder. After all, people who meet secretly are nervous about that secret, regardless of how innocent their motives may be. Darn these bumps! It will be a good thing when we finally pave these roads."

Schultz spent the rest of the trip lecturing on the history of Washington roads, and the need for a comprehensive transportation plan for the city including covering the dirt roads with cobblestones or corduroy surfaces. The rain backed off to a fine drizzle, and the cabbie had no problem finding the address. Hunt felt disappointed with what he saw when they arrived. Carlisle's old wooden house needed paint and nails, and the adjacent office looked the same.

A man well into his fifties answered their knock on the office door. Carlisle was a rolypoly man. A tight seamed, button popping, tailor's nightmare of a man with an unfixed collar and dirty cravat. A fine head of sandy hair crowned his moon face, and an impossibly small pair of pince-nez balanced on his ruddy, pockmarked nose. "Yes?" he asked in a tiny voice out of all proportion to his size.

"Morgan Carlisle?"

"I am he. How may I help?"

Schultz dismissed the cabbie with a wave of his hand before continuing. "It is the matter of a bequest."

"A bequest? You need a will made?" purred Carlisle. "Please come in. Hum. Yes. Mind the step. A plank is loose."

Loose planks were the least of Carlisle's problems with the house. A threadbare carpet lay over the creaking floor, and Hunt thought he spied a rat scuttling in the dark corner of the room. Dark wallpaper peeled away, to hang from the mold-blackened plasterwork in great strips. Carlisle seemed oblivious to all of this, and seated himself behind a desk overflowing with papers and journals. A dusty painting of a prosperous and stern-faced farmer - perhaps Carlisle's father - hung on the wall behind him.

"Please be seated. Hum. Regrettably, I can spare you only a short time today, but next week I can make a will if you require. I am an accountant, but I turn my hand to many things."

Hunt perched himself on the edge of a cloth chair. The fabric felt damp to touch.

"I fear we are at cross purposes," said Schultz. "Are you acquainted with John Anderson, the late editor of the Washington Herald?"

Carlisle wasn't an actor. His eyebrows furrowed intently, straining to meet each other over the bridge of the pudgy pink nose while his porcine eyes darted back and forth between Schultz and Hunt. "Anderson? I... ahhh... no... that is, yes, I have heard of the name."

"We represent his daughter," dissembled Schultz convincingly. "John Anderson had a group of friends he met with on Wednesday nights to play cards, and his daughter wishes to honor them with a bequest from his estate."

Morgan Carlisle fixed his eyes on Schultz. "Indeed! Hum. What kind of bequest?"

"Perhaps there is money involved. We will come back to that point," demurred Schultz. "Our first need is to ascertain the cardplayer's names, and ensure these are the right people. That is the point of our investigation here."

"Investigation? What do you mean investigation?"

"You must understand that the names must be proven. The gift cannot be given to anyone. I'm sure you appreciate the need for delicacy. If word of this bequest got out, then all persuasions of fortune seekers might claim Anderson's acquaintance."

"Yet you start with me? How do you know my name?"

"Anderson's daughter remembered your name. Apparently John Anderson didn't speak much about these Wednesday card evenings, yet his daughter felt he attached great significance to those times, thus she wished to honor the friends who meant so much to her father. Your name came up once in connection with another trifling matter, now beyond recall, and he said he would see you on Wednesday night about it. Thus she recalls your name, but nothing else."

"I see," said Carlisle, somewhat mollified.

Hunt admired his colleague's gift for improvisation, although a nagging voice chastised him for his complicity in taking Jane's name and money in vain.

"Did she misremember? Did you play cards with John Anderson on Wednesday nights?"

"Cards? Yes. We met on Wednesday nights. Hum. A small number of us every Wednesday."

"Excellent. This task is less difficult than we feared. If we could trouble you for the names of the other gentlemen, then this whole matter can be wrapped up to everyone's satisfaction."

"Names? Oh no! Hum. I couldn't do that. I mean, this is a matter of confidence. The members of our lod... our group would not care to be the subject of gossip. Hum. I will contact them and seek their permission."

Schultz tightened his lips and looked at the floor. "It won't do Mister

Carlisle. Please consider our position. Some might believe you sought time to find accomplices who would agree to your story in return for a share of the proceeds. I have no doubt you are an honorable man, but we must discharge our duty to the lady and protect her interests."

Schultz's audacity amazed Hunt. Men had been challenged to duels for less. Yet Schultz seemed to have picked his mark carefully. Carlisle slumped like a deflated balloon.

"You place me in an impossible position sir. I cannot name my friends without their permission."

Schultz's right hand snapped to his chest, and he gave out a faint moan. Then, with a sharp intake of breath, he bared his teeth in a grimace of pain and his left hand scrabbled in his jacket pocket.

"My pills!" he gasped, almost inaudibly. Hunt sat paralyzed for a second. Schultz made no previous mention of a heart complaint. Hunt jumped out of his chair and knelt at Schultz's side. "What is it?"

"It will pass," grimaced Schultz gamely. "Mister Carlisle, might I trouble you for... for a glass of water?"

"Certainly! Certainly!" replied Carlisle, rising to his feet and waddling through the door leading to the adjoining house.

The instant Carlisle left, Schultz made a dramatic and miraculous recovery. "Delay him," he hissed. "Tell him I need sugar in the water or something! Warn me as you return."

Hunt stumbled after their host, once again impressed by Schultz's ingenuity. He found it easy to delay Carlisle. The search for sugar found only molasses, which Hunt, after some deliberation, deemed as acceptable. Then Hunt managed to drop the glass on the way room necessitating the drawing and mixture of a second draught. When the two men returned to the other room, to the accompaniment of Hunt's loud apologies, Schultz sat calmly in his chair.

"Here is your water and sugar. I can supply an antifogmatic if that will help. Whiskey or rum or both. Hum."

"My fault. All my fault," offered Hunt gallantly. "How are you feeling?"

"Better, thank you," replied Schultz, taking the water from Carlisle and then seeming to swallow a pill before draining the glass. "These attacks are painful when they come, but the pills fix them. Ah, that's good."

Hunt guessed Schultz used the time to make a rapid search of Carlisle's desk but he could see no difference in the piles of paper. They were untidy before, and they were untidy now.

"Mister Carlisle, we respect your confidences," Schultz continued. "If you feel you cannot provide us with the names of your friends, then we will consult with the lady and determine her wishes. Naturally we ask that you don't discuss this matter with anyone."

"Hum. Yes, I see. Was the bequest... ah... significant?"

"We cannot comment further," said Schultz, rising to his feet. All trace of his medical emergency had gone. "We have delayed you long enough."

"Does it need our entire group? Would half of the number do? There were five... four of us now. I cannot say more."

"That must do for now," said Schultz, walking to the door. "Thank you for your time."

Hunt followed Schultz out of that damp pit of suffocating humidity. His last view of Carlisle showed the man standing on the doorstep wringing his hands in anxious frustration. The two detectives walked half a block before Hunt spoke.

"That heart complaint of yours must come in handy at times."

Schultz laughed. "Carlisle seems such a caricature, doesn't he? Nervous as the fattened turkey the week afore Thanksgiving."

"Did you search his desk?"

"It'd take the Corp of Engineers a good month to work their way through that labyrinth. I got a start on it, and I did find what I feared."

Schultz spoke with an even and conversational tone, but his words worried Hunt. How could that inoffensive little butterball hold anything that would cause Schultz any concern?

"In the top drawer of his desk Carlisle keeps a diary," continued Schultz. "It seems he is attending the White House charity ball tonight."

Schultz stopped and faced Hunt. "Let me point out for you that Morgan Carlisle is a financial failure. His house speaks for itself. He has no clients worthy of the name, yet he holds a fifty dollar ticket for tonight's dinner."

"Anyone can buy a ticket," protested Hunt.

"A man wearing a ten year old coat with a drawer of unpaid household accounts doesn't easily part with those sorts of dollars. Mayhap someone bought him the ticket, but for whatever reason our friend has some pressing need to attend that event. Greeley will be there and so will the imposter who bought Banker Singleton's ticket. Everyone will be there."

"The three suits on the ship! That's why the suits were there."

"Exactly. Three Confederate spies and three clawhammer coats. The men on the *Angelique* held her in port because the second half of their plan involves them appearing at the charity ball this evening."

Hunt whistled softly. "Then Owens told the truth. This plan does involve Lincoln. Kidnapping, or murder."

Schultz consulted his watch. "It's half past the hour. I don't know what they plan, but I'll lay huckleberries to persimmons it's happening tonight at the Executive Mansion. We'd best get there."

Cabs were hard to find. The Friday afternoon shift change for the drivers combined with the need to ferry partygoers to their Friday night events rendered cabs scarce, and the lurking thunderclouds gave many a traveller the nudge to take a cab rather than walk to their destination. It took a good thirty minutes to find a cab, and Hunt needed to wave his police badge in the nose of a competing voyager to achieve that victory. The defeated pedestrian retired in bad grace, and the two detectives headed for the Executive mansion.

The evidence showed that the rebels planned to kill, or kidnap, Abraham Lincoln, yet a nagging thought reminded Hunt that he had been badly mistaken before. He couldn't escape the fear that on this point he might, once again, be completely and utterly wrong.

At the White House

The roaring log fires within the White House warmed the rooms to a comfortable temperature as Horace Greeley and Arthur Merivale moved through the growing crowds, carefully avoiding each other. They would record the events of the evening, one to tell his political masters in Britain, and one to tell the rest of the world. Neither felt any compunction about the impending removal of Abraham Lincoln from the world stage. Hannibal Hamlin would succeed Lincoln as president, and the United States would take a different path than the one it travelled for the previous four years.

Greeley could see Vice-President Hamlin now, talking with the French Ambassador. Hamlin had been a Democrat until 1856 when he, like many other antislavery politicians, left that party after it endorsed the Kansas-Nebraska Act, potentially allowing slavery into those new territories. The complex issues of slavery would probably be far easier to resolve than the political whirlwind about to descend on him. Greeley felt a pang of sympathy for the man, but dismissed it. He turned away, and for a handful of minutes traded meaningless comments with a liquor merchant and a colonel. Through the windows, he could see a procession of carriages bringing new guests to the party. Somewhere in this room were the men from the south who would change history. Greeley would wait and watch.

Schultz and Hunt dismissed their cab on the corner of 17th Street, and gazed across Pennsylvania Avenue at the presidential estate. Numerous oil lanterns, affixed to poles pushed into the earth, spotted the grounds, and light blazed out from the main building and conservatories. Dozens of people strolled through the grounds of the Executive Mansion.

"That's odd," said Schultz. "There's always extra security at these banquets, but this is a bit extreme."

"Extreme?"

"The soldiers! Look there."

Hunt scanned the grounds. The White House grounds remained unfenced, and citizens could freely enter and leave the gardens. Indeed, complete strangers would sometimes enter the House uninvited, and engage the President in unexpected conversation.

The arrangements were quite different tonight. Hundreds of soldiers stood twenty yards apart from each other in a perimeter completely encircling the grounds of the White House. The soldiers could challenge anyone who tried to avoid entering by the gates. Another two soldiers stood at the driveway, inspecting the invitations of the arriving guests.

"That'll be because of the warning we gave about Owens," said Schultz.

"You gave them the warning. You said we needed to alert them!"

"They did need to be warned. Trouble is, all this added security is now working against us."

Hunt leaned against a hitching post. "Not good, Schultz. Not good."

"Normally the Speaker of the House holds a reception on Friday evenings but I recall the *Intelligencer* noting that Colfax had cancelled his get-together for tonight. Probably did that as a favor to Lincoln to give a boost to the attendance numbers for this event. Colfax, Seward, Lincoln, mayhap even Stanton will all be here. If the rebels strike tonight then they could decapitate the government."

"This just gets better and better."

"And look there," said Schultz, pointing at another group of soldiers standing closer to the Executive Mansion. "More of them. This is a nuisance."

"Maybe those southern boys won't be able to get in there either."

"They'll be there. They'll have that invitation that Singleton missed, and doubtless another three or four more to be safe."

"We know Singleton's name. We could have the imposter stopped at the gates."

"That won't work. When we stop one of them, his colleagues will know we are wise to their plan. They may not arrive in the same carriage, but they'll see each other arrive."

"All of these soldiers make a kidnap attempt pointless. It must be assassination."

"It looks that way," replied Schultz, sitting on the edge of the horse trough and stretching out his injured leg. "Look at the facts. The rebels chose this night. They could have struck anytime this week, but they waited until now. Tonight's levee will have... does have... additional security, so their task is tougher than if they struck earlier in the week. There must be someone else there tonight who is of prime importance to their plan."

"Greeley? Owens said Greeley would be a witness."

"So you said. I'm still wondering, does Greeley know what is happening here, or is he an innocent witness?"

"Pearson's Paper could be the name for the document detailing their plan of action."

"Possibly. Pearson is still a mystery."

"Whatever it is, unless we get onto the grounds we won't be able to stop it. If we show our badges at the gate..."

"No point trying that. Even if I talked to Monohan, we have no proof of anything, and he'd have no reason to let us in."

218

The task seemed hopeless. The detectives possessed neither invitations nor formal wear.

A detail of soldiers marched up 17th Street. Their bowed shoulders and hangdog expression showed that they were only now ending a long day of work. An idea came to Hunt's mind. He looked down at his clothes; the old army uniform he pulled on that morning while his work clothes were recovering from their much-needed laundering. It might work. He pulled out his revolver and pointed it at Schultz. "I'll get us in," he smiled.

At the sight of the drawn weapon, Schultz opened his mouth and half-raised his cane in defense, but before he could comment Hunt called out in a voice of command. "You men! Halt!"

The infantry obeyed the order, with nine left boots smashing to a synchronized stop. The corporal commanding the troop looked over at Hunt. Before the man could comprehend the sight before him, Hunt barked out his questions. "Report to me, corporal! Where are you taking these men?"

The corporal looked at Hunt holding the gun and wearing a Union army uniform.

"Yes, sir! Corporal Withers taking a guard detail back to the F street barracks!"

"No, you're not," countered Hunt, putting his revolver back in his pocket. "I'm Lieu... Captain Hunt and I need your men to guard this here prisoner. Bring him along."

The corporal's mind struggled with the new situation for a few seconds, but Hunt's voice of command, well polished by his time in the army, won the day.

"Detail! Fall in 'round the prisoner," ordered the corporal.

The enlisted men responded to the order, and Hunt became an officer again. He turned and led his little company across Pennsylvania Avenue. He could hear the men marching behind, but he couldn't risk turning around to see how well Schultz adapted to the situation. An officer gave the orders; it fell to the corporal to enforce them.

The steady marching steps suggested Schultz cottoned on to the gambit, and now played the part of a compliant captive. The company neared the driveway to the Executive Mansion and Hunt lengthened his stride to gain some headway on the marching troops. It would be easier to finesse their entry if the men didn't have to stop marching. The guard at the gate watched their approach. Hunt considered demanding a salute as befits a superior officer, but appealing to the guard's bored indifference might have a greater chance of success.

"Captain Hunt with reinforcements for the security detail. Stand aside."

"Reinforcements?" asked the guard, looking from Hunt to the approaching soldiers. Not surprisingly, the new arrivals puzzled the guard, but with any luck, Hunt's matter-of-fact approach would merely make him presume that his own commanding officer failed to advise him of the change. The other guard came out of the guard box.

"I don't want to be here either. I'd sooner be inside where it's warm and I'm sure so would ah… Mister Pinkerton."

Hunt jerked his thumb at the approaching group, conscious the 'prisoner detail' would be at the gate in barely ten seconds time. The guard's eyes widened.

"Pinkerton!"

"The same. Don't go telling anyone. It's one of his surprise inspections on the security arrangements."

The guards didn't seem to notice the not-so-subtle change in Hunt's story. The ruse worked. They stepped to the side of the driveway, and watched Pinkerton's reinforcements march through their checkpoint. Neither of them commented on how 'Mister Pinkerton' seemed unusually heavily escorted for the head of a world famous Detective Agency. Hunt stood back to let his detail through, juggling his time carefully.

"That corporal's one of Pinkerton's best men, not that you'd know it," warned Hunt. "Make sure you stand to attention when he's leaving, or he'll have you up on charges."

He sprinted to catch the detail before they reached the Executive Mansion. They followed his next set of orders without question, and accompanied him to the rear of the Conservatory.

"Detail, Halt! All right corporal, I'll take it from here."

The corporal seemed mystified by the unexpected events, but Hunt's drawn revolver pointed at Schultz's midsection neutralized any potential threat from the prisoner. "I need to wait here for the others. You get your men back to camp. No point you standing around also."

The prospect of an early end to this unexpected duty pushed all questions from the corporal's mind. "Yes sir! Detail, about face! Forward march!"

The two detectives watched the men march back towards the guard post on Pennsylvania Avenue.

"Proper little general, aren't you," commented Schultz with a smile.

Hunt permitted himself a satisfied grin. "Soldiers are the same everywhere. They'll hold a hill 'til the death, but if you order them off it, chances are they'll leave their trenches, form road column and march wherever you tell them to go."

The dismissed soldiers were out of sight now. Hunt's trick gained them entrance to the grounds, but much harder work lay before them. By mutual unspoken consent, the detectives moved into the cover of nearby bushes to discuss their situation.

Schultz spoke. "Let's think this through. If they planned on completing their work during the public reception, there would have been no need for them to obtain the dinner tickets. I'd say they'd wait until the public reception is over and then strike during the charity dinner. Dinner is probably planned for eight, so we've got maybe an hour to find them."

"Without being found ourselves."

"True enough."

"Might they be hiding?"

"A good point. They may have gained admittance and be concealed somewhere, rather than face the danger of casual conversation with a Washington local."

Schultz peered out from behind the bushes, and surveyed the grounds around them. "I doubt they'll hide in the grounds. Too many chances for an encounter with a patrolling soldier. Speaking of such things…"

Schultz ducked back into cover and crouched behind the bushes, trying and failing to suppress an exclamation of discomfort. Hunt burrowed close in beside Schultz, taking care not to bump the injured limb. Two sets of rapid footsteps approached their concealing bushes. Hunt's fingers inched towards his Bowie knife, until he felt Schultz's calming hand on his arm. The footsteps stopped no more than five paces away. Hunt felt like an overwound clock ready to bust a spring. The sound of rustling cloth reached their ears, and a whispered voice revealed the intention of the intruders.

"Oh, my love! My love! How much longer need we wait?"

"Hush! We are together now. Let's not waste the moment."

The unmistakable sound of lips meeting lips in the throes of passion came through the bushes. Hunt looked at Schultz, and the two of them broke out in soundless grins. The rustle of clothing indicated the rising of the newcomer's desires.

"No! Not here! If we are discovered…"

"We are alone! Kiss me again."

"Ummph! Oh, yes. Touch me! Touch me!"

"Ahhh, so soft, so lovely."

A nearby sound came to the ear of the lovers. It may have been a bird in a tree, or a fox in the bushes, but the disturbance moved the couple to immediate action. With a whisper of warning, and an adjustment of apparel they left.

"How very interesting," whispered Schultz. "I'm sure that was the Senator's wife, but that certainly wasn't the Senator! Not our problem though. They've gone now. Follow me!"

Schultz limped his way between the trees and Hunt followed him. He knew their clothes would be in stark contrast to the formal dinner suits and expensive wraps of the proper guests. Moving carefully from tree to tree, the two detectives made their way around the conservatory. It struck Hunt that if the patrolling guards saw them, then they would rapidly become the people under arrest. A fine ending for their mission to save the President.

The Executive Mansion stood bathed in light. Some couples strolled along the paths, but the chill of the night air persuaded most of the visitors to stay inside.

"Over there!" Hunt followed Schultz's gaze and saw the lower level entrances to the building. The service doors for supply of food and fuel, and the carting out of garbage were potential entry points into the building.

"I wouldn't like to try the coal chutes. Our clothes are poor enough quality without covering them in soot. My guess is our adversaries won't arrive until there is a sufficient crowd to guarantee anonymity, and neither will they arrive so late they are the subject of comment. I would expect them here within half an hour."

"You're guessing!"

"For once that is true," admitted Schultz. "If you have a better estimate then I'm happy to hear it. Until then, we'll work with my timing."

"So how do we get into the actual White House? I don't think my trick with the gun will work a second time."

"I'd agree with you there. Our badges won't get us through the vestibule, and I suspect our street clothes and lack of an entry ticket would be sufficient for us to be escorted off the grounds with a minimum of formality."

"It's looking like unless we waylay a few guests and steal their invitations this might be as far as we go."

"Look there!"

Schultz's outstretched finger indicated a crook in the wall at the base of the Executive Mansion. A solitary red light flared in the darkness, then dimmed to a dull glow.

"A cigarette", mused Schultz. "Mayhap a kitchen hand having a break."

"Could it not be a guest?"

"Not likely that a guest would walk down to the gardens for a solitary cigar. The upper levels have the music and the wine. Even if two guests wanted a private discussion, I doubt they would go so far from the upper levels. Let's get a closer look."

The two men moved through the bushes. After they had advanced twenty yards, Hunt could see Schultz had been right. A negro dressed in white kitchen hand clothes stood admiring the trees in between deep pulls on his tobacco.

"There's a doorway behind him. Stand up and follow my lead here. We're guests now. Hey! You there!"

Schultz strode across the sodden lawns towards the smoker. They caught the man unawares. In an instant, the cigarette light faded, doubtless pinched out between callused fingers and stored away for future use. Tobacco remained a luxury in the north, and half-used butts were still precious currency.

"Yassah! Fine evening, suh."

Schultz reached the negro, a young man of twenty or so years dressed in the white cloth of a kitchen menial, and standing outside a doorway leading to the cellars.

"Never mind that," retorted Schultz, leaning on his cane. "I have a problem. My stomach, it... ah, fails me at times. Where is a privy?"

"Upstairs, suh. Round the corner there and..."

"No, you don't understand," interrupted Schultz in a more measured tone.

224

He moved his hips in apparent discomfort. "I can't go up there now. I need to... ah... I need a place I can clean up."

Light dawned in the negro's eyes, and he stared keenly at the dollar bill Schultz held up.

"Find me a washroom my man! I can't meet the President in this condition."

The negro nodded as he pocketed the money. "This way suh."

Then they were inside, moving through dark corridors and into a kitchen where harried chefs and menials sweated in the heat of the room. Roaring fires tormented the glowing bottoms of countless pots, preparing the meals for the official guests. Two of the staff there gave them a passing glance, but the presence of their guide gave them the required authority, and they passed through the kitchen without challenge. They turned into a corridor, and the negro showed them into a cramped and poorly lit washroom. The tub of water on a stand, and the open drain in the floor gave them what they asked for. Schultz turned to the negro. "Good work, my man. I'll be fine from here."

The negro hesitated for a moment, as if considering the consequences of his action, but Schultz shut the door and Hunt stood in the corridor with his arms folded. "Run along now," urged Hunt. "He'll be fine. We'll get back upstairs by ourselves."

"Yassah."

The negro disappeared back into the kitchen, and Hunt waited. A movement in the shadows further down the corridor caught his eye, and Hunt saw the face of a small black kitten observing him. He took a step towards it to shoo it away, then realized the cat presented no hindrance to their plans. Best to leave it alone to chase down its dinner amongst the rats and mice that surely scuttled through the storerooms here. A second look showed the cat as much bigger than he first thought. He turned, and tapped on the door. "Schultz?"

The door opened a crack and Schultz peered out. "All clear?"

"All clear. Nice move."

"That evens the score for getting us onto the grounds. Follow me."

Hunt risked a final backwards glance at the cat. It had moved closer towards them in the corridor. Either that, or it had grown remarkably larger within the space of a minute.

Schultz limped down the corridor away from the kitchen, and through a door into a small room with a wooden staircase leading up to the main floor of the Executive Mansion.

A single oil lantern hung from a wall hook near the bottom of the stairs. At the top of the stairs, a crack of light and the murmur of voices penetrated under the door, and into the stairwell. Schultz stopped at the bottom of the stairs and turned to Hunt.

"I've got to rest this leg, Hunt. The wound is bleeding under the bandages."

That statement came as no surprise to Hunt. A man with an injury such as the one Schultz received should be lying in a hospital bed, rather than zigzagging across the city in search of criminals.

"This is where it gets difficult," Schultz said, sitting on the bottom step and stretching out his wounded leg. "We need to find our three Confederates and then we have to disarm and interrogate them."

"We're through the hen-coop door, but how do we find the right chickens? There could be hundreds of people here."

"For the moment mayhap. Less than a hundred would stay for the banquet in the State Dining Room."

"Damn! It's hopeless!"

"Difficult, but not hopeless. Tell me what we know of these people."

Hunt looked at Schultz. The situation called for action, not talking. All of his senses cried out to arrest every man he could find, and search each one until he found their quarry. The sheer impossibility of that task didn't lessen his desire to carry it out. Schultz's cool gaze forced Hunt to curb his emotions and look for other answers. Schultz said nothing, and the silence spurred Hunt to additional thoughts. "There's three of them!" he announced with satisfaction. "Three men with no women."

"Yes, three men. I'd venture they'll be fit, athletic men, between twenty and forty years old, and anxious to avoid conversation. It's unlikely that they will be prominent men. The risk of a northern cousin recognizing a southern blue blood is too high. They'll doubtless have stories to explain their presence here. Corn traders from Missouri, or businessmen from Canada or the like, but far better for them if they don't have to talk with anyone. Their southern accents might give them away. What else?"

Else? Hunt could see little light here, either physically or intellectually.

"Tell me."

"They are tired and on the run. The loss of the *Angelique* doubtless took away many of their preparations. The fine suits they planned on wearing to this event are now in the hands of the Union Navy."

"They might have purchased new suits."

"They probably have. The fact they could get Singleton's invitation means they have contact with a confederate sympathizer somewhere in the city who could perhaps obtain new suits for them. Carlisle comes to mind as a possibility. Allowing for their journey from the wreck of the *Angelique*, and the necessity of finding safe quarters, they have had less than two days to get the necessary clothing. The strain of that timetable may show in their outfits. Hence they may be poorly dressed, and in need of a barber."

"Something like us then," said Hunt, with a glance down at his own clothing. The detectives were dressed neatly enough, but their clothing wasn't a patch on the dinner suits and top hats of the other guests.

"That's true also. We are perhaps a little underdressed for the occasion."

"We'll have to make our best guess then," said Hunt decisively, drawing his Bowie knife and flipping it in the air. "If anyone goes anywhere near Lincoln, I can nail him. Guaranteed."

"Put that thing away, you fool! Suppose a waiter offers a menu to the President? Or an aide delivers a message? Would you attack them? How will you know?"

Hunt sheathed his knife and didn't answer. He knew Schultz spoke wise words. This time, he could accept that rebuke without anger.

"I'm thinking that despite their fancy suits those Confederates will be as out of place as we are," continued Schultz. "They may well need a place to..."

The door above them opened, and Hunt felt Schultz's hand pushing him into the shadows under the staircase. Footsteps progressed down the stairs. Hunt could not see the newcomers.

"Get down there! Half an hour to wait."

"I'm sorry, sorry."

The voices displayed an undeniable southern twang. Hunt felt Schultz's hand grip his arm.

"You're a dang fool, Cletus. I told you to talk about religion and the weather."

"I'm new at this stuff! He asked me where I came from."

"And you told him! What's a Yankee going to think of a North Carolina preacher wandering through Washington? Dang fool! Get in there."

The footsteps approached their hiding place.

Questions are answered

The fight took less than a second. As the two men came around the bottom of the staircase, Hunt hit out at the first man's chin while Schultz's cane swung a short arc into the second man's temple. Both intruders fell to the floor.

Hunt pushed his knee into his man's back, and dragged the head back by its hair. The point of his Bowie knife floated close to the man's eye. "Move a muscle and you're blind!"

The stranger didn't hesitate. "Don't kill me!"

The Bowie knife near his face persuaded the prisoner to allow Hunt to frisk him, and relieve him of the revolver in his pocket. Finally, satisfied that the prisoner had been disarmed, Hunt removed his knee from the prisoner's back and stepped away. "You're under arrest. Don't move."

"Arrest? There's some mistake. I'm a…"

"We're arresting you for the murder of James Anderson. What's your name?"

A gasp came from the prisoner, and he slumped forwards. He took his time to answer. "MacMaster, James MacMaster. What about Cletus?"

"I'm sorry, Hunt. I misjudged my aim. This one's dead," answered Schultz, stooping over the other body.

"Then he can't help us. Tell us then, Mister James MacMaster, where's the third man?"

"What third man?"

"The third man who came into Washington on the *Angelique*. The third man who tied up and killed John Anderson at the Washington Herald on Sunday. The third man who escaped the shipwreck on the Potomac two days ago. The third man who's part of this plot involving the President."

MacMaster tensed for a breath, then closed his eyes and his body relaxed. At length he spoke again. "There's only the two of us now. Wolfsberger broke his arm when we lost the boat. He'd be back in Richmond by now."

The prisoner looked over his shoulder at Hunt. "I'd fancy sitting up if you don't take it amiss."

"Go on," replied Hunt moving away from the prone captive. "Best you do it slowly, and keep your hands out wide."

MacMaster followed instructions, and turned over to sit with his back against the wall and his legs stretched out in front of him. The light of the flickering wall-lantern showed his face clearly. Hunt watched him for any sign of fight, but the man seemed defeated. Hunt saw no reason to take chances and lifted the confiscated revolver to point it at the survivor's face. As if on strings, the man's hands raised themselves out wide in a gesture of surrender. "Another half-hour," he murmured.

"You were almost there," agreed Schultz, sitting back down on the step with a grimace of pain. "Which one of you... aaargh... has Pearson's Paper?"

MacMaster's head jerked up, and his energy returned. "You know about it?"

"Only by name," conceded Schultz massaging his wounded leg. "I've been looking forwards to reading it."

MacMaster laughed weakly. "Everybody wants to see it, except I suppose, the man it's meant for. Kind of funny really."

"So, who is Pearson?" asked Hunt.

"I'd guess that's the easiest question I'll get all night," replied MacMaster. "Mumford Pearson's the Chief Justice of the Supreme Court of North Carolina. Appointed in '58 and still there. He's the one who signed the Paper."

The prisoner appeared willing to talk freely. That gave them a good start. Private Pemberton wouldn't be needed here. Hunt settled down on his haunches with his back against the staircase and kept his gun pointed at MacMaster. The gurgle of water through nearby drains served as a reminder of the dismal weather outside. The cold of the cellar reached through his clothes. Hunt wore his buckskin coat and army trousers, yet he would have been happier with a thick coat like the one Schultz wore. "So what's in this darn Paper that's got everyone so all-fired up?" he asked.

"It's a summons," answered MacMaster heavily. "A summons commanding Abraham Lincoln to appear at the bar of the Supreme Court of North Carolina twenty-eight days after service of said document. The charge is treason."

Hunt laughed. He glanced across at Schultz, but to his surprise, saw Schultz listening intently, concentrating on every word MacMaster said. For some reason, Hunt found that disturbing. "You're saying Lincoln committed treason?"

"That's what's on the summons."

"Treason? How?"

MacMaster cocked his head and looked up at Hunt. "You really want to know?"

Hunt knew they should take MacMaster back to the station, but he wanted answers first. He looked over at Schultz who shrugged his shoulders. "I'm in no hurry to walk anywhere on this leg. Let the man talk for a minute, then you go upstairs and find Monohan."

231

That made sense. The criminal sat helpless before them. It wouldn't hurt to listen to the man's explanation. Hunt nodded, eager to hear the details.

"Easier if you read your Constitution," said MacMaster. "Article Three Section Three. There's a copy of it in my bag there."

A burst of distant laughter from the top of the stairs reminded Hunt that they sat not fifty yards from where the President stood. He tightened his grip on his revolver and looked at the prisoner. A calico bag dropped by MacMaster in the earlier scuffle lay on the ground halfway between them. Hunt considered the likelihood of a trap, and kept a careful eye on MacMaster as he leaned forward to grab the bag. The flap fell open, and Hunt used his free hand to fumble inside the bag. His gun stayed trained on MacMaster. Finally, he gave up and passed the bag up to his partner.

"You're the brains here, Schultz. You do the reading."

MacMaster and Hunt looked at each other while Schultz searched in the bag. At length, the senior detective drew out a thin set of papers clipped together. The single wall lamp gave a poor light and it took a while for Schultz to find an angle that gave sufficient illumination for reading. When he achieved that, he turned to the correct page, coughed, then read. "Treason against the United States shall consist only in levying war against them."

Schultz looked at Hunt. "That's why Anderson kept those treason cases in his desk. He needed to check the legal precedents."

Hunt looked at each man in turn. Their faces were serious. "Oh, come on!" Hunt exploded. "The President's fighting a rebellion! Those rebels are destroying the Union!"

"Go read your newspapers, Detective," replied MacMaster. "North Carolina was still a loyal member of the Union on April 14th 1861 when Lincoln called for volunteers."

MacMaster cleared his throat. His attitude changed from that of a defeated prisoner into the lecturing tone of a teacher. Hunt watched MacMaster's movements carefully, but the man seemed intent on talking rather than tensing for a fight. "Two weeks after that there call for volunteers, Lincoln issued specific orders to the Union Navy to blockade North Carolina's ports. Your Supreme Court's already held that to be the date of the declaration of war. Some case about naval prizes it was. North Carolina didn't secede until a couple of weeks later, in the middle of May. Therefore, Lincoln declared a blockade, an act of war, on a loyal Union State. Pearson had every right to charge him with treason."

"The President can't commit treason. That's impossible!"

"I suppose his harp never needs tuning neither. He swore an oath to protect, preserve and defend the Constitution, not to destroy it. Now get it through your head that Abraham Lincoln isn't above the law, and then perhaps we can move things along here."

MacMaster glared at Hunt, and the detective returned the favor with equal venom. Despite the revolver in his hand, Hunt felt the other man winning this battle of words. He felt a blinding urge to pistol whip the prisoner for his arrogance. "Congress let him fight the rebels. They didn't see a problem with it."

"Congress isn't above the law either. It can sell its soul to Lincoln, but it can't authorize him to commit treason. According to the Constitution, levying war on the state of North Carolina is treason, whether it's done by the president or by anybody else."

The light above them flickered, and MacMaster moved a little to ease his legs. The distant murmur of conversation from the social event above them floated down the cellar stairs. Hunt decided he wasn't going to play this man's game. "You're pissing in the wind here. Show me where the Constitution says the President can't fight this damn rebellion."

"That's not the way it works! If the Constitution doesn't talk about something, then the individual states retain that authority, not the federal government. Check the amendments. Number nine or ten or something. It's in there I know."

"But treason IS in the Constitution. You said it yourself. So the Supreme Court tries that case. Not North Carolina."

"That's for treason against the whole United States. Not for treason against an individual state. Believe me, better minds than you and I have been through all of this. I'm a lawyer by profession, and I can tell you that it's not as simple as you think it is."

"Mayhap it's not a war," ventured Schultz thoughtfully. "As I remember it, Lincoln's call for volunteers said he needed to suppress an insurrection."

MacMaster held up his hands apologetically. "I been there also, but there's nothing about insurrection in the Constitution. It does say the Union has to protect the state against domestic violence, but that needs North Carolina to ask for help first. Don't recall Governor Vance requesting that. Anyway, looks mighty like a war to me, and Lincoln's wanted in Raleigh to explain why he started it."

Schultz's soft chuckle broke the tense mood of the conversation. "Raleigh, not rally! Hunt, remember I wrote 'rally' in my notes of Picard's interrogation? Picard remembered the word correctly. I spelt it wrongly."

"Yes, Raleigh," confirmed MacMaster. "Capital of North Carolina. Where else would you expect the Supreme Court of that state to sit?"

Hunt looked at Schultz for help. He knew how to lead bayonet charges and drill troops, but he had no idea how to fight a war using words on paper as weapons.

"So you came to Washington looking to serve this summons on the President," said Schultz. "You chose tonight because there'd be plenty of witnesses. Anderson somehow got wind of the story. He planned to run a headline on it and you knew that would send Lincoln into hiding for the rest of the war. So Anderson needed to die."

"No! We never planned to kill him. We were thinking to take Anderson to the ship till we served the summons. We tried for him at his house on Friday and Saturday, but he never came there. It took us until Sunday to realize that he sometimes stayed at his office for the night. We caught up with him there, but he wouldn't tell us where he kept his notes. We persuaded him to open the safe in the end, but his heart gave out so we smashed a window to fake a burglary and left him there. Anderson's wife came from Raleigh..."

MacMaster stopped talking, and gazed stone-faced at Hunt. The detective stared back. He had to ask. "Was Anderson's daughter your contact in the north?"

"Didn't know he had a daughter, and that's the truth," replied MacMaster. "Anderson's brother-in-law is still in Raleigh, and those two wrote to each other through some friend in England. Anderson found out about the Paper, and let slip that he planned to publish it. You can figure out the rest."

"Raleigh to Washington?" asked Schultz. "That explains why you needed a ship. An agent coming by road might be stopped and searched with no time to destroy the Paper. You'd lose the element of surprise. At least with a ship you'd have time to burn the Paper before you were boarded, and the Union would be none the wiser as to your scheme. Who served as your contact in Washington?"

"Ah... I don't think that matters."

"Oh yes it does!" challenged Hunt. "You got berthing rights for the *Angelique* on the Washington docks when she should have been upriver. You stole Singleton's invitation and a couple of others to this here party tonight. The three of you wandered through Washington killing and thieving, and you're telling me there's not some Big Bug protecting you?"

"You'd have to ask Cletus then. Cletus was in charge and Wolfsberger provided the muscle. I'm only the attorney sent along to make sure they served the Paper correctly. Wolfsberger's the one who did the dirty on Anderson if you want to know. I'd gone downstairs to look through the safe. When I came back upstairs with the paperwork, I found Anderson dead on the floor. Not that it matters now."

"Did Greeley help you in this? Is he your protector in Washington?"

MacMaster shrugged. "I followed along and did what Cletus told me to do."

Hunt realized he wouldn't get a better response. The time arrived to put MacMaster behind bars. He turned to look at Schultz and raised an eyebrow. Schultz nodded, then slowly pulled himself to his feet, favoring his injured leg.

"Time to go MacMaster. Hunt, you head upstairs and ask for …"

"Wait!" interrupted MacMaster. "I've got to tell you now, I've been doing this talking for a reason. You said you boys are Washington police?"

"Fifth Precinct," confirmed Hunt automatically.

"In that case, you and I do the same job. I've been deputized to serve that paper on Abraham Lincoln. Now I've explained the situation to you, I'd say you boys should be working with me rather than shooting at me."

Hunt raised his gun towards MacMaster. "You got one hell of a gall there mister."

"Why?. Any other summons and you'd be helping me serve it. That's a police officer's job isn't it?"

"If President Lincoln touches that paper he's a gone sucker," objected Hunt.

"So how come you get to choose which summons you serve and which ones you ignore? Were you hired to uphold the law or to make up your own?"

"You rebels can't leave the Union and then call on us to help you."

"Yet according to Lincoln the southern states never left the Union, and he can't have it both ways. If Lincoln says North Carolina is still part of the Union, then he has to respect North Carolina law."

"Lincoln didn't commit treason!"

"That's for the courts to decide. Not you or me."

"The Supreme Court maybe, not some judge in North Carolina. And hey! What about sovereign power… immunity… whatever. You can't sue the government."

"But that's not what's happening here," countered Schultz thoughtfully. "The summons names Abraham Lincoln as an individual, not in his capacity as president."

"You don't get it do you? Any State or Federal court can convict Lincoln of treason, though I'll grant only Congress can impeach him. That's for them to decide after Lincoln's trial, and I daresay his conviction, in North Carolina. So I ask again, are you going to do the right thing here or not?"

Hunt wrestled with that choice. The rushing of the stormwater through nearby pipes echoed the blood pounding through his head. He knew he had to work this out for himself. However, whichever way he added it up, it seemed MacMaster had an airtight case.

If the evidence showed that Abraham Lincoln committed treason against North Carolina then Pearson, as Chief Justice of North Carolina, had the right to summons him to Raleigh to answer those charges. Now MacMaster asked Hunt to serve that summons for him. If that happened, then Lincoln would lose his freedom and without its warrior president, the United States would lose the war. No wonder the Confederacy risked so much to get the Paper to Washington. In school, his teachers told Harrison Hunt that the Union and the Constitution amounted to the same thing.

Today, he needed to make a clear choice between them.

He tried a middle course. "Lincoln could say he never received the summons."

"Then he's in contempt of court," broke in Schultz. "Come the election, the Democrats would have a wonderful time with that."

"It would certainly stir things up," agreed MacMaster. "That's why it's happening here, with a crowd watching. When you serve that summons on Lincoln in front of everyone here tonight, the whole story will come out. Every newspaper in the world will cover it and there's a few big ones standing around upstairs who already have their headlines written and ready to print. The Treason Trial of the Century they'll call it. However, you're missing the point here. No one's expecting Lincoln to go to North Carolina. You sign an affidavit that you served the summons, and the trial will proceed without him. He'll be found guilty for sure - hell, he is guilty - and then you stand back and watch Lincoln try to argue to the Senate that he doesn't need to follow the Constitution. I'll grant you he's done that before, but there's a world of difference between keeping some small-time political opponent locked in a cell for a few months and committing treason. What northern senator wants to face his voters in November and admit that he supports a politician who's been convicted of treason? They'll abandon him quicker than the rats off the Hesperus!"

"Owens said you were going to kidnap Lincoln," said Schultz.

"Owens?"

"Jimmy Owens, the deckhand", confirmed Hunt. "We caught him. He said you were planning to take Lincoln back south."

MacMaster chuckled at the thought. "Never part of the plan. The crew might have talked it up big among themselves, but how in Hades would we kidnap Lincoln? You've got half the Union Army in Washington. Better to let him make his own choice. He'd stay in Washington for sure. If Lincoln decides to travel anywhere in the north, then you can be sure Governor Vance will be asking the northern Governors to arrest him. That's in the Constitution too. Once Lincoln is served, then there's nowhere for him to hide. When the newspapers start hollering that Lincoln refused to face the courts on a treason charge, you can bet the farm he'll lose the election in November. No two ways about it. Lincoln's out, one way or another, after he gets that summons."

"The Democrats might win the election, but there's no guarantee they'd let the southern states go," pointed out Schultz.

"I reckon they would. You've still got the Constitution there? Read out Section Four and tell me what you think."

Schultz looked at the prisoner for a long time then held the document up to the light. He rustled through the pages until he found the required section. "The United States shall guarantee to every state in this Union a republican form of government, and shall protect each of them against invasion."

MacMaster stretched his legs out in front of him. Hunt lifted the gun an inch, but their prisoner seemed sure he'd won without the need for violence. "Shall protect each of them against invasion? Note that word 'shall' in the sentence? Quite inconvenient isn't it? The Constitution orders Lincoln to protect North Carolina, and all of the other southern states too by the way. So what will happen when North Carolina formally asks for protection against the invasion of Lincoln's volunteers? That would set the regular Union Army fighting the volunteer Union army. Lincoln would refuse of course, so there's another case for the Supreme Court. Take it from me, once Lincoln gets this summons, the war will be over in sixty days."

"Let me see that," demanded Hunt, standing up and pulling the document from Schultz's hands. He glared down at the prisoner, but MacMaster didn't move. With one eye on their captive, Hunt read the words that Schultz spoke. He had to admit that MacMaster won each point of this discussion.

"So where is the Paper?" asked Schultz.

"Now we get to the brass tacks," answered MacMaster. "If I give it to you, what will you do with it?"

Hunt snorted and raised his gun. He still held the weapon, despite all of the southern laywer's high-faluting arguments. "I don't rightly know that yet, MacMaster. But I do know what I'll do if you don't give it to me, and trust me, you won't like it. For the moment, though, we'll take it to the station and record it as evidence. It'll be available at your trial, and you can take up your arguments with the Judge then."

"There won't be a trial! Lincoln suspended habeas corpus last year, remember? I'll be thrown in a cell, and that'll be it until the war is over."

"That may be," conceded Hunt. "But for now we're arresting you for the murder of John Anderson. We still have our regular job to do, and if you want us to serve a summons later, then you'll need to get our captain's approval first. You can talk to him at the station. On your feet!"

The prisoner looked despairingly at each of the police officers in turn, but their stony faces gave him no hope. He rose to his feet and faced his captors.

"I've still got your gun here. Now let me see that Paper unless you'd like your bullets back one at a time."

MacMaster pursed his lips with a look of resignation. "Can't argue with that."

He held up his left hand as a warning of his intention, and moved it to his jacket pocket. A crackle of paper, and then the hand returned with a folded document. A flick of the wrist and the Paper fell halfway between them.

"Sorry. I'm right handed."

"Most people are," agreed Hunt, bending for the Paper.

The knife came from nowhere, slashing upwards with the full energy of MacMaster's desperate weight behind it. Hunt reacted instinctively, pushing his arm upwards and sideways, all the time knowing his buckskin coat wouldn't stop the blade. The knife sliced through the sleeve, grazing the skin as a shot rang out and MacMaster pitched forward onto the ground, left hand grasping for the Paper.

A thin wisp of smoke trickled upwards from the muzzle of the derringer held in Schultz's right hand. MacMaster coughed once, and tried to raise himself from the ground.

"Give me that," shouted Hunt, snatching the Paper from the dying man's hand, and feeling the acrid powder of Schultz's deadly shot grating in his nostrils. The Paper felt surprisingly flimsy. Such a little thing to control the destiny of a mighty nation. Hunt passed it across to Schultz. MacMaster rolled slowly onto his back. A small knife, which Hunt missed in his hasty search of the prisoner, fell from MacMaster's right hand. He gazed up at Hunt. His voice sounded frail, but clear. "That's the summons, detectives. I'm deputizing you... both of you... to serve it on Lincoln."

Schultz drew a sharp breath as if to speak, but Hunt spoke first and firmly. "I'm no confederate agent, MacMaster! I'm an American citizen and I'm sworn to uphold the Law. That's American Law I'm talking about, not some damn Confederate summons."

MacMaster coughed feebly. A bubble of blood grew on his lips and his voice weakened as he spoke. "You still don't see it... that paper is North Carolina law. That's American Law whether... whether or not the Confederacy ever existed. The North Carolina Court issued a... issued a valid summons for Lincoln... you're... you're choosing to ignore it."

"I won't do it."

Hunt saw the other man's pain. He failed, and he would die in sight of his goal. McMaster's voice softened to a whisper now. "It's your duty, officer."

Hunt raised his face to respond, but MacMaster had gone. He felt Schultz taking the Paper from his hand.

Duty. That word returned to haunt him. Lukey spoke of it. Schultz spoke of it. Now MacMaster spoke of it.

Schultz leaned against the wall reading the Paper. "Look here," he breathed.

Hunt stood, and peered at the papers in Schultz's hand. The words were hard to read in this dim light, but the second page showed the name of Abraham Lincoln and the seal and signatures on the final pages made it look official enough. A half-dozen sheets of paper held the fate of the United States.

"It's legal all right," Schultz said softly. "Far as I can make out, this summons is valid. God's Blood! This is a perfectly legal summons!"

Hunt took the Paper from Schultz, and angled it under the dim light to read the pages. The words were clear enough. The state of North Carolina charged Abraham Lincoln, citizen of the United States, with treason. If MacMaster served the summons, then Abraham Lincoln's presidency would be destroyed and the war would be lost. The thought overwhelmed Hunt, and he heard Schultz's quiet voice only faintly.

"I'm thinking that mayhap he's right about this, Hunt."

Schultz takes charge

Like most men of his generation, Ignatius Schultz knew a hard life. He had risen to his current position through his own efforts and for him, the Law served as the foundation on which society depended. The politicians wrote the legislation, but the police force found the miscreants and brought them to justice. In the eyes of Schultz, that responsibility became a sacred obligation, and an officer who ignored a crime became no better than the criminal himself.

He considered the question of Lincoln's alleged treason as a matter for the courts to decide, and he had no desire to usurp that authority. While MacMaster remained alive, serving the summons on Lincoln had been the southerner's duty, but his dying words of deputization thrust that responsibility onto the two Washington detectives. Now Anderson's killers were dead or back in Virginia, the newspaper case could be closed. Pearson's Paper remained as the only outstanding question. What should be done with that document?

Schultz could no more ignore his professional responsibility in the matter than he could choose to stop breathing. With all of the pieces of the puzzle now on the table, he knew what he had to do. It didn't take much thinking to realize that Hunt wouldn't like the solution.

"He's right? Right about what?"

242

"That's a legal summons. Serving it on Lincoln is our duty."

"Now wait a minute!"

"No, Hunt. I'm running this case remember? We do it my way."

"You can't do that."

"I can do that Hunt, and if you knew your duty you wouldn't argue about it."

"Schultz! We're…"

"That's enough! Right now, I think you're not sure where your loyalties lie so I need to take some precautions. Give me your gun."

Schultz's right hand still held the double-barreled derringer pistol that he used to kill their prisoner. He reached across and took MacMaster's gun from Hunt's unresisting fingers. "I'll have your knife also."

"Steady on Schultz. We're Washington police. That's a North Carolina summons. We don't have to touch it."

"You can't, or don't want to, acknowledge the facts here Hunt. MacMaster spoke the truth. This matter is for the courts to decide, not you and me. Now pass over your knife. Slowly. Use your fingertips."

"What about your country?"

Schultz laughed derisively. "Don't talk to me about those things Hunt! You're in it for the glory. I'm saying that being a detective means upholding the law, all of the law, not just the parts we like. That's a legal summons, and we have a job to do. Now pass me your knife."

The demand could not be refused. Schultz took the knife from Hunt, and slid it into his coat pocket along with MacMaster's gun.

"Now the Paper."

A new voice spoke from the top of the cellar steps. "You down there! Come out with your hands up."

The words of command were a complete surprise to both men. Schultz whirled to face the possible threat, but the stairs were empty.

"Come out I say!"

Still no-one coming down.

"We're police officers here," yelled Schultz. "Schultz and Hunt from the Fifth Precinct."

A new voice. "Schultz? That's you? It's Bill Monohan."

A grin broke out on Schultz's face. "Bill? You still drinking gin at the Coachman? I thought that stuff would have killed you by now."

Relieved laughter broke out from above. "Come on out Schultz. I'll tell the boys not to shoot this time."

Schultz jerked his thumb up the stairs. "I know those people, Hunt. You try any tricks and you're dead. Now give me the Paper."

Hunt paused, then in one slow movement held out the document. "Alright Schultz. We'll do it your way."

"You go first, Hunt. Keep your hands visible when we get to the top. Those boys are a mite twitchy at the best of times."

Schultz crammed the document into his coat pocket, and stowed his weapon. Hunt ascended the steps with Schultz limping behind. A pang of sympathy for Hunt passed through Schultz, but their duty remained clear. Perhaps one day Hunt would understand what duty meant. At the top of the stairs, Schultz stopped to retrieve his badge from his pocket, then stepped past Hunt and extended his free hand out of the door so the watching police officers could see his authority. Two halting steps forward and they could see all of him framed in the doorway.

The ground floor corridor of the Executive Mansion created a wide passageway. Supports for the vaulted ceiling ran down the walls to create regular pillars along the hall. Two agents were standing behind those pillars, both in good firing positions. Schultz figured other officers he hadn't yet spotted kept him in their sights, but he had no problem with that situation. He didn't plan on starting a gunfight. Hunt stood beside him. The wounded leg gave way for an instant and Schultz grabbed the door frame for support.

"Schultz! Your leg!"

"Don't panic there Bill," said Schultz. "That's only a splinter wound, and we fixed it up some days ago. Tell you what though, some of your gin'd come in right handy."

"Don't carry any gin on the job. You know that."

Monohan holstered his gun as he came up to the two detectives. At that signal, the rest of the police relaxed slightly and Schultz felt safe enough to put away his badge. Two more policemen appeared from their vantage points behind nearby furniture and joined the group.

Guests standing in the corridor spoke among themselves in hushed tones. Such a thing to happen in the Executive Mansion! Monohan caught a subordinate's eye and jerked his head at the guests. The subordinate got the message, and moved to disperse the audience.

"That's the presidential detail for you, Hunt," commented Schultz. "Overstaffed and underprepared. Stick with the waterfront beat."

"So, what've we got down there? Murray heard a shot."

Schultz looked around to confirm all of the guests were out of hearing before he replied. "Two dead boys of southern sympathies. We've been chasing them all week for the murder of John Anderson."

"The editor fellow? How'd his killers wind up here?"

Schultz glanced at Hunt for a second, then shrugged his shoulders. "We went where the evidence took us. We followed them here and they put up a fight. They died. We didn't."

"Can't ask for more than that," agreed Monohan, looking over Hunt. "This fellow with you?"

"This is Detective Hunt. I'll vouch for him. For now."

Monohan looked at the two men. Schultz could see the man's suspicion of a deeper story here, but he also knew that Monohan didn't have time to ask for more details. Two men came up the stairs; a detachment of Monohan's men sent via another path to secure the stairwell's exit to the kitchens. "No-one else down there sir."

"Alright. Murray, you clean up down there. Bartlett, get outside and check the perimeter patrol. Schultz, I should put you and Hunt under arrest, but right now, I'm putting you on punishment detail. We're short staffed and the cussed army's as bad as the civilians. Turn your back for a second, and they're stealing the silverware and the napkins. Put your badges on your coats and wander round for a bit until Murray gets back. We'll sort out the paperwork on Monday."

"We'll do it," said Schultz abruptly, and then moderated his remarks with an explanation. "I guess we haven't made your life any easier."

"Fine then. Do it 'till Murray and Bartlett get back. Walk around and keep your eyes on anyone standing by themselves. They'll be the ones looking to put the silverware in their pocket."

The head of the Presidential Guard walked off in search of another crisis to resolve, and the two detectives busied themselves pinning their badges to their coats. Schultz's heart thundered fit to burst. Somewhere in this house stood President Lincoln, and Schultz would not shirk his duty. He glanced at Hunt. The younger man waited there quietly. He appeared somewhat different now, but Schultz couldn't put his finger on the difference. Like a coiled spring, but with a measure of self-control that Schultz hadn't seen before. Could he be planning something? "You don't have to like this Hunt. I don't much like it either, but this is the job we're paid to do."

Hunt nodded. The meek acquiescence of the junior man disturbed Schultz, but he let that thought slide past. He held the Paper now, and Hunt could do nothing about it. "Let's go then."

Small groups of guests moving down the passage dotted the wide, thickly carpeted hallway Schultz self-consciously smoothed his crumpled clothes as he moved haltingly down the corridor, gritting his teeth against the pain from his leg. An elegantly dressed couple walking towards him cut him up with their eyes. He could see their thoughts, their disdain at his clothes, their questioning of his presence in this House. He avoided their gaze, and moved to the side of the corridor to let them pass.

The end of the passage opened into a wider room, and music from the room drifted down the corridor. A negro servant holding a tray of wineglasses stood in the entranceway of a vast room. Schultz stopped in the doorway to take in the scene.

Gold and blue paint picked out the elaborate patterns of the ornate twenty-foot high ceiling. Three crystal chandeliers hung in a row down the center of that ceiling, each one trimmed with brilliant colored glass that sparkled and glittered in the light. A single enormous rug covered the center of the room, reaching to all four walls with a rich pattern of gold and blue. The walls were covered in thick gold-toned paper; exquisite, expensive and tinted to let the eyes move from the ceiling to the floor without detecting any abrupt change in color.

A polite cough from the servant brought Schultz back to earth. He realized he still stood motionless in the doorway, impeding guests wanting to advance into the room. He stepped inside, and pressed his back up against the golden wall. A fine crowd graced the Executive Mansion. Parties of men and women decorated in jewels and finery stood in small groups scattered unevenly around the room, but most people congregated around the four fully stoked marble fireplaces set around the walls.

Massive gilt-edged mirrors hung above the fireplaces. The women used the mirrors to admire themselves, and the men used the mirrors to admire the women. The arrangement suited everyone. In a corner of the room the United States Marine Band - 'The President's Own' - softly played 'Lorena' underneath the buzz of conversation, while the Big Bugs and their partners swapped casual conversation about the price of corn and Who had been seen with Whom during the week. People moved with grace between the small clusters of conversation. Schultz's heart continued to pound with the tension of the moment.

An ornate bar took up the other end of the room. Neatly dressed negro servants replenished their empty trays at the bar before setting out on another circuit of the room to supply the attendees with their wine. The stacks of fresh crystal glasses on the bar gleamed in the light. Hunt stood beside him, surprisingly quieter than Schultz had ever known him before. The confrontation in the cellar seemed to have blunted his partner's arrogance somewhat. Perhaps they could discuss it at another time.

The two detectives moved into an empty space between two fireplaces. Schultz checked his badge for the fifth time since entering the room. It protected him from being asked to leave. He forced his eyes to methodically search through the crowd for a sign of the President. Surely General Grant stood there, talking to two other officers and a bewhiskered, big-bellied civilian wearing a fur-edged suit and string tie.

Women in silken dresses and adorned with fur boas caught his eye at every turn. Could that be that Jane Anderson in the flowing crimson dress and ostrich feather bustle? Schultz's eyes searched her back, willing her to turn and show her full face. A passing waiter masked the lady for a moment, before moving on and revealing her as an older woman, coldly returning Schultz's stare with the contempt nobility reserved for menials who dared to gaze upon their betters. Schultz's eyes refocused on other guests.

"Schultz?" Hunt's hushed voice demanded his attention.

"Schultz!" Hunt still stood beside him. Schultz needed to move. One or two people glanced at them standing there, but otherwise paid them little attention. He pushed off from the wall and threaded his way through the crowd, careful to avoid brushing up against the guests. A spilt glass of wine would be a distraction that could have him removed from the room. Horace Greeley stood talking with an officer dressed in a red-coated military uniform. British perhaps, or possibly a Russian. It didn't matter.

What did matter was the sudden realization that Hunt still had a gun! Schultz knew he'd taken one revolver from his partner after the battle downstairs, but that would have been MacMaster's gun. Hunt would still have his service issue revolver. Schultz knew that his oversight was serious. Would Hunt use the weapon? He needed to stay away from his partner.

As he watched the group, Greeley turned and caught his eye. The man recognized him instantly. His reaction proved that. The editor muttered something to his companions, then quickly moved to another group where he buttonholed a man in urgent conversation. It was Morgan Carlisle. Carlisle glanced once at Schultz, then nodded in affirmation to Greeley.

Schultz's thoughts were moving faster now. What did Greeley have to do in planning the whole affair? He couldn't know that Schultz now carried Pearson's Paper. Did Greeley want the summons delivered, or could all of this be a plan within a plan, with Detective Schultz as the unsuspecting dupe? That didn't matter. Schultz had a job to do. Where could Lincoln be? Could he be in one of the other rooms?

There!

Near the window opposite the Marine Band.

Lincoln didn't stand out from those around him as Schultz expected he would. Two men and a woman were with the President. As Schultz watched, one of the men bowed his farewell and left the group, and another man immediately took his position.

Now Schultz looked more closely, he could see a pool of sycophants, fawners, and political parasites milling in an untidy barricade, each waiting for a turn to press forward and present his idea or request to the Great Man. The human barrier seemed impenetrable. Where had Hunt gone? No matter. Greeley's conversation with Carlisle became more animated. The time arrived.

Schultz moved forward as quickly as his injured leg could carry him. His hand stayed in his pocket, closed around the reassuring feel of the Paper.

John Parker, the appointed bodyguard, stood beside and slightly behind Lincoln, watching the crowd. His wandering gaze fixed on the purposeful approach of Schultz.

Schultz tapped the badge on his coat with his free hand, and received an affirming nod from Parker in return, a greeting between professionals that acknowledged Schultz's authority and allowed him to approach.

The human barricade wasn't so easy. Each of the people there had a desire to see the President, and wouldn't easily give up their position to a newcomer. Schultz's shining badge gave him a key to the logjam. The protests died when the closest people saw his insignia, and then other guests, alerted by the sound of his approach, turned and comprehended his rank and sense of mission.

They parted in turn, none willing to make a bad impression on President Lincoln by hindering a police officer in a hurry. Lincoln stood three yards away. The man conversing with Lincoln stopped talking and glared at Schultz, clearly angry at having his private dialog disturbed. The Great Man turned in his direction. Everything fell into place. A woman approached from the right dragging a man by the hand. Her face wore a politician's smile, and her lips were opening with some platitude and probably a request for some favor. Schultz took two painful steps and stood before Lincoln. His sudden approach drew many eyes, and doubtless, more would follow. Lincoln could never deny this event.

"Abraham Lincoln! I'm Detective Schultz and I... I..."

Words failed him. He pushed the Paper at the President. Lincoln's hands moved instinctively to protect himself from Schultz's sudden thrust, and the two men stood there holding the Paper between them. Schultz let his own hand open and fall to his side.

Abraham Lincoln had been served.

Lincoln's eyes locked with Schultz as the tall man opened the document. A small smile played on the President's lips as the standard greeting of polite politics that hid the real emotions. Schultz could see the strength there. Strength and determination. An inexplicable worm of guilt ate its way into the detective's stomach.

The tableau froze itself as a picture in Schultz's mind. He could see all of the characters around the President at that moment. The delicate pink flowers in vases around the room. The coalscuttle beside the fire. The trickles of rainwater sliding down the windowpanes. All were there in his mind forever. Schultz's mind registered that the band had stopped playing.

He turned to see the people pressing closer. Boiled shirts and cravats surrounded him. Barely an arm's length away stood Horace Greeley.

Morgan Carlisle stood behind Greeley. Schultz could hear the unravelling of the Paper in Lincoln's hands. He turned back, and looked at the President. Lincoln's eyes dropped and travelled the length of the Paper. Schultz could see the lips pursing as the man read his political death sentence.

No emotion showed his face, but that wasn't a surprise. Schultz knew that Lincoln possessed excellent self-control. The President flipped backwards and forwards through the sheets of paper before looking up at Schultz. "Our Constitution is an important document, Detective. Did you want me to autograph it for you?"

Schultz's eyes jerked to the paper in Lincoln's hands. He could see the words *"and shall protect each of them against invasion"* displayed between the man's spindly fingers. The President stared kindly at him.

Schultz spun his head around. At the side of the room, Hunt stood before a fireplace, staring at tiny charred fragments of North Carolina Bond paper that fluttered and danced in the roaring flames. Hunt straightened and turned to face Schultz. Their eyes met, but Schultz could read nothing of the other man's thoughts. It didn't matter. Hunt's actions spoke for themselves.

The band started playing again, and the group around Schultz and Lincoln retreated. Muttered comments percolated through the group. Schultz knew what they were saying. Dismissing him as a common autograph hunter. A plebian chaser of greatness. None of them knew what they witnessed. Greeley stood there, oddly perspiring despite the coolness of the room. Perhaps he knew what almost happened.

"The Declaration of Independence and our Constitution are the foundation documents of our country, Detective Schultz," continued the President. "Did you know that not all of the original signatories of our Declaration of Independence signed it on the same day?"

Schultz managed to nod. Lincoln walked to a desk at the wall, reached for a pen and with a practiced hand, dipped it into the inkwell before scrawling his signature at the bottom of the page. Lincoln blotted the text and held out the document with a paternal smile. "Guard this well, Detective. It's what makes our country great."

Schultz swallowed. "Thank you sir." Hunt stood at his side now, respectfully taking the document from Lincoln's hands.

"It's a pleasure for us to meet you, Mister President," said Hunt. "Thank you for talking with us. Good night to you, sir."

"Wait! Detective Schultz? Of course it is! We spoke about that man from Spain and the Mexican war. Heavens, that must be years ago now. We meet under easier circumstances this time."

"Yes sir Mister President," said Hunt. "We need to go now. Good night sir."

Lincoln smiled his farewell, and his eyes moved to the next supplicant who began an impassioned monologue on the difficulties of shipping corn along the recently liberated Mississippi river. The buzz of conversation started again. Hunt guided Schultz through the crowd and out of the Executive Mansion. Schultz felt the eyes of Greeley and Carlisle follow them to the door.

A few minutes of slow walking brought them out onto Pennsylvania Avenue, where Schultz subsided onto a bench to rest his aching leg. A negro wheeling a dung cart walked slowly past them, and the detectives watched him push his load across the street.

Schultz broke the silence. "You switched the papers."

"In the cellar after Monohan called down to us. You were looking up the stairs. I didn't want it this way, but I didn't see an alternative."

"You fooled me. Damn you for that!"

"I figured you weren't going to talk about it, and your friends were more than I could handle. It seemed simpler to let you follow through with your plan while I disposed of the Paper."

"Double damn you, Hunt! You set yourself above the law. Where are your limits?"

"I did my duty to my country Schultz. Even if it costs me my job. That Paper and Greeley's editorials would tear the rest of the Union apart, and prolong the war. We'd be facing rebellions and State factions and more wars and death for the next hundred years. At least this way Lincoln gets to finish the job and restore the Union, and then all of the killing and dying can stop. I'll tell you straight, I'm not looking to see my country stay forever at war because of some stupid point of law."

"Your country hey? What about the people of North Carolina and the other states in the south? What about their country?"

"You want me to decide whether state rights are more important than the rights of the whole USA? I can't do that. I'm not a lawyer. I swore an oath to defend the Union, and I won't walk away from that. Maybe one day I'll regret this. Maybe I won't. Anyways, Pearson's Paper is gone now. You and I are the only ones here who know the story."

"There's Greeley," corrected Schultz. "Greeley knows more. So do Carlisle and the rest of their crowd."

"Doesn't matter. They can't do anything without the summons. I did what I had to do."

Schultz knew that Hunt spoke the truth. They both did their duty as they saw it. Schultz looked at the younger detective, and saw a more mature person than the angry and arrogant catastrophe of an individual he first met five days ago. He recalled the amusement he felt arriving at the Herald office, and listening to Hackett describe how a young detective had already investigated the murder and arrested Picard.

"So tell me then. What did the Illuminati want out of all of this?"

"The Illuminati?" Schultz dragged his thoughts back to the present. "Mayhap that's another mistake you can chalk on my slate. Don't get me wrong here. They're a dangerous crowd. I daresay they were useful in getting MacMaster the tickets for tonight's ball, but that may well be the only reason they were involved. Pearson could well be a member of a southern lodge, and they called in some favors from their brethren in Washington. No doubt, the Illuminati want the Confederacy to win this war. Far easier for them to manipulate two small nations than one large one. Pearson's summons would do the job. They could just stand back and watch."

Schultz looked up at his partner. His resentment cooled somewhat. "I'll grant you this much, Hunt. You did a clever job in switching those papers. I never suspected a thing."

Hunt nodded, graciously accepting the compliment. "I think I'd call it lucky rather than clever, Schultz. If you'd looked at what I gave you…"

"My fault there, Hunt. You were wrong in what you did, but I'll allow that you did what you believed to be right. Mayhap there's more to you than bayonet charging. Mayhap Colonel Lukey was wrong about you after all."

"Maybe he was. I still don't know this thing is over though. What if that Pearson fellow writes out another summons?"

"That's possible, but I'd say unlikely. It took them long enough to set up this first summons and get it to Washington. This whole treason thing sounds like a legal long shot anyway. Hell, Lincoln wasn't even born in North Carolina so I don't see how their State Court can stick him for treason. I guess that's why lawyers earn more than we do. Since they don't have anyone left to swear whether the original summons has been served, then I think they need to wait three months … or is it six months? Either way, they need to reissue the summons, and then find a new way to get it to Washington. Lots of effort with no guarantee of success. I'd say their plan focused more on getting bad publicity for Lincoln rather than having him impeached. Once the election is over in November, there'd be no point in it. I'd be surprised if they tried it again."

Schultz chuckled. "Mind you, if they do send another summons I won't ask you to deliver it."

"That would be wise," replied Hunt with a grin.

Less than five hundred yards away the guardians of the United States continued their wheeling and dealing, mindless of the events that almost came to pass.

"What do you think of Jane?"

The change in topic took Schultz by surprise, but given the hints of the last few days, he should have expected it. Schultz pulled himself to his feet to give himself more time to think. On reflection, he decided that not much thinking would be required. Sometimes you had to be cruel to be kind. "She's part of another world Hunt. Let her go."

"I reckon I could…"

"You're not in her league, my friend. I'd advise you forget you ever met her."

"You're a bastard Schultz."

Schultz laughed. "Mayhap I am, Hunt. However, I'm your partner. So I'm allowed to be a bastard." Schultz's arm draped itself across Hunt's shoulder as the older man sought relief for his leg. The two men broke into a slow walk along the sidewalk.

"I'd be interested in your comments on the Spaulding case, Hunt," said Schultz. "I've found a woman who worked with Mary Macmillan in her previous position. Now, we know that Spaulding had a passion for billiards. One of Macmillan's tasks as Spaulding's housekeeper involved keeping the billiard room neat and tidy."

Far above, the clouds of the past week had almost cleared away, and stars shone down from the night sky. The voices faded down Pennsylvania Avenue as Schultz and Hunt returned to their work.

###

HISTORICAL FIGURES

Abraham Lincoln won re-election as President in November 1864 despite earlier predictions that he could not win. The capture of Mobile Bay (August 5th 1864) and Atlanta (September 2nd 1864) changed the public perception that the war had stalemated, and those military victories helped swing popular support behind the incumbent.

In September, the Radical Republican ticket of Charles Fremont and John Cochrane, aware that many of their supporters were switching back to support Lincoln, withdrew from the electoral race while the Democrat candidate, 38 year old Union General George McClellan, remained politically compromised by his refusal to personally endorse the Democrat's stated platform of seeking a negotiated end to the war.

In the end, Lincoln won the election with 55% of the popular vote in the Union states (the Confederate states didn't submit any election results) and secured 212 electoral votes to McClellan's twenty-one. After the election, Lincoln maintained the military pressure on the southern states until their final collapse in early 1865.

John Wilkes Booth assassinated Lincoln on Friday April 14th 1865 while the President watched a play at Ford's Theatre.

*****

Horace Greeley built himself into one of the leading newspaper editors of the 1860s, becoming as influential then as William Hearst would be in the 1920s, or Rupert Murdoch in the 1990s. Greeley corresponded with Lincoln on a number of matters, and he opposed to the war on practical grounds rather than issues of political ideology. In mid-1864 Greeley informed Lincoln that Confederate delegates were in Canada, and available for discussions about ending the war. The President appointed Greeley to meet the emissaries, however the discussions went nowhere.

After the war, Greeley supported a policy of letting the southern states control their efforts at reconstruction, and in 1867 controversially offered to provide bail for the captured Jefferson Davis. In May 1872, the Liberal Republican party selected Greeley as their candidate for the presidency, running against the incumbent Ulysses Simpson Grant, but the editor's life went rapidly downhill from there.

He lost money in the Diamond Hoax of 1872, and then his competitor Whitelaw Reid, owner of the New York Herald, gained control of Greeley's flagship newspaper, the New York Tribune. Greeley's wife died in October that year shortly before the election, which Greeley lost with 43% of the popular vote and 66 Electoral votes compared to 55% of the popular vote and 286 Electoral votes for Grant.

Greeley himself died on November 29th 1872 in Pleasantville, New York less than a month after the election.

*****

Richmond Mumford Pearson served as lawyer, state legislator, and Superior Court judge, before being elected to the North Carolina Supreme Court in 1848, and then becoming Chief Justice in 1859. His prewar political leanings were with the pro-Union Whig Party which included Abraham Lincoln as its leader in Illinois, until the 1854 Kansas-Nebraska Act split the Whigs along sectional lines and effectively destroyed the Party.

Pearson's legal judgments reveal him as a strong supporter of individual rights, which makes his own impeachment crisis somewhat ironic. The electorate perceived him as a political ally of North Carolina's first postwar Governor, William Woods Holden, who was impeached in 1870 for "high crimes and misdemeanors", including suspension of the writ of Habeas Corpus. Holden's opponents made an effort to impeach Pearson as retribution for his support of Holden, but the effort failed and Pearson continued as Chief Justice until his death in 1878.

*****

COULD IT HAVE HAPPENED?

The Second Continental Congress adopted the Declaration of Independence in July 1776. That action is rightfully remembered as a landmark event in the process of removing the Thirteen Colonies from the control of Great Britain, yet there remained much work to do in order to Perfect the Union of the states. Mindful of the administrative vacuum created by that declaration, the states then adopted the Articles of Confederation to provide for a form of common government between them.

That Confederation possessed a number of fatal flaws. Apart from having no Judiciary and no power to directly levy taxes, it provided no penalty for a state which ignored the financial requisitions set by the central government. Consequently some states (looking at you New York!) did not contribute to the cost of running the country in some years, so the value of the Continental dollar plunged dramatically, leading to the expression 'not worth a Continental'.

Within the 'Committee of the States', which served as the Confederation's government, no individual could serve as president for more than one year in three, making continuity of executive policy impossible. Since the individual states retained their power to negotiate international treaties, it proved impossible to create a common foreign policy, because the European powers could use discriminatory trading arrangements to play one state off against the other. Another complication arose from the proviso that the individual states were responsible for raising their own army regiments, and for appointing all officers with or under the rank of Colonel. That policy might have been adequate for dealing with suppressing Indian tribes or a local insurrection, but it would make the Army unworkable as a tool of foreign policy.

In order to fix these and other problems a constitutional convention met in Philadelphia in May 1787, and by September had produced the United States Constitution.

The framers of this new Constitution wisely provided a process for amending the document, and in the time preceding the events of this story there were twelve accepted amendments, the first ten of which are collectively known as The Bill of Rights. The ninth and tenth amendment specifically reserved undocumented rights to the people and the member states respectively ie. if something wasn't mentioned in the Constitution, then the individual citizen or state retained that power - not the Federal Government.

The tenth amendment stated:

"The powers not delegated to the United States by the Constitution, nor prohibited by it to the States, are reserved to the States respectively, or to the people."

but did that mean *expressly* delegated or *implicitly* delegated?

For example, the Constitution explicitly gave Congress the power to fund and maintain an army and a navy, but it did not mention an air force. It is perhaps inapt to rebuke the Founding Fathers for this oversight, since aircraft would not be invented for another hundred and thirty years, but the omission did raise the question of whether the Federal Government had the implied authority to fund an independent Air Force. That question is still debated today, despite the words of Douglas J. in *Laird v. Tatum* 408 U.S. 1 (1972), who noted in passing that the Air Force is *"comprehended in the constitutional term 'armies'."*

The issue of membership in the Union required more significant hair splitting. Article 4 Section 3 stated:

260

"New States may be admitted by the Congress into this Union"

Unfortunately there was no corresponding clause explicitly covering how a state could *leave* the Union. Did this Right to terminate a state's membership come from an implied subset of the power of Congress to admit new states, which would therefore require the approval of Congress? Alternatively, could that Right be seen as an explicit right not covered within the Constitution, thereby reverting to the individual states, meaning that a departing state could leave on its own authority?

The attempted secession of the individual Confederate States, focused the attention of the world on this section of the Constitution, and it took over six hundred thousand deaths for the Union to prove that the Supreme Court did not need to rule on that point of law.

This issue did not disappear with the surrender of the last Confederate forces on land (General Staid Watie on June 23 1865), or at sea (CSS Shenandoah on November 6, 1865), but continued onwards in the minds of many, despite the ruling of the Supreme Court in *Texas v. White*, 74 U.S. 700 (1869) where the Supreme Court held that:

"... the ordinance of secession, adopted by the convention and ratified by a majority of the citizens of Texas, and all the acts of her legislature intended to give effect to that ordinance, were absolutely null. They were utterly without operation in law."

At that time, the Supreme Court consisted of the following eight Justices, five of whom received their appointments from Abraham Lincoln:

- Nelson, Samuel - Born in New York - Appointed by Tyler on February 4, 1845.
- Grier, Robert C. - Born in Pennsylvannia - Appointed by Polk on August 4, 1846.
- Clifford, Nathan - Born in New Hampshire - Appointed by Buchanan on December 9, 1857.
- Swayne, Noah H. - Born in Virginia - Appointed by Lincoln on January 21, 1862.
- Miller, Samuel F. - Born in Kentucky - Appointed by Lincoln on July 16,

1862.

- Davis, David - Born in Maryland - Appointed by Lincoln on October 17, 1862.
- Field, Stephen J. - Born in Connecticut - Appointed by Lincoln on March 6, 1863.
- Chase, Salmon P. - Born in New Hampshire - Appointed by Lincoln on December 15th 1864 - Chief Justice of the Supreme Court.

Abraham Lincoln's work in holding the Union together while it defeated the Confederacy, and in appointing a Supreme Court that would decide *Texas v. White* in the way that it did, changed the path of history.

Could the southern states have successfully defined any Union military action against them as treason? If so, then since the U.S. Constitution mandates the removal of the President, Vice-President or any other Civil Officer of the United States from office following a conviction for treason, it would be impossible for the Union to conduct the four year campaign it took to subdue the Confederacy.

The starting point for that enquiry is the recognition that treason is not, and has never been, exclusively a Federal offence. The US Constitution acknowledges the category of treason against a state, specifically in Article 4, Section 2.2 which states:

"A Person charged in any State with Treason, Felony, or other Crime, who shall flee from Justice, and be found in another State, shall on Demand of the executive Authority of the State from which he fled, be delivered up, to be removed to the State having Jurisdiction of the Crime."

Historical evidence of the acceptance of this dual jurisdiction is shown in the convictions of Thomas Dorr (1844) and John Brown (1859) for treason by State courts. During Dorr's trial his defense team argued unsuccessfully that ratification of the U.S. Constitution removed the crime of treason from the prerogative of the State, however Presiding Justice Story rejected that line of reasoning. Dorr's subsequent release from jail came about through a charitable Act of the state legislature, which in no way impugned the legality of his original conviction.

According to J. Taylor McConkie [1], in 2012 forty-three states still had constitutional provisions or criminal statutes defining treason against the State. The State Convention of North Carolina passed their first treason law at their State Convention in May/June 1861, to wit:

"Treason against the State of North Carolina, shall consist only in levying war against her, or in adhering to her enemies, giving them aid and comfort."

The lack of an applicable North Carolina statute prior to this law prevents any State charge against Lincoln for treason, unless that treason law is interpreted to operate retrospectively or the charge is bought under Common Law.

In 1859, the Commonwealth of Virginia allowed that the Virginian citizenship of John Brown could be presumed from Brown's simple act of setting foot in the Virginia during his raid on Harper's Ferry, but such a line of reasoning is irrelevant here since Abraham Lincoln was born in Kentucky and lived in Illinois. He never visited North Carolina, therefore even under the extreme 'John Brown' interpretation, Lincoln could not be viewed as owing civic loyalty to that state.

If Lincoln's civic responsibility to North Carolina does not exist, then Article 3 Section 2 Clause 1 of the US Constitution, which extends the authority of the Federal Supreme Court to controversies between a State and citizens of another State, effectively disenfranchises North Carolina in the matter.

However once the case is moved into the Federal jurisdiction then the situation becomes more complicated. One line of legal reasoning could proceed as follows:

1. Article 3 Section 2 of the US Constitution states: *"Treason against the United States, shall consist only in levying war against them."* Note the use of the plural *'them'* indicating that treason is an offence against the individual state(s) rather than against the singular Federal authority.

---

[1] Kentucky Law Journal, volume 101 2012-2013, p.281, State-Treason: The History and Validity of Treason Against Individual States

2. On 27th April 1861, Lincoln proclaimed a blockade of North Carolina's ports. Since the declaration was one of blockade rather than an administrative closure of the State's ports, this action constituted an exercise of war powers.

3. In *Prize Cases*, 2 Black 635 (1862), the US Supreme Court held that the proclamation of blockade was, in itself, official and conclusive evidence, that a state of war existed.

4. North Carolina did not secede from the United States until 20th May 1861, therefore Lincoln's orders to blockade her ports occurred while she was still indisputably a member of the United States. In the absence of a prior attempt by North Carolina to secede, Lincoln had no legal right to refuse her all of the rights and protections guaranteed to the individual states under the Constitution.

5. Since the power to declare war lies with Congress (not the President), Lincoln could not claim that his proclamation of blockade/declaration of war against North Carolina had been done in the discharge of his official duties. Ergo, he was acting as an individual and was therefore not entitled to the legal protections otherwise afforded to a Head of State in the execution of their duty.

6. If Lincoln's proclamation (and subsequent enforcement) of the blockade constituted an act of war against North Carolina, then the accusation of treason is proved.

Of course, the challenge here would be to persuade the Federal Supreme Court to hear the case. However once that hurdle is overcome, then the words of Chief Justice Marshall in *Cohens v. Virginia*, which are also quoted at the start of this book, should persuade the Court to see the case through to the end:

"With whatever doubts, with whatever difficulties, a case may be attended, we must decide it, if it be brought before us. We have no more right to decline the exercise of jurisdiction which is given, than to usurp that which is not given."

In summary, North Carolina's only meaningful chance of playing the treason card to force a constitutionally imposed end to hostilities appears to be if they follow through with that accusation in the Federal jurisdiction. Unfortunately, that approach requires an acknowledgement that North Carolina remained subject to the authority of the U.S. Supreme Court, and such an acknowledgement is fundamentally incompatible with the act of secession. This would lead to the ironic situation that the best method for the southern states to achieve Union acquiescence to their acts of secession would be for them to refrain from those acts of secession in the first place.

***

THE DC DOCKS CRIME SERIES

YOU'VE JUST READ "PEARSON'S PAPER", the third story in the DC Docks crime series.

The first story is "Hobart's Hogsheads". Percival Hobart faces financial disaster when an eagerly awaited shipment of illicit alcohol from France is somehow replaced by 200 crates of brandy. The unexpected blessing is quite welcome, until the owner of the brandy comes calling and the original hogsheads are nowhere to be found. Hobart's customers won't wait forever - if he can't provide them with their liquor then his whole business is bankrupt. Thaddeus Noble's quick thinking solution to the problem shows he is a man with a future in Hobart's organization.

The second story is "Reardon's Reward". Managing the day to day operations on Percival Hobart's waterfront keeps Thaddeus Noble busy and pays his bills. He'd like to move up in the organization and displace Reardon, the company accountant, as Hobart's right hand man. The opportunity arrives when Hobart's enforcer, Alex Jackson, is caught forcibly extracting money from a delinquent creditor. Hobart looks after his men, but the police have the proof he needs to send Jackson away for a long time. Noble needs to save Jackson and to advance his own career. If Reardon can be taken down a notch or two in the process, then that's fine by Noble. He's been preparing a surprise for quite a while now and this might be the time to give Reardon the Reward he so richly deserves.

You can find more details at www.grahamdodge.com

Acknowledgements

No story springs fully grown from the mind of the author. There is a period of gestation, which takes many months or years, or in the case of this story, decades. Throughout the gestation there are kind words, provocative inputs and other essential commentary from a variety of sources, many of which I have doubtless forgotten. For the moment though, let me thank the following people:

- Lizzie Vosburgh, chief proofreader and emotional confidant.
- My fellow authors at Scribophile who refined this story through many months of mutual critiques.
- Janet Hankins and other members of the Association of Retired Police Officers in Maryland who kindly reviewed my draft manuscript. Their assistance was extremely helpful; any lingering factual mistakes in this story are mine.
- Sergeant Slater and my other friends from University days including the long forgotten law tutor who said "They would never do that".
- Wolfsberger and the other reprobates from the Fairfax Rifles whom I would love to meet some day.

Book Cover Credits
- **White House:** National Archives photo no. 111-B-4246 (Brady Collection)
- **Richmond Mumford Pearson:** *"Representative men of the South"*, published by Charles Robson & Co., Philadelphia 1880

Legal

www.ingramcontent.com/pod-product-compliance
Lightning Source LLC
Chambersburg PA
CBHW022154170626
46807CB00005B/2202